STAR TREK: THE NEW VOYAGES 2

IN THE MAZE: Kirk, Spock, and McCoy become guinea pigs for an alien scientist investigating human intelligence.

SURPRISE!: Lieutenant Uhura helps the Enterprise crew organize a surprise birthday party for Captain Kirk . . . but an unexpected guest surprises everyone.

MARGINAL EXISTENCE: A dead city turns into a living nightmare when a landing party unintentionally awakens its sleeping inhabitants.

THE SLEEPING GOD: The Nagha was a computer brain of gigantic capabilities . . . the Sleeper the most powerful human mind in the universe . . . and the Enterprise the vehicle that brought them into fateful confrontation.

STAR TREK:®
THE NEW VOYAGES
2

EDITED BY SONDRA MARSHAK
AND MYRNA CULBREATH

BANTAM BOOKS
TORONTO • NEW YORK • LONDON • SYDNEY • AUCKLAND

STAR TREK: THE NEW VOYAGES 2

A Bantam Book / January 1978

2nd printing .... March 1978	6th printing ...... June 1982
3rd printing ...... July 1978	7th printing .... March 1983
4th printing .. September 1979	8th printing ...... June 1984
5th printing ... January 1981	9th printing .. September 1985

ISBN 0-553-23756-X

Published simultaneously in the United States and Canada

Bantam Books are published by Bantam Books, Inc. Its trade-
mark, consisting of the words "Bantam Books" and the por-
trayal of a rooster, is Registered in the United States Patent
and Trademark Office and in other countries. Marca Regis-
trada. Bantam Books, Inc., 666 Fifth Avenue, New York, New
York 10103.

PRINTED IN THE UNITED STATES OF AMERICA

H   18 17 16 15 14 13 12 11 10 9

Dedication to
Star Trek: The New Voyages 2

These voyages are for Terry,
whose own was too brief,
We do not speak of grief ...
He might have gone
voyaging—
He was that kind:
"Let's go."
He sailed the seas of earth, not stars,
stood sentinel against night and silence,
between home and danger
no less than on some nighted veldt, or starship.
Jungle or tall ship,
home seas or where-no-man—
it is much the same:
young faces, undiscovered promises,
small boys barely grown,
ever thinking of themselves as daring,
not counting costs or risks.
"Let's go!"
And those who love them—
always wanting them home
from whatever voyage. ....

This is for Terry, who served in the Navy, loved
it, loved home, family—who knew the fierce protectiveness of family—mother, father, three sisters, a brother.
He was a firstborn son, first grandson, first nephew—
barely three years younger than his mother's youngest
sister, who used to tell him her stories, share books she

loved with him. She would have liked to share this one —and STAR TREK—and man's voyages to the moon, the stars.

She would have liked to share Terry.

He just barely missed the first giant step. But he knew that we were on our way—upward, outward— And he would have said; "Let's go."

That much of him we *can* share. This is for Terry Shore, 1944–1968, and for those who loved him, especially two very special people to us: his parents Regina and Artie Shore. And for his grandmother, Mrs. Anna Tornheim Hassan. Regina is the oldest of her five daughters, and Sondra is the youngest. For all of them and all the family . . . with all our love.

Acknowledgments

Very special acknowledgment must be made to Carol Frisbie, who has had her own part in the space connection, and an enormous part in the New Voyages connection—searching for good material for us, helping fan writers write better—and helping us, beyond telling. Thanks Carol—again beyond measure.

Our acknowledgments to Nichelle Nichols are apparent throughout this book, as are our appreciation of her, our thanks, and our love. Nichelle—voyage in delight, always.

Our acknowledgments to Jesco von Puttkamer, and our thanks, permeate the book—and still are not sufficient. Thank you, Jesco, beyond measure, not only for what you did in this book, but for what you will do to the future.

You'll find also our acknowledgments to writers, readers, fanzines, their editors, and everyone who has made NEW VOYAGES 2 possible.

Two people who must receive very special acknowledgment here: Frederik Pohl and Sydny Weinberg of Bantam. Once again, there are editors and editors . . . You have not heard our last word on that subject.

Finally, the Merlin of our particular Camelot, Sondra's husband, Alan, is still working his practical sorcery to make our voyages possible. Without him, we wouldn't get off the ground. Trips, deadlines, his advice needed—all while he teaches electrical engineering at LSU, and devotes far more than full time to his students and his own creative work: fundamental research in electronics. This is perhaps the proper place to acknowledge that without that kind of work done by teachers and researchers all over the world, nobody would get off the ground or to the stars.

Alan's particular field is theory of semi-conductors and solid-state devices—transistors and the like—which are, of course, essential to any space hardware. His work results in a steady stream of scientific papers which he is invited to give at conferences around the country and internationally. He is part of the Camelot connection in that sense, too.

Yet with all his twenty-four-hour-a-day dedication to his work—like Spock to that starship—Alan will take time, for us, to take care of Jerry, and everything which has to be taken care of when we are away. That is the kind of thing which is beyond acknowledgment—but we must keep trying.

What Alan doesn't do, Mama—Mrs. Anna Tornheim Hassan—does, and she'll do it first before anybody if we don't watch out. She is such an enormous help that we couldn't function without her. Not one of our books could have been done without her practical help, limitless inspiration and boundless love.

Contents

Editors' Preface:

The Once and Future Voyages 2—
The Camelot Connection

> . . . and *Star Trek* is our new dream, the *possible* dream—to reach for the reachable stars.
> . . . If this be our new Camelot, even more shining—make the most of it.

> STAR TREK: THE NEW VOYAGES
> *March 1976*

February 1977. The *Enterprise* flies.

As we write this, on the road in San Francisco and Los Angeles, as Jesco von Puttkamer writes his magnificent introduction in Washington, D.C., the *Enterprise,* our first true non-expendable space ship is aloft for first atmospheric tests.

The reality bears the name of the dream—and they both fly, in our real skies.

A handful of *Star Trek* fans spearheaded what became a nationwide movement which persuaded President Ford to change the name of the orbital shuttle, creating the moment when the *Enterprise* rolled out, fact and dream together, before the eyes of the creators of the dream, and the creators of the reality—and into the history books.

"The dream is father to the fact . . ."

Star Trek continues to make the impossible seem inevitable.

In another impossibility which now seems inevitable, Jesco von Puttkamer, Program Manager for Long-Range Planning Studies for NASA, one of the principal architects of the future of the reality, has also become an architect of the dream, and of what we privately think of as "the NASA connection."

He has written for *Star Trek: The New Voyages 2* his beautiful introduction, saying everything which we wanted to say on that subject. (Well, almost. There are a few things about himself which he couldn't say, and about NASA's plans for new voyages—which we want to say.)

And he has written—out of his love for *Star Trek,* his experience as part of the Apollo team and the development of the orbital shuttle and, incredibly, as a professional science-fiction writer (in his native German; not, until now, in English)—a *Star Trek* novelette, "The Sleeping God," also for *New Voyages 2.*

Nichelle Nichols, since our NASA trek with her last year to Huntsville, Alabama, has become a *NASA contractor,* with a contract to help put women and minorities into space.

She has written the epilogue for this book—and, with us, from her idea taken from her life, the story "Surprise!" (It shouldn't happen to a starship captain . . . especially not in such a skimpy towel . . .)

Quite a number of things shouldn't, and most of them *do,* in this collection of where-no-man (and where-no-woman) voyages. Not to mention where-no-Vulcan. We've tried to make it so that you never quite know what to expect on the next page—as our voyagers never know what to expect beyond the next star.

In short, it's another *New Voyages.* A touch of humor, maybe a touch of tears, some surprises . . . A kind of thank-you bonus for your response to *The New Voyages* (1) in Nichelle and Jesco's contributions, adding their magic and the touch of *Star Trek* and the star-bound reality of NASA to our ongoing Camelot-to-the-stars.

. . . a living legend of heroes and high deeds—
man's truest legend, seen at last; the legend not of
a golden age lost, but of one yet to be found . . .

That's what we said, and did, in *New Voyages*
(1)—and you wrote to tell us—in spades—that we
got it *right*.

Thank you. And—thanks to you—*New Voyages*
(1) is in its sixth printing by Bantam. We've also received copies of the British edition put out by Bantam's affiliate, Corgi—with a different cover. (Bright
colors. Kirk and Spock.) We think it's only a matter of
time before the Martian edition comes in. Or the Vulcan edition . . .

You even made the most of the box number we
published for manuscripts and comments. Did you
ever! Our box runneth over. Boxes. Bales. File draw-
ers. There are stories, poems. Epics. Tomes. Volumes.
Sagas. Trilogies. Soliloquies. Elegies. Eulogies. Sonnets
from the Vulcan.

Letters. Letters. Letters. From all over the world.
Every state. Many foreign countries. An Israeli kibbutz.
A Polaris submarine. Air Force bases. Ships at sea . . .
From somewhere behind the Iron Curtain . . . From
places where someone voyages, or stands sentinel . . .

One or two of them broke our hearts (". . . We
cannot here receive *Star Trek* . . . Your books are our
only contact with it . . . Please do not delay . . .")

There were one or two in languages we didn't
think we could read. (We managed. There seems to
be a certain universality to what they are saying.)

We read them all with great interest and appreciation. You *have* reached us. And touched us. We are,
literally, overwhelmed, both by the volume of mail and
by its content. It is a profound tribute to *Star Trek*—
and a gorgeous way of saying "thank you" to us—
which virtually every letter, even from the youngest
fans, did. (We even received some very special "thank
you" mementoes or things people wanted to share
with us—a fanzine, a book—a lovely "clear casting"
plaque: an artform made from the cover painting of

New Voyages (1) cast in lucite on a black background —with a tiny note from the artist, just saying, "thought you'd like to have this." Yes.)

Thank you. All of you and each of you.

We wish that we could answer each letter personally. We do answer what we can—sometimes by phone. Our "Mama"—Mrs. Anna Tornheim Hassan—who loves *Star Trek* fans, has answered some, especially from Israel—and has to be restrained from tackling the entire stack of boxes which is moving us out of home and house. It's just impossible . . .

A German group of *Star Trek* fans writes:

> Please do not answer this letter. Do not take time from future books. We are desperate for them here. They are all we have. You cannot imagine what *Star Trek Lives!* and *Star Trek: The New Voyages* have meant to us. Thank you. We want to say you must be working on new books, and ask when we can expect them. But do not answer. Answer in the books. That will be our reward . . .

Naturally, we put that one aside to answer. That recognition that it can come down to answering the letters or writing the books—and the thoughtfulness of telling us not to answer—really touched us. It went on our "most immediate" pile.

Our new German shepherd puppy, "Omne"—named for the villain in our new *Star Trek* novel, *The Price of the Phoenix*—promptly broke loose in the wrong part of the house and ate the letter. (For an appetizer. The main course was the seat of our favorite chair. A side dish: the telephone wire. Dessert was three straight pins. Omne lives. It's a phenomenon—or *he* is. Maybe we shouldn't have named him for the *villain*. Especially not *that* villain.)

People have written to thank us for letting them have glimpses of our personal lives and our particular home Camelot in our introductions, dedications, acknowledgments—Sondra's husband Alan, their son Jerry (five now), Mama. Add to that a puppy who may get mad at us when he reads that novel. And who eats letters.

Actually, the puppy ate only 86.2 percent of the German letter's envelope. Inside with blessed Teutonic thoroughness, the German fans had included two return addresses. The rescued fragments are carefully preserved on our "yesterday" pile, with a stack of other letters, traveling with us to San Francisco and L.A. where we knew we would be writing this answer to all your letters.

Please do, each one of you who wrote, accept this as our personal answer to you. We are delighted *that* you wrote and with *what* you wrote. Your comments are extremely thoughtful and thought-provoking, and they are helping us to shape *New Voyages*.

Many of you offered detailed, highly literate analyses of each story, showing a profound understanding and love of *Star Trek* and its characters.

Curiously, every single story was ranked as the top favorite by a substantial group of fans, and some were blockbusters. You've been saying that the funny stories were funny (". . . I laughed until my jaw ached . . .") and the serious ones touched you and moved you, sometimes to tears . . .

From a professional woman who gave a professional-quality analysis of all the stories: ". . . I will tell you right now that I used up three Kleenex . . ." (On one story.)

A male physician writes us stiffly: "You have the honor, if one can call it that, of being the first to make me cry."

A seventeen-year-old female, who gave a startlingly thoughtful analysis, started with a bang: "Wow! I feel as if I've just been stunned with a phaser. You could knock me over with a feather (or, as Mr. Spock would say, 'the horny epidermal outgrowth of a bird.') In case you're wondering, I just read *Star Trek: The New Voyages*."

In case you're wondering, we read her letter with equal delight. She finished by speaking of "the profound depth of love and caring between Kirk and

Spock . . ." and the caring among all the characters. And she thanked not only us and the writers, but the actors and creators of *Star Trek* for the introductions which they generously wrote for *New Voyages* (1).

We thank them again, too, and have, many times, whenever we see them. There have been magnificent comments on those introductions and on the fact that the creators would take the trouble to do that.

Interestingly, there was essentially *no* negative mail. We received *two* letters which were mildly critical, in the sense of: "Couldn't you have picked this instead of that?" Two.

The rest, in essence and spirit, were essentially like this:

> I just finished reading *Star Trek: The New Voyages*. What a beautiful, beautiful book! I wish I could tell you exactly how I feel about it. It made me smile. It made me laugh and dream. It made me think—and cry . . .
>
> I found it hard at first to believe that fans— people not too different from me—wrote such excellent stories, full of fantastic adventure and warm, genuine feelings—feelings they have toward the characters, feelings the characters have toward each other. I thought that could only be done by the pros. But once I read them, once I believed, I began to wonder if I could do the same. I now hope to try, very soon . . .

Please do. We do consider all manuscripts carefully, and they have been, or will be answered, although we do like to keep them long enough, unless otherwise requested, to give them full consideration for more than one volume. (Please continue to send two copies, and be certain to keep one. Box 14261, Baton Rouge, La. 70808) Our space for any one volume is so limited, and the volume of stories and mail so unlimited . . .

The writers are of all ages, both sexes, all walks of life: doctors (including doctors who are women), scientists, engineers, Ph.D.'s, businessmen and women, coaches, nurses, lawyers, teachers, students, actors, professional writers, truck drivers, servicemen . . . Infinite diversity—and infinite delight:

> To be hungry, and know it, is bad. To be hungry and not know it is worse . . . I realized only when reading *Star Trek: The New Voyages* that I was on the edge of starvation for new stories about the crew of the *Enterprise*. Thank you for your masterpiece, for it is truly a masterpiece.

We read what you have written also with delight. And almost every letter stresses: ". . . You have captured the characters . . ." ". . . You know the meaning of the true bond of love and caring between Kirk and Spock . . ." ". . . I was glad to see that you and the writers understand the real friendship between Spock and Dr. McCoy . . ." ". . . You got them all *right*—this is the real *Star Trek*. In some ways I was moved even more deeply than by aired *Star Trek*."

That is praise, indeed. And we do feel that the writers of the stories in *New Voyages* (1) did a magnificent job. We thank them, and you. We are proud of our choices. May you enjoy these as much. We've listened to what you've said. And some of these have come through Box 14261.

Almost every letter also had a tone toward us which we found profoundly touching, a tone of friendship, a sense that we were friends:

> Please put together another book of New Voyages. We've been waiting so long for more voyages that now that we've got eight, we want more. (You've unleashed a monster!) I would send you the only *Star Trek* story I've attempted, but I'm afraid that it wasn't very good, and slightly X-rated.

> P.S.   My English teacher would kill me for not making this a business-type letter, but I feel as if I know you from your books, and who writes a business-type letter to friends? In case you're

wondering, I'm fifteen and a sophomore in high school.

Um-hmmm. And we're wondering what a sophomore in high school is doing writing a "slightly X-rated" story. And what are you doing *holding it back* from *friends?* Come on. Give.

And that goes for each and all of you. Send us your stories, your comments. We can't always answer —but we do listen. And much of what you are saying is finding its way into our books in one form or an-other—not only *New Voyages,* but the books we're co-authoring with William Shatner, with Nichelle Nich-ols, and others. We're in L.A. to work with him on the book we are writing with him, and we've interviewed Nichelle for that book, spoken with her about *Uhura!,* which we are writing with her.

We had to catch her in mid-flight—in San Fran-cisco where we were guests together at Space Con Three, in L.A. as she came back from NASA in Washington and headed out again on a tour for her contract with NASA. Last week, Nichelle Nichols, *Star Trek*'s communications officer Uhura, spoke in the U.S. House of Representatives on the real space program.

We couldn't know a year and a half ago, when we suggested to her that we collaborate on a book, that it would help to set her and us off on a NASA trek which helped to shape not only *Uhura!* but this *New Voyages,* with its NASA connection.

We are deeply touched and honored that Jesco von Puttkamer has brought the magic of NASA's Camelot into these pages. NASA and the reality of the space program today are the possible dream of which *Star Trek* is the longest-range plan.

The coalesence of the forces of dream and reality, *Star Trek* and the space program is perhaps the most important thing which could happen to make the real future of *Star Trek* possible.

When we visited NASA in Huntsville, Alabama, a year ago, and met Werhner von Braun's old Apollo team and many NASA scientists, we found a magnificent effort going on. But we found a NASA which was trying valiantly to recover from triumph.

NASA and the space program were punished for their greatest triumph—for mankind's greatest triumph—the Apollo program which answered the challenge to put man on the moon within a decade.

Apollo Eleven flew. Mankind took the giant step onto the face of the moon. And the next day self-styled intellectuals and self-appointed pundits said that the triumph was *"only* technology"—meaning: only *greatness*. They said: Pour the money down the ratholes. Save the slums. (Never mind getting people *out* of the slums—to the stars.)

NASA, with the generosity of its innocent greatness, could not believe that it could be punished for greatness.

It was. It was cut off at the knees, starved for funds, forced to fire and retire many of its irreplaceable personnel, denied any comprehensive long-range plan—let alone a where-no-man plan for manned flight to Mars and beyond. (It could have been well underway by now. A distinguished scientist from von Braun's original team told us that 1983 would have been an excellent year, when Mars would be in a more favorable close position than it will be again for years. If we had started right after the moon shot in 1969, with a comparable effort, we might have reached Mars in 1983.)

NASA was not allowed even to think of that. It struggled on with what it had, and with brute courage —and it struggled well: *Skylab, Orbiter, Viking, Soyuz-Apollo,* and the orbital shuttle now named *Enterprise.* But it was not the Camelot of the Apollo years, and not the direct route to where-no-man.

We found NASA still stunned, unbelieving, seven years later, wondering if the public could really support such injustice, or be so uncaring.

We said: No. We said: The people don't know. They assume, as we had, that the pundits had crawled back under some rock, and NASA lives—on time, on schedule, to Mars, to the stars, as quickly as it can be done. They don't know that NASA lives at a fraction of its strength, that NASA now has its own new long-range plan—but needs approval even for the next necessary step.

That step: Star Harbor. It might or might not have that name. It would have that function: Harbor, home, haven, space-port, shipyard in orbit, industrial district, work-place, living-space, construction camp, permanent foothold for man in space—serviced and built by the orbital shuttle—a stepping-stone to space colonies, to Luna City, to Mars and the stars—a jumping-off point for where-no-man. It could begin simply—a space frame to which units could be added.

The cost? The increased cost for NASA's whole new plan—less than a penny on the dollar of the national budget.

We said: People don't know.

We said: It is not possible that there are tens of millions of people who love *Star Trek*—and that they would knowingly stand by and see the real space program held down like a chained giant.

Support for the dream *is* support for the fact.

When we said that to certain NASA people, it was almost like a benediction, as if we had said what they had always known and needed to hear: Yes, it was greatness.

And we said: People need to know—especially the people who *do* know that those who act on an idea can move the world. One man *can* summon the future. Every man can. Every woman. And certainly a movement which can revive *Star Trek*—and name the fact for the dream—can.

It occurred to us that NASA could use a fandom like *Star Trek*'s. And that it would find one. The same one. Nobody will have to be told what to do or how to do it. Paramount listens. Politicians listen. Presidents listen.

We went home with that thought. Within a few weeks we sent in this volume of *New Voyages,* with its NASA connection.

But the later process of publishing takes time. And meanwhile the space connection, NASA connection, Camelot connection has been developing.

At San Francisco we were guests of Space Con Three, a combination *Star Trek,* science-fiction, and real space program convention—drawing 8,000 fans of all three, and guests with names like a roll call of honor in all three. (This was the third Space Con in a year, with a fourth planned for Los Angeles, brain-children of Terry Terman, President of Space, The Final Frontier.)

We felt as if we had walked into Camelot.

There we met the once and future dreamer of the possible dream, Robert Heinlein, properly called the dean of science fiction, and such a gallant, magnificent man that he would take your breath—and did ours. As Theodore Sturgeon properly said to the convention, Robert Heinlein is really the father of the dream, science fiction and Star Trek—and even the reality— it's all his. Yet as it happens Robert Heinlein never wrote for *Star Trek,* he has no personal stake in *Star Trek*. What he said about it hit home.

We interviewed him, and talked with him late into another night and Robert Heinlein told us:

Star trekkers *alone* can make the difference between a future in which mankind will fall back
into a dark age that will last a thousand years,
and one in which we will go upward, outward—
to the stars. The turning point is *now*. We make
it now, or we don't make it. But I believe that
we will.

We sat silent for a long moment, feeling a chill, a hope, a sense of urgency . . . and something in the throat which a Vulcan wouldn't care to admit . . .

We thought of this man, standing sentinel these many years to summon the future. Somewhere, like a low music, words echoed, and we knew that they did name both the spirit which was his and the spirit which can make that difference:

. . . man's truest legend, seen at last—the legend not of a golden age lost, but of one yet to be found . . .

. . . if this be our new Camelot, even more shining—make the most of it.

And like a counterpoint . . . "upward, outward —to the stars . . ."

SONDRA MARSHAK
MYRNA CULBREATH

February, 1977

Introduction by Jesco von Puttkamer

Let me tell you about that magic moment out there in the high desert of California when dream and reality came together in a spark of greatness and purpose for humanity.

The year was 1976, the day—the 17th of September. Out there among the tumbleweeds, on the lot of Plant 42 run by the Rockwell International Corporation, two thousand invited guests from all walks of life were assembled to witness the roll-out of the first U.S. Space Shuttle. Special guests on the red-draped dais, framed by the Stars and Stripes, included Senator Barry Goldwater, Congressmen Olin "Tiger" Teague, Don Fuqua and John Tunney, NASA Administrator Dr. James Fletcher, and others.

The eyes of the distinguished crowd fixed on the corner of the main hangar when John Yardley, NASA's head of Space Flight, gave the signal for the long-awaited moment. The motor of a low-slung tow truck growled into the expectant silence, punctuated by a muted drum roll from the military band: The bow of Orbiter 101 nosed slowly around the corner. On both sides of it was painted the ship's name, *Enterprise*.

And in that instant when time seemed to freeze, the band—clear and triumphant—struck up Alexander Courage's rousing theme from *Star Trek*.

A moment never to be forgotten! For many, the impact was visceral. Like one, those two thousand were on their feet, yelling and clapping with delight. Up front, in the first rows of seats reserved for VVIPs (very, very important persons), a small group of special people stood petrified: there was Gene Roddenberry, Leonard Nimoy, DeForest Kelley, Nichelle Nichols, George Takei, James Doohan, and Walter Koenig. They, who had portrayed the "beautiful crew" of the Starship *Enterprise,* now witnessed the birth of the Shuttle named after their fictional vessel.

Nichelle and Walter had climbed on their chairs. Gene Roddenberry held Nichelle's right hand, unconsciously crushing it in a vise-like grip. On her left, her son Kyle, caught in the unbearable emotion of the moment, did the same to her other hand. I looked at Gene—his head was cocked to one side as he listened to his music, and he clearly had tears in his eyes. Dee told me later about the goose bumps and the tingling down his spine when the *Enterprise* made its appearance. Tears burst from Nichelle's dark eyes when she saw it—that gorgeously beautiful white space machine in the brilliant sunshine there underneath the gigantic deep-blue canopy of the Mojave sky. Later she told me about her feeling of being part of history in the making, of glimpsing destiny, of so much more that words could not describe.

Star Trek and the Space Program . . . What brought them together? Why had thousands of fans of the TV series petitioned their government to name the first Shuttle after their dream? And why had two thousand guests at the roll-out applauded the choice? Was it just the "Space Connection" between the two? Or was a deeper chord struck? Is it that *Star Trek* reflects the hopes of people for a brighter, open future for humankind, and that the Space Program, with its inherent potential to bring out man's greatest qualities, holds out the promise of upward/outward growth, both physical and mental—of a true humanization of the world we live in, of space?

Alfred Adler, the great pioneer of modern psychiatry, once said, "Fantasy is but another creative faculty of the soul." As an essential, deeply engrained part of the mobility of the human organism, fantasy is nothing more than a method of pre-vision, pre-judgment, and prescience. The fantasy world of *Star Trek,* a vision created in a miraculous, once-in-a-life-time burst of inspiration by one man, is undoubtedly contributing to forming a forward-looking attitude in its fans. It can heighten your awareness of your own future and the future of all humankind. Out there, centuries from now, there may indeed exist a Kirk, a Spock, a Uhura, a world of infinite diversity in infinite combinations, a better "you."

As a form of science fiction, *Star Trek* teaches us that our future is represented by an infinity of options or alternatives. Some possible futures are positive, others negative—but none of these options is predetermined or predestined. It is up to you and me to decide on a direction for the future and work toward making it more probable than the others. *Star Trek* fans are often asking what they can do to make the future they want come about. Let's not ignore that dream, nor any other upbeat vision of the future, for there is something self-fulfilling in all visions. The energy of the soul, focussed on such fantasy, should not go to waste.

And there is the Space Program . . . As long as there is the determination to build a Space Shuttle, as long as there is growth, there will be hope of a positive future for humanity.

In this sense, *Star Trek* holds out a mirror to our present world—with some adventure thrown in. It actually glorifies humankind and its future. It is not "escape literature." From that moment in time when science fiction leads the reader/viewer to consider that it is not enough to ask what the future will do to us, but that we must ask what we can do to the future, it is no longer mere "escapist" literature.

Star Trek visualizes that the Space Program is an attempt by man to stretch his arms and open up the world—the world of the future that can be an open future. In such a future, without the fear of living in a shrinking "water droplet" world, there will always be New Voyages for humankind.

It is difficult to believe that the coincidence in time of the explosive growth of the world's population and the advent of space exploration in the twentieth century, should be an accident. Life is a force which has persisted on Earth for two to three billions of years, which has spread across this planet like a grass fire—which has already gone out to touch the moon and the planet Mars, and is even now stretching its tendrils and sensors out toward the galaxy. This life, evolving under the pressures of its own making, will survive for many millions of years more—and to do so it will continue to expand and to weave its way out. Almost instinctively, man will follow this push and settle on other worlds ". . . to boldly go where no man has gone before." The dreams of science fiction will then no longer be dreams, just as the fictions of Tsiolkovsky, Jules Verne, H.G. Wells and many of today's most imaginative science-fiction writers have been turned into fact. Shades of a starship, aloft today in the Space Shuttle *Enterprise . . . ?*

With its over-arching program of Space Industrialization, NASA's intent is not only to put humans into space but—more importantly—to bring space to humans on Earth. This humanization of space is made more understandable for the young in mind by such media as *Star Trek*. If the stories in this anthology series succeed in contributing to this goal, the New Voyages of *Star Trek* will be more than just entertainment.

A book on *Star Trek* voyages must draw from widely differing sources and should reflect the thoughts of widely different writers. Hence, the diversity of stories in this volume. Ten years of *Star Trek* have involved millions of fans and semi-fans, not just in the United States, from all walks of life, with all sorts of education, of all ages and all pigments, of all religious and political backgrounds, in all kinds of climate and in many languages—in no particular order: just like those guests at Palmdale.

The fans are being entertained and stimulated by it, have drawn from it according to their own needs, and are being offered hope for a better future of their particular aspiration. Even today, through reruns on

TV and New Voyages in short-story form, they are being touched and enriched by *Star Trek*. If fantasy is indeed a creative faculty of the soul that may provide prevision and prescience and—thus—insights to problems in our day-to-day routine, then such dreams are necessary for our metabolism, or else we would be human robots, androids.

In one of *Star Trek*'s seventy-nine episodes*, Chief Ship's Surgeon Dr. Leonard McCoy, in a moment of desperate command decision by the Captain, utters that marvelous opinion, "I recommend survival." *Star Trek* fans are survivalists. They possess a creative courage very definitely, and they project in their creations a positive mental force very much like the crew of the *Enterprise* itself.

Fantasy and purpose—that magic moment out there in the Mojave Desert—illustrated this powerful combination vividly. The message is especially clear for young *Star Trek* fans and readers, female and male, who are still free to choose what they want to do with their brand-new lives: Fantasy *plus* purpose can involve all levels of experience and provide the challenge to seek out those answers that one *must* find by oneself, for human beings cannot be fed with answers. With an orderly mind, an early commitment and persistency, they can be found. This, incidentally, is also the very basic make-up of a genius.

Yes, *Star Trek* recommends survival. Who would not join in old Doc Bones' recommendation and especially extend it to *Star Trek* itself and to these New Voyages, presented to you, gentle reader, by two of *Star Trek*'s most devoted and soulful ladies, Sondra Marshak and Myrna Culbreath.

Keep on trekking!

March 1977

---

*"The Immunity Syndrome."

STAR TREK:®
THE NEW VOYAGES
2

Nichelle gets the first, and the last, word—here and in her Epilogue.

That's only proper. We always knew that there was a powerhouse of a woman at that communications board, with a lot more to say than "Hailing frequencies open, Captain."

What we didn't quite expect was a philosopher, a writer, an imp, a mother to small boys and starship captains, a NASA consultant, and a great many other things about which books could be written, and will be, by us, and her.

We were surprised to find out what kind of team that made.

Meanwhile, she absolutely laid us away with the idea of this story, which, by the way, was taken from life—hers. The ending is absolutely authentic. We'll say no more about that here, but we trust no one will write us saying, "Aw, that couldn't happen." It did, if not exactly aboard the *Enterprise.*

Translating it aboard the *Enterprise* ultimately became a blending and melding of the three of us, with ideas crackling back and forth sixteen to the minute, Nichelle acting out all the parts and rolling us in the aisles, drafts being written at white heat and read to each other, and so forth.

We won't forget moments like watching Nichelle act out a certain inauspicious meeting of a communications officer with her captain . . .

You'll know which meeting when you get there. And we doubt if you'll forget it, either.

This one is for fun, and was fun for us—a voyage in the sunlit universe of *Star Trek,* with just that startling touch of danger which is never missing against the unknown. The *Enterprise* is a home, but it is far away from home . . .

SURPRISE!

by Nichelle Nichols, Sondra Marshak, and Myrna Culbreath

Spock turned as the transporter effect released them, with some thought of how to hustle the Captain off to bed, not too obviously.

But Kirk was saying, "You won't forget that lullaby you just composed, will you, Uhura? It was a smash—not only with little Mori. I think you just lulled another planet right into the Federation. His grandparents are very influential, you know."

Uhura stepped down from the transporter, pleased. "I can't say I was thinking of that, Captain. Just of a very bright, very brave little boy who said that he wasn't lonely all that time on the wrecked ship when his parents were in a coma. He did seem to enjoy that belated birthday party, but still there was a loneliness about him."

Kirk smiled as they moved through the corridor to the turbo-lift. "Yes, there's something special about your very own party . . ." For a moment he was silent, and Spock stepped in with a voice command to the turbo-lift. It shot them to the level of officers' quarters with suitable alacrity. The Captain had very nearly been killed this day on what should have been a relatively routine rescue of the boy and his parents from a damaged ship. And Kirk had been under such stress for so long that it was a source of amazement to Spock how he kept on his feet, let alone took such obvious delight in the little boy, the impromptu party, the lullaby. Although it had to be admitted that the little boy was rather special, perhaps quite a lot like James Kirk had been . . .

They stepped out of the lift. "You make a terrific mother, Uhura," Kirk said.

She turned with a lift of eyebrow that was almost Vulcan. "Indeed? Thank you, Captain. But then, I always am. The ship is just full of little boys."

Kirk did a small double-take as she vanished through the door of her quarters, a "Good night, gentlemen" floating sweetly after her. Spock was not quite sure whether he heard correctly, "Sleep tight." It did not seem quite logical, nor, if the Captain's expression was any indication, quite safe.

"When is *her* birthday?" Kirk muttered. "I think the traditional spanking might be in order."

Spock raised an eyebrow. "Fascinating custom, Captain. Do you really want to inaugurate it among the command crew of the *Enterprise?*"

Kirk shot him a look of mischief, with just a touch of speculation on whether the Vulcan implied that someone might try to inaugurate it on the Captain of the *Enterprise.*

"No," Kirk said firmly, in answer, or in rejection of the speculation. "But—" he looked back at Uhura's door, "there's no law against being sorely tempted."

"Indeed," Spock said blandly, and collected a small double-take himself.

Kirk paused beside his door, his mind visibly shifting to his ship. "I think I'll just check the bridge. It's a quiet night, but—" There was that look in his eye as when there was some odd mood among the crew or an engine running imperceptibly rough, some anomaly waiting to make its presence felt. Spock knew the look—and the feeling. He'd had a touch of it himself today, but it was doubtless only from the kind of day they had had. He could tell himself that and dismiss it with logic, but the Human could not.

"Jim, would you mind taking a look at my last move in our chess game? I'll take a turn around the bridge."

Kirk gave him the long-suffering look of being coddled too transparently. "Mother's little helper," he said with the look of a self-satisfied *morgril.*

"I trust you will find the move helpful, Captain," Spock said in his best Vulcan manner.

"Mate in three moves," Kirk challenged.

"Two," Spock said innocently, and Kirk began to look worried. He laughed, with the look of giving in gracefully.

"All right, Spock. You hooked me. Sure you wouldn't like to tuck me in?"

Spock allowed himself to brighten visibly. "Quite a logical suggestion, I believe." He inclined an eyebrow toward Kirk's door. "Mother's little helper," he said helpfully.

"I'd just like to see you try it . . . No, belay that," Kirk said hastily. "I'm going, already. Before you decide to sing me a lullaby. Good night, Spock."

Spock resisted the temptation. It would ruin his reputation for Vulcan decorum—which was none too secure with this particular Human, in any case—to say, "Sleep tight." Besides, Kirk looked as if he had read the thought without benefit of telepathy. "Good night, Jim," Spock said.

Spock watched the Captain go through the door. Vulcan decorum might have suffered, but Vulcan discipline had made it through one more time of seeing that man go through this door after a day on which he had very nearly died. They both knew that, too.

Spock headed for the bridge. It had been too early to wish James Kirk happy birthday, and Spock was not quite certain that the Captain had fully realized that tomorrow *was* his birthday. But Kirk would discover, eventually, that Spock's last chess move was a special birthday present, planned for weeks for this night, and made this morning in the chess alcove which had been Spock's present to Kirk on his last birthday. The snap-in bulkhead doors had turned a little-needed access corridor between their quarters into a private sanctum-sanctorum where they kept their game-of-games. Their bathroom doors opened onto it, and the Captain of the *Enterprise* had taken to the custom wholeheartedly, finding it a convenient challenge to working out a move or two between showering and shaving.

But when Spock eased in stealthily after a late

tour of the ship, Kirk had not made an answering move. Small wonder. Spock had made a move which a galactic grand master might not answer in a week.

Spock went contentedly to bed. That would occupy Kirk's worry circuits for the better part of a day. However, Kirk would see through it, if Spock knew his Kirk. And he did.

Kirk strolled onto the bridge the next morning, a bit late—some 47.234 minutes—looking a little sheepish, a little lazy, a little expectant, probably not quite certain whether he had rolled over and gone back to sleep after the soft computer call.

Was it Spock's fault if there had needed to be a certain adjustment to the computer, and he had made it at a certain moment in a certain way with a certain predictable but unavoidable result?

There were routine morning greetings from the day-shift bridge crew—except Uhura, who had assigned a relief for an hour, and Sulu, who had excused himself on some errand in the botany lab, leaving the navigator to cover. Spock presented status reports on a clipboard display, showing all quiet.

"Good morning, Captain. You appear rested."

Kirk shot him a small look of wondering whether he was being deviled. "Yes, Mr. Spock. I gather it's been a slow morning at the store."

"Indeed, Captain."

Kirk sat down to dictate the Captain's log. His voice was just an imperceptible fraction off as he said the stardate, Spock perceived. No one had wished Kirk happy birthday.

The navigator flinched, not so imperceptibly, at the date, and Kirk caught it. Plainly, someone had forgotten. Kirk settled his shoulders and dictated the log in the voice of the Starship Captain. But once he glanced up toward Spock's station. He would know that the Vulcan would not forget, but he was Human enough to be a little hurt if others had. And Uhura had not been wrong. There was a certain element of the little boy—very prevalent among Humans, of course, but rather more evident in the Captain at times, since he permitted it to show through. Fortunately, of course, Vulcans. . . .

There was a signal from the intercom and Kirk answered, "McCoy here, Captain. I want you down here first thing for that overdue quarterly physical, and another check-over after your stunt of yesterday. Ten minutes, Jim."

Kirk made a small face. "Pulling medical rank, Bones?"

"If necessary," McCoy grumbled, keeping it light but with just an edge of warning. Spock knew that the Doctor had been shaken by Kirk's narrow escape of yesterday.

Kirk relented a little, knowing it, too. "Can't do it right now Bones. Couple of things to check on. I'll try to fit it in."

"Jim—"

"*Later,* Bones." Kirk softened the tone. "I'll stop by for a quick check at least. Kirk out." There was a grumbled "okay," and Kirk turned to Spock as the elevator doors opened behind him to admit Uhura. "All right, Spock, let's drum up a little business. The planet Arcos is of strategic importance between the Federation and the Klingon Empire. It's been stand-offish to both sides except for limited visitation rights. Now, we didn't ask to rescue the grandson of a Triumvir of Arcos, but we did, and now we have a friend here who has promised to lay our case before the other two members of the Triumvirate. We'll stay here and follow up on that. And—I want a Class One check on all systems on the ship."

Spock felt his eyebrow rising. But it was Uhura who said, in a faint tone of protest, "Class One, sir?"

Kirk whirled the command chair to face her. "Does my Chief Communications Officer have some objection?"

Uhura swallowed and stiffened. "No, sir. I was just thinking that it would take most of the day."

Kirk nodded. "Well, that's what we signed on for,

is it not? Another day, another dollar, just like any other day." Kirk eased off a little. "We don't know what damaged the Arcosian ship, or why its automatic equipment threw everything in the book at me. But since we went through the same region in space and were exposed to an unknown phenomenon, there is, as Spock would say, a finite probability that we have been exposed to some danger. We will check it out. Since you are late, Uhura, you had better get started."

"Yes, sir," Uhura said stiffly, displacing her relief at her board. There was a slight squawk as her relief hit a switch. He had been trying to answer a light, and the signal came through suddenly on audio. Sulu's voice filled the bridge, in a loud, strained whisper. "Uhura, you'd better get back down here fast——"

Uhura moved to cut it off, but not before some searing, screeching noise assaulted Spock's Vulcan eardrums——a symphony of discordance not unlike certain Earth music——or the dismemberment of a starship.

"What was that?" Kirk demanded, coming out of the chair. "Where——?"

"Rec, sir," Uhura said, almost as if reluctantly.

"I *heard* the wreck," Kirk snapped. "Where—— Main Rec? Get Sulu back."

"Yes, sir." Uhura bent over her board in a rather odd position. Spock couldn't see her hands. "No answer, sir."

"From Main Rec?" Kirk said incredulously, already halfway to the elevator and gathering Spock with a nod. "Take the con, Uhura."

Spock was on his way, but Uhura seemed to be in his way. They tangled unaccountably. Uhura was *never* in his way. Then her voice was in his ear, pitched only for a Vulcan ear. "Keep him out of Rec, Mr. Spock, *please*. For me. For h——"

"Spock!" Kirk was looking at them unbelievingly.

Spock lifted Uhura and set her back on her long legs. "Your pardon," he said. "Clumsy of me." She closed her eyes with an expression of such astounded relief and pure love for a Vulcan who would cover for

her that for a moment Spock would have thought she
was going to faint—if he had not known her better.
Then Spock joined Kirk in the elevator, blocking
Kirk's view of the Chief Communication Officer's frantic dive for her board.

"Doubtless some minor malfunction of the recreation or food equipment, Captain," Spock said. "I
can check it out. Why don't you stop for that quick
check you promised the doctor?"

"Whose side are you on?" Kirk complained. "Mc-
Coy wants to glom me for a physical. Half my bridge
crew is late for duty. I thought your report said Sulu
was in the lab? Uhura has her nose out of joint and
manages to fall all over you. And the Main Rec room
won't answer after giving a convincing imitation of a
disaster area. I suppose somebody dropped the set out
of his ring?"

"The metaphor—" Spock began.

"Metaphor, shmetaphor." Kirk turned to him
more seriously. "Spock, am I getting—" he broke off
and finished with "—space nerves?" But had Spock almost heard the word "old"? "Spock, do you have any
feeling that there's something a little bit *off* on the ship?"

That was something, of course, about which there
could be no question of covering. It touched on the
Captain's command intuition, which grew more un-
canny by the year and must not be shaken. "I have had
a trace of some such subliminal awareness," Spock
said gravely. "However, I hypothesize that it is merely
some odd mood of the crew after long stress." Odd, indeed. A Human custom which was becoming totally
clear to him now, without being any less illogical.

"I suppose so," Kirk sighed. "God knows, they've
got every right . . ."

– The elevator decanted them on the recreation
level. Kirk cut a straight line for the door in question.
Spock saw no practical means—

He took a hasty step, caught a toe on the heel of
his boot, and fell in front of Kirk. But he had mis-
estimated the Human's speed and singularity of drive.
He had hoped only to delay Kirk with picking Spock

up—possibly Spock could manage a wrenched ankle, sickbay—

Instead Kirk fell over him, and the Vulcan was hard-put to break the Human's fall. They wound up in a tangle, Kirk's breath going out of him in a grunting wheeze. And then Spock was rising, the Human in his arms like a child. "You've hurt yourself, Captain. Unforgivably clumsy of me. I will get you to sickbay. One moment now. Hold on . . ."

"Spock!" Kirk roared—although it came out rather more as a gasp. "Spock!" he whispered through his teeth, seeing crew members observing them from all over the rec level. "What do you think you are doing? Put me *down*." He started to wrench himself free, but he hadn't really quite reckoned with Vulcan muscles. He never quite did.

"Assisting the injured, Captain," Spock said rather loudly. "You will recall Dr. McCoy's last lecture on not walking on an injury. Only yesterday . . ."

"I'm not hurt, Spock. *Put me down.*" It was a whisper. Otherwise it would have rocked the *Enterprise* from bow to nacelles. Figuratively, of course. It was one thing for the Captain to be carried home with his shield or on it, or even by Vulcan muscles, when he was truly hurt. It was quite another to be carried through the *Enterprise,* knowing that he didn't even dare to struggle, and would look feeble if he did. "Spock . . ."

"Quite all right, Captain—"

Chief Engineer Scott popped out of the elevator as they reached it. His eyes did not even widen. "Morning, Captain. Mr. Spock."

"Mr. Scott, see to the Rec room," Spock ordered.

"Aye, Mr. Spock," Scott said, looking a little crestfallen. "I believe my poor wee bairns of food automats may have been into mischief. I'll see to it."

"*Mister* Scott—" Kirk began.

"The Captain has had a fall," Spock said. "Have you hit your head, Captain?"

"I have *not.* Have you hit yours? Or are you just out of your mind?"

"Neither," Spock said, privately doubting the veracity of the latter denial. But his Vulcan hearing was in working order, and he was hearing other doors of the Rec room opening and closing, as well as a certain amount of noise within, rather odd, unidentifiable noises. But possibly the stalling was working and the bodies were being buried.

"In that case, Mr. Spock," Kirk said very quietly, evenly, "you will put me down. That is an order."

"Certainly, Captain," Spock said. "You might have said so in the first place. However—" the elevator doors whooshed open again, "—it is against my medical judgment."

"*Whose* medical judgment?" Dr. McCoy said, stepping out of the elevator, medical scanner in hand. "I had a report of an injury." He ran the scanner over Kirk.

"Put me down, Spock," Kirk whispered silkenly.

"Of course, Jim," Spock said innocently and swung Kirk to his feet. It was in the lap of the gods now, as the Humans would say. Kirk was looking rather like the god of war. He didn't even splutter. He marched to the Rec room door. It opened and he sailed through under full impulse power.

And fell, not on his head.

Spock charged in ahead of the others, treading lightly on the goo on which Kirk had slipped, and retrieved him off the floor once again. There was a small gobbet of goo—something like frosting?—on his face, and what looked rather like a fat, red cherry sliding gently down the Captain's nose.

Kirk disposed of it with vast, monumental, longsuffering calm as another gobbet sailed past from the food dispensers. Spock scooped him up and made for the door, recognizing only then a dejected figure completely covered with goo: Sulu.

Sulu managed to get one eye open and winked at Spock. The Vulcan gathered that the bodies, at least, had been buried. He put Kirk down outside the door without order.

Kirk turned one of his looks on him. "Thank you,

Mr. Spock," he said with infinite patience, and turned the look on Scott and McCoy. "Do you gentlemen have anything to say?"

"Nary a word, Captain," Scott said, looking as if he had swallowed a tribble.

"Can't think of a thing, Jim," McCoy said, with an equal look of cat-on-a-canary-diet. " 'Course, that's only a medical opinion."

Kirk turned, *"Mister* Sulu?"

Sulu dripped white and grinned through it sheepishly, and swallowed hard, "I—just stopped in for coffee and cake on my way from the lab, sir. I—got the cake."

"I see," Kirk said. "While you were more than an hour late for duty?"

"Yessir," Sulu said stiffly, stoutly.

"You're on report, Mr. Sulu. You, personally, will clean this mess up. Mr. Scott, fix the machinery. Class One check on everything aboard." He turned to Spock. "Mr. Spock, if you will be good enough to concentrate on using the muscles between your elegant ears and determine what caused this debacle . . ."

"Certainly, Captain."

"Mr. Spock, did you see anything—odd—in there?"

Spock raised an eyebrow. "Practically everything. Did *you?*"

Kirk shook his head. "I didn't see it, either," he said definitively. "Bones, I think I *do* need to be examined."

McCoy started to run his scanner near the area of impact. "Not *that* end, Bones," Kirk said, and marched to the elevator. "And," he said over his shoulder, "nobody better venture to tell me not to walk on the injury!" Nobody did. Even Spock maintained a prudent silence. McCoy shot after Kirk into the elevator just as the doors closed, but Scott turned to Spock with a look of deviling appraisal.

"Beggin' your pardon, Mr. Spock," he said in his best Scots manner, "but would y' mind tellin' me— what kind of a performance was *that?*"

Spock gave him his best Vulcan eyebrow. "Performance, Mr. Scott? Are you under the impression that you saw anything but the routine performance of my duties?"

Scott tried not to break up. "Aye, laddie, that I am. Your Vulcan cover is blown forever. Welcome to the human race, Mr. Spock."

"A dubious honor, Mr. Scott, but well-intended, I'm sure."

Scott could stand it no longer. He grinned all over his face. "You old fraud, I always knew you had it in you. Happy Captain's birthday, Spock."

Spock resisted an impulse to sigh. They had all known, then—a fact of which he had remained in some doubt—and they had not told him, doubtless supposing that he could see no logic in it. Or perhaps that he couldn't help "spilling the beans" to Jim Kirk. Well, they were not so far wrong. "Birthday?" he said blandly. "Surely you wouldn't want me to assume that this has anything to do with a birthday? Let us say that I was merely being—mother's little helper. Carry on, gentlemen."

He left them looking stupefied and made a proper Vulcan exit to the elevator. "Bridge," he told the elevator, and did not quite mutter—"I have to see a certain mother about a party."

Even so, Spock was not prepared for Uhura. She popped into the elevator as the doors opened, took his face, ears and all, firmly between her hands and pulled him down, and herself up, enough to kiss him. He felt the warm silk of her lips for one moment on his and then brushing his ear, whispering, "Mr. Spock, I'm sorry, I love you, you were gorgeous, will you take the con?"

Spock extricated his ears, not too hastily, by clasping her wrists firmly and looking down at her sternly as the doors closed behind her. "Do you consider this proper, logical behavior for a senior officer —and a mother, Lieutenant?"

She laughed breathlessly and put on her best

officer's face, with only a trace of imp. "Oh, *yes,* indeed, Mr. Spock."

He nodded. "I have the con. Carry on."

Her eyes sparkled. "Yes, *sir!*" Then the worried frown collected between her eyebrows. "We'll never get him to a Rec room now—let alone *that* one. It has to be someplace where he'll just walk in . . . Do I have your permission to use any suitable area on the ship, sir?"

"I forbid you nothing," Spock said. "However, do you wish me to assume that you have a purpose which requires—?"

She stretched her fingers up to stop his lips. "What you don't assume can't hurt him," she said thoughtfully. "Is that it?" She chuckled. "Mr. Spock, if you will release my wrists, I will ask you no questions, and you will tell him no lies."

He unlocked the light grip of his fingers. "I was sure that you would see the logic of my position."

He moved to activate the door control again and moved crisply onto the bridge wearing his Vulcan face, but wondering whether anyone would notice a slight green flush at the eartips.

Spock started the Class One check, covering the area of his special responsibilities and Uhura's. She, presumably, would be preoccupied. The Doctor would doubtless see to it that the Captain was the same. Where would she move the event about which Spock was making no assumptions? Never mind. The check must proceed. There was, obviously, something wrong with the computer control of the food equipment. Was there more? Had Kirk believed he had seen something? If he did, he had. The Captain did not "see things" unless they were there. If he had glimpsed something which could leave him in some doubt, it had to be extremely subliminal, or the Captain himself would know for certain that he had seen it, and be taking the ship apart. Kirk did not doubt his own mind.

Spock felt a kind of leaden sensation somewhere in the region of his stomach. Had his own improbable behavior thrown Kirk off? The Humans had a word for it—several: "Oh, what a tangled web we weave . . ."

This was the Vulcan's first practice to deceive Jim Kirk—apart from those transparent deceptions which were intended as such and known as such by both of them. "Merely my quite logical concern that Starfleet not lose the services of an excellent commander . . ."

"Would you mind taking a look at my last chess move . . . ?"

Was there really any logic in the illogical Human custom about which he was making no assumptions? He could visualize Kirk's stunned delight if they pulled it off . . .

"McCoy to bridge," the intercom cut in. "Uhura, he's on the loose."

"Spock here. Loose, Doctor?"

"Oh, uh . . ." Spock could hear the wheels clicking. Was Spock really in the know, or had he just been solicitous on his own account? And how far would the Vulcan go? "Uh, I just meant to say, the Captain decided to shower and change before the exam."

"Message understood, Doctor. I shall give it top priority. Spock out."

The bridge crew was staring at the Vulcan, but the Vulcan was busy having a sudden prescient vision of catastrophe. He had never fully believed in intuition. Intuition was normally the lightning sum of things known but not analyzed. This was, but that did not stop it from being intuition. He heard Uhura's voice saying "Someplace where he'll just walk in . . . do I have your permission . . . ?" And his own, saying "I forbid you nothing." He must have known, even then. Of course Spock's quarters, or Kirk's. It was well known that, by Vulcan convention and in declaration of equal trust of his shipmates, Spock did not leave his door locked. Through his quarters and into Kirk's one could . . .

Spock was trying the intercom in his cabin, silently, not daring to call out, merely looking through the viewscreen. He caught a last glimpse of Uhura tiptoeing through his bathroom door, reaching the door to the connecting alcove.

"Uhura!" Spock said in a strangled whisper. But she didn't hear him. And it was much too late.

The door from Spock's bathroom to the alcove whooshed. Uhura jumped as if caught, then gathered herself and peeked through the door—not resisting a look toward the famous chess game. If this be invasion of privacy, make the most of it. Well, she had permission, didn't she—of a sort? The thought was written in her tiptoeing stance.

Spock shifted to the alcove camera pickup which recorded their chess game for posterity.

And at almost the same moment catastrophe presented itself for posterity's inspection.

Kirk's bathroom door opened and he stepped out, dripping.

"Sp—" he began, the towel barely gathered around him, and finished "—ock . . ."

"Captain!" Uhura squeaked in a high, emaciated coloratura.

The Captain of the *Enterprise* attempted to gather the towel and his dignity around him. Neither seemed to cover the situation.

The Chief Communications Officer was attempting the same—without benefit of towel. And she was attempting to keep her eyes front and center and up, also without complete success.

She stood caught between officer and woman, and Spock could see it coming to her that she was also well and truly caught with cream all over her face. There was no conceivable explanation which she could give for being in Spock's quarters, let alone the chess alcove, let alone confronting a nearly naked male specimen who just happened to be her Captain.

Her coloring did not betray her, but Spock judged that his heat sense would have registered the deep blush from three paces. Kirk's coloring, of course, required no such delicate perception.

Uhura drew herself up. "Sir," she said.

"Sir!" Kirk exploded quietly. *"Madam*—would you *mind* explaining what you are doing here? I won't even mention a little item such as the fact that I left you the con. Just kindly explain what you are doing in Mr. Spock's quarters, not to mention—"

"Captain," Uhura said with cold and fiery dignity. "Obviously there is a logical explanation." She looked as if she were still trying to think of one, but she plunged on with dignity and decorum. "Obviously Mr. Spock relieved me of the con. You cannot suppose that I would leave my post without proper relief."

Kirk sighed. "I said I wouldn't mention it. Although during a Class One check . . . But—*Spock's* quarters? Vulcan privacy . . ."

Uhura took refuge in offense. "You cannot suppose that I would not have Mr. Spock's permission."

"To come into our private—" Kirk broke off. "I've never known him to give permission . . ."

Uhura gulped and drew cool self-possession around her. "Does it not occur to you, sir, that I might be on an errand for Mr. Spock? For example, that your Class One check would keep him on the bridge, but he might be humanly curious to see whether you have made a move? Perhaps to answer it?"

Kirk's eyebrows lifted. It hadn't occurred to him for the simple reason that Spock would not have done it, not in that way. But to question Uhura's word . . . Nor did it quite occur to him that she had phrased it as a question.

She struck before it did. "You aren't supposed to be here, you know."

"*I'm* not," Kirk said indignantly. "This happens to be *my*—"

"You might at least stay where you're supposed to be," Uhura said, "and not come bursting in on people in a towel. Not much of a towel, at that. And here you are being the Captain in a . . . a *towel*. Well, Mr. Spock can make his own chess move, and I'll make mine. If you will excuse me, *sir*—"

She turned to march out through Spock's quarters —a brilliant retreat in good order, Spock thought, having the look of an attack. Kirk stared after her. But some devil made her turn over her shoulder. "Sir—you're dripping."

Spock saw the flush gather in Kirk's face, not of embarrassment. "Uhura," he said sweetly, softly, almost sensuously.

Uhura's back tightened and she stopped in midstride, almost as if her knees threatened not to cooperate. Kirk was calling her back. That tone . . . It wasn't possible . . . ? Speculation was written in her body, and she shivered slightly as she turned back slowly.

Kirk surveyed her deliberately. "Uhura," he began in the same soft, slow tone, "I am not a little boy —or a captain—all the time."

Uhura's composure was faltering. "I am—fully aware of that." She swallowed a "sir." Her turn had put her close to him again in the narrow alcove. He reached out a hand and tipped up her chin. "I also am fully aware—" he went on without a break in the tone, "—that there is something going on on my ship. I don't know whether my senior officers, not to mention the computer, are going bonkers—or whether it's something really serious. You are an utterly reliable officer, and you are off station—and in the soup—during a Class One check. I would consider it a great personal favor if you would give me a sensible explanation—or make Mr. Spock's chess move—or confine yourself to quarters."

Uhura blinked hard. "Confine to quarters?"

Kirk held her eyes. "I trust that will not be necessary."

Spock snapped off his screen and was moving. He was in the turbolift before it occurred to him that he had forgotten to designate who should take the con —something he could not remember doing in his lifetime.

The turbolift took interminable seconds, and he ran to the snap-in bulkhead door and keyed the emergency release to step into the alcove. They were still in the same pose, Uhura fighting back tears of frustration and outrage.

Spock raised a Vulcan eyebrow. "Your pardon, Captain," he said as if he had accidentally burst in on an assignation. "And yours, Uhura. When you did not return from your errand, I feared you had encountered some difficulty. If you will excuse me . . ." He started to turn—

Kirk jerked his hand away from Uhura's chin. "Spock!" Spock turned back. "It's not—" Kirk cut himself off. "Did you actually—?" He stopped again. "Uhura was about to make your chess move." He did not quite challenge them to prove that they had not both been lying to him, covering for each other in some inconceivable conspiracy.

"Of course," Spock said blandly. "Uhura, would you mind?" She looked at him, a little panicked. She? Make a move in their game-of-games? But Spock held her eyes steadily and she covered and moved toward the board.

"Of course, Mr. Spock," she said steadily. Kirk watched for some signal between them, but Spock gave none. Uhura would have little time to analyze the board, but it was an endgame, reduced to a few pieces. Spock had seen at a glance that Kirk had made the one and only brilliant move he could make, and it left essentially only one move which did not result instantly in checkmate. Uhura was an accomplished player, and progressing. If she saw it . . .

"I of course was anxious to reply to your . . . rather irritating . . . move, Captain," Spock said, to give her time. "Naturally I didn't suppose that you would be . . . in your towel . . ."

Kirk flushed. "Spock—"

"I see what you mean, Mr. Spock," Uhura said sweetly. "Thank you for doing me the honor of letting me see it. Your instruction in chess has been most valuable, and to see a game which is a masterwork . . . You're sure you wouldn't rather make the move yourself, now that you're here?"

"You may have the honor, Uhura. My pleasure. You have been a most apt pupil." *I hope,* Spock told himself silently and fervently.

She reached out decisively and made the move—

the right one. Spock considered fainting. Kirk looked as if he might. Uhura looked cool, almost smug.

"May I return to duty—*sir?*"

Kirk wavered between breaking up and exploding. "Get out of here, both of you," he said, "and leave me in my towel in peace."

"Yes, sir," Uhura said, sidling past him, and Spock bowed her out the door, cocked an unreadable eyebrow at Kirk, and stepped after her, closing the bulkhead door behind him.

Uhura almost collapsed into his arms in a silent pantomime of relief, laughter, shock. Someone passed them with climbing eyebrows. Spock lifted one in reply, daring anyone to see anything other than the routine performance of his duties. He hustled Uhura around the curve of the corridor.

"Oh, Mr. Spock, it *was* the right move?"

He bowed gravely. "You are an apt pupil."

She giggled, then tried to regain decorum. "It was the only move I saw."

"Precisely."

She grinned. "So that's why you gambled on it. But you took an awful chance." The imp took over her face. "You are an apt pupil, Mr. Spock, sugar."

He was still raising an eyebrow when she turned and ducked into her quarters.

He went back to the bridge. And he sighed.

Spock didn't hear much more for a time. Uhura remained conspicuous by her absence. Christine Chapel came on the intercom to remark to no one in particular that the Captain was in sickbay. Spock checked the computer. There was nothing wrong with it. Records showed a slight, untraceable power surge at the moment when Sulu had tried to program it for birthday cupcakes. Cupcakes? Spock traced another slight power surge to the main food processing area, and tuned in the intercom to see Uhura watching a conveyor belt deliver one extra-large birthday cake and fourteen smaller ones all in a row, like a Mother Goose with goslings. Uhura traded looks with a bedraggled Sulu and turned her eyes ceilingward.

Spock switched off the intercom and rechecked the computer. What is real is not without cause. However, there was no known cause which could be responsible. Class One checks of all systems also showed nothing. But Spock's intuition was joining the Captain's in going off like a bell. Yet it was still probably only the infectious mood of the crew.

Chapel chimed in again to say that the Captain was about to leave sickbay. Spock could almost feel the scurry throughout the ship.

Uhura and Sulu scooted in, wearing the twin expressions of somewhat exhausted partners in crime, and scattered their reliefs like startled geese. The reliefs recovered and busied themselves ostentatiously at auxiliary boards just as the Captain strode onto the bridge.

Kirk looked it over, a sedate, businesslike, orderly, innocent bridge. His eyes raked over Uhura, saying silently: "Innocent?" She looked at him with her best Vulcan face. A remarkably good imitation, Spock noted.

"Mr. Spock, report," Kirk said crisply, all business.

"Class One check shows nothing abnormal except two power surges in the computer, affecting the food processing equipment," Spock said.

"Two?" Kirk groaned. "Don't tell me that the mess halls are up to their knees in chicken soup?"

"No, sir. Everything under control," Spock said —truthfully, he hoped. Where had they stowed the large cake?

Kirk sighed. "Don't tell me. I don't even want to guess. All right, we'll get back to it. Uhura, get me Mori's grandparents. Main screen."

Uhura busied herself, and momentarily it came through. The patrician couple, still in their prime, exchanged greetings with Kirk, obviously delighted at his call.

"How are Mori's parents?" Kirk asked.

Triumvir Moraan smiled with relief. "As your Dr. McCoy said, they are in an odd coma, as if induced by electrical stimulation of the sleep centers of the brain. However, our physicians concur: They will recover completely. We cannot thank you enough."

"Their recovery is already our thanks," Kirk said. "But if you wanted to please a starship Captain, you could let me say hello to Mori."

A slight frown gathered on the distinguished features of Duela. "Captain, I'm not certain that is a good idea. Mori is well, but he is not happy. He keeps talking about missing his 'friend.' He won't say who, but I'm afraid it is you, and since you will have to be leaving soon, I am afraid he would only become more attached and find the good-bye harder."

Kirk's face fell. Every good-bye seemed to get harder. He tried to smile, but it was an effort. "You may be right. I'll check with you before we leave."

Triumvir Moraan answered the question Kirk had not asked. "I may have news of thanks of a more practical nature, Captain."

Kirk nodded his thanks and they ended the call on a satisfactory diplomatic note, but it had not made the Captain happy. Nor was he happy with his crew.

They got through a bad afternoon.

Toward evening Spock was wondering whether the conspirators were scheduling the main event for before or after his birthday dinner with Kirk. Spock hadn't exactly issued the invitation, but Kirk would expect it, and if Spock didn't say something soon, the silence would become thick enough to cut with a *lirpa*.

Spock rejected that metaphor. Cancel and erase. However, the logic remained impeccable. He must ask. But would the Captain even go? He was still feeling the uneasy sense about the ship. For that matter, should he go? Should Spock? The Vulcan did not care to admit to a case of the nervous jitters, but he *knew*, allegedly, what was going on on the ship, and it did not seem to help his case.

There was the subliminal sense of something

else. Spock did not reject that as illogic. They had run into stranger things.

Spock moved down to the Captain's chair. "Jim," he said in a low voice, "about tonight . . ."

Kirk brightened visibly.

There was a sound from Uhura's board. Spock wondered whether she had manufactured it. He looked up. She shook her head frantically at him behind Kirk's back, then as Kirk swung the chair she was instantly into her "hailing frequencies open" suit. "Incoming call, sir. Mori's grandparents."

Kirk nodded, and turned back to the main viewscreen while she put it on the screen. "Captain, I don't wish to trouble you," the grandfather said, "but it appears that Mori is truly inconsolable for his friend. I wonder if you could—"

Kirk's face lit from the inside. "Absolutely. Tell him—he's invited to a party. No—don't tell him." He stood up as the grandparents beamed all over him. "Alert the transporter room," he said to Uhura. "Take the con." He inclined his head toward the screen. "On our way. Kirk out."

He turned to Spock as the screen went dark. "Mr. Spock, we have checked everything that moves, including your king. Is there anything on this ship that cannot wait while one lonely little boy sees a friend and has a party?"

Spock straightened up and looked down at his Captain. "No," he said, and after a moment, "sir."

"You're invited, Spock." Kirk turned toward the turbolift, not waiting for an answer. Spock was at his shoulder, but he looked back over his to Uhura.

"Stall him!" she mouthed silently and urgently. "Spock, please!"

Spock lifted the wrong eyebrow at her and almost bumped into Kirk as he turned back to see where he was going. Kirk steadied him as the doors closed behind them. "Something wrong with you today, Spock?" he asked, not concealing a tone of worry.

"No, sir," Spock said, truthfully. Not unless you count needing my Vulcan head examined, he added silently. "Preoccupation, possibly. Jim, would you mind stopping by my quarters?"

Kirk nodded to him with just a trace of the small, secret look of the little boy. Trust Spock, it said. He would have some surprise up his Vulcan sleeve.

Indeed.

Spock bowed Kirk into his cabin, trusting hopefully that there were no guilty traces of comings and goings, stray bits of decorations or the like, and that Uhura would have the sense to use the bulkhead door which he had left unlocked.

The tray which he had set out on the desk that morning was undisturbed. Kirk saw it—the Vulcan glasses and decanter, the package gift-wrapped in a Vulcan adaptation of the Human custom.

Kirk laughed softly in simple delight. "Thank you, Spock. I guess I'm not very grown up at that." He stretched and eased some of the tension out of his shoulders, looking suddenly very young.

Spock stopped with the decanter poised over a glass. "I would not want to contribute to the delinquency of a minor."

Kirk smiled threateningly. "I wouldn't want to have to continue the education of a Vulcan in minor delinquency—just now."

Spock raised a bland, slightly regretful eyebrow. "I believe that education may be nearing completion," he said cryptically, and poured the drink. Then his hand froze. His Vulcan hearing was picking up sounds from beyond his bathroom door. Surely Kirk wouldn't hear. Spock clinked the glasses unnecessarily.

But Kirk suddenly cocked his head alertly toward his cabin. "Did you hear something?"

Spock hastily handed him the glass. "The sound-proofing is excellent. Health and long life, Jim."

Kirk raised the glass, trying to pull his attention back. Then there was a fatal sound which sounded very much like a suppressed giggle—faint, but unmistakable, even in direction.

"I *did* hear something," Kirk said. "From my cabin." He started to swing around the desk.

"Surely not, Jim," Spock said, stopping him with a look. "If you could hear something from your cabin from here, then I of course would always be able to hear—much more." He fixed Kirk with possibly the best transparently unreadable Vulcan look he had ever managed. He saw it go through Kirk like slow ice, distracting him completely, as intended.

Spock needed no telepathy to read the thoughts. This was a very private man, and very much a man, and there had been times when he had counted on the excellent soundproofing. There had been times when he had needed it badly. Not all of their guests were soft-spoken schoolteachers from Iowa. Kirk looked as if he could not offhand recall one who had been. Aliens, Princesses, Doyens—no, that had not been his cabin. The Petruskan Empress with the custom of . . . ! Had Spock been on duty then? No.

Kirk looked at Spock helplessly, a slow flush rising into his face, radiating across the distance.

"You didn't," Kirk said, for once not having a quick comeback. Then he pulled himself together. "You're absolutely right, Mr. Spock, I didn't hear a thing. I couldn't possibly have heard anything. Could I?"

Spock looked at him innocently over the rim of the glass. "It would be Humanly impossible, Captain." He lifted the toast again. "Infinite diversity in infinite combinations, Captain."

"Spock," Kirk said dangerously.

"Well," Spock said, finding the perfect echo of Kirk's long-ago tone. "There's no need to be embarrassed about it, Captain. It happens to the birds and the bees."

Kirk looked at him, stopped, realizing that the Vulcan must have been wanting to say that for years. Spock was only just realizing that himself.

Kirk lifted his glass with the ultimate look of long-suffering. "The birds and the bees," he said slowly, "are not starship Captains. If they were, with certain diplomatic obligations, they might have rather more than logic ripped from them at times." He touched his glass to Spock's and the starship Captain's boyish eyes were wickedly innocent over the rim of it, and still set in hot cheeks.

"I haven't heard a word you've said," Spock quoted, and they drank the fiery Vulcan drink, celebrating how far they had come since those words were in dead earnest.

Kirk made a face over the fire of the drink or the fire in his own face. "I certainly hope not. And if you *did*—where were you when I needed you?"

Spock was trying to think of a logical answer to *that* when the fatal sound came through again like the dropping of the other shoe.

Kirk set the glass down swiftly, very deliberately, softly. Spock almost dropped his. The Captain moved very fast to and through the bathroom doors, and came rebounding back from the alcove even faster to throw an arm in front of the Vulcan, almost around him, blocking his way. "Don't go in there! *I didn't leave that door open!*"

Spock saw the door to Kirk's bathroom standing open and the inner door into his cabin standing closed, even as Kirk moved. Spock was slow by a fraction, the fraction of knowing in shock what was wrong, while Kirk knew only that there was some unknown presence on his ship—and that it was in his quarters.

Kirk yanked the antique handgun off Spock's weapon wall and was back through the doors, and across the alcove and bathroom to the closed door, with Spock's "No, Jim!"—and Spock—after him, helplessly one step behind tragedy. The gun was in perfect working order—and loaded.

The inner door of Kirk's bathroom opened into his cabin—and Kirk leaped in, slammed his hand on the light switch, and leveled the gun at every alien intruder he had ever faced. Except—this alien had the very same face as Uhura. A dozen bright voices started to chorus a *"Surprise—"* They choked on it in mid-screech. Everybody froze.

By some miracle of reflex or training Kirk's finger did not close on the trigger in the first instant, and by no miracle Spock's hand closed over Kirk's in the next instant and bore his arm down, as Spock braced him with the other arm.

The gun did not—quite—go off.

Spock found himself standing with an armful of Captain while everybody considered fainting.

Particularly the Captain. Spock could feel him shaking.

Uhura swallowed. "Surprise . . ." she squeaked voicelessly—and managed to pale visibly.

"Would you kindly unhand me, Mr. Spock?" the Captain whispered.

"Certainly, sir." Spock recovered sufficient aplomb to unhand the Captain and unhand the gun from the Captain and put it down.

Kirk turned on him, "You, too, Spock?"

Spock raised both eyebrows. "Me, sir?"

Kirk groaned. "You, sir. Mother's little helper." He turned on Uhura. "And *you* . . ." He moved toward her slowly, like a stalking *morgril*.

"Sir? Sir . . . Captain . . . ? Happy birthday, sir . . . ?" Uhura retreated slowly until she ran out of room against the packed group and found herself backed up against Dr. McCoy.

"Captain . . . you wouldn't," she faltered.

"Wouldn't I just?" Kirk said wickedly, his hand flattening in anticipation. He bent a little toward her, reaching.

Suddenly Spock caught some odd little flicker of motion, almost like a heat shimmer, subliminal, barely there—behind Kirk—almost as if it were reaching . . .

Kirk straightened abruptly, explosively, almost yelping—his hand reaching back involuntarily as if someone had swatted him—and whirled on Spock behind him. "You wouldn't," he said incredulously. And then, his eyes suddenly hardening. "No, you wouldn't."

"No," Spock said very quietly. "Everyone will remain quite still. There is an alien presence in the room."

"The power-surges," Kirk said, "some kind of energy being . . ." Unknown, his voice said, capabilities, perhaps almost unlimited, loose on his ship . . . here . . . "Spock . . . any telepathic impression?"

Spock was reaching—

A small energy being—about four years old—burst from between the legs of the frozen surprise party. "I want my friend," Mori announced and ran toward Kirk.

Kirk caught him practically out of the air and hugged him hard while bending to shelter him from the alien shimmer with his own body and starting to hand him to Uhura. "I can't now, Mori. Get him out."

"Not *you*," Mori said indignantly, and performed one of those improbable wiggles only possible to Humans and broke free between Kirk's handing over and Uhura's taking possession to scramble between Kirk's legs.

Then the little boy was kneeling and hugging the alien shimmer, which was coalescing into a slightly more visible shape—and wriggling.

Kirk started to dive to pull the boy away, but Spock stopped him with a hand. "Captain . . ." He reached his other hand steadily to the alien.

It felt furry.

He set himself in the Vulcan disciplines so far as he could and opened his mind to it. Kirk was holding his arm. After some interval of time which he did not quite measure, Spock realized that the Captain was shaking him.

"Spock!"

Spock snapped out of it and realized that he was smiling. He straightened his face. "Captain."

"What is it, Spock?" The tone was worried.

Spock almost allowed the smile to creep back. "Mother's little helper," he said.

Kirk stared at him. "Mr. Spock, report," he said, reading Spock to know that there was time. Also, he was kneeling close to Spock with an arm around Mori, and catching some of the wriggle of small boy and—something else.

"It is—a warm puppy," Spock said. "An invisible playmate. A—teddy bear. A *sehlat*. A nurse. A nanny. A firm hand on selected anatomy, when needed."

McCoy snorted. "You mean that the big, bad alien is some kind of an energy entity adapted for children?"

Spock raised his best eyebrow. "I believe that is what I *said*, Doctor."

There was a collective sigh and groan in the room. Spock looked innocent—with his Vulcan half. There was a Human in him somewhere who was considering sitting down very quietly and having hysterics.

Kirk put a hand on Spock's shoulder. "It's completely harmless?"

Spock sighed confirmation. "It is even disposed to take care of adults—particularly those who rush in where children fear to tread." He looked at Kirk. "It stopped Mori's parents from pushing into a dangerous storm, but didn't know its own power."

"It wouldn't hurt anybody," Mori announced. "It's only a sniggly. It's *my* sniggly. Sniggly, meet my friend the Captain. And Mr. Spock and Uhura. I love her, you know. But why didn't you follow me home? You took care of me . . ." The little boy's eyes grew abstracted and Spock felt the child's easy link with the alien. Then Mori looked at Kirk. "Oh. It's sorry. It made the machines on Daddy's ship throw things at you because it thought you wanted to hurt me. Then it realized it had made a mistake and hurt you. And then it wanted to take care of you. It wanted to help with the party. It thought you got into a lot of trouble . . ." Tears started to come to Mori's eyes. He threw his arms around the Captain's neck. "Oh—you need it more than I do. You keep it. I love you. Besides, it's your birthday."

The child's lips were quivering with loss. It was the last present he wanted to give, but for that moment he wanted to give it.

Kirk hugged him and the Captain's eyes were suspiciously bright and his lips none too steady either.

"Thank you, Mori, but it's yours. It has to take care of you for me."

Mori tried to steady his lips, but it was the voice of the very little boy which came out. "You want me to keep it? Can I?"

Kirk looked up at the grandparents, who seemed to have materialized out of the crowd. Uhura had thought of everything. They nodded warmly. And Kirk looked at Spock.

"It transferred to you when you were almost killed," Spock said, "and it wanted to help when it saw people trying to make you happy, but now you are, and it *is* his."

"You can keep it, Mori," Kirk said.

And then there was a certain amount of purely Human sentiment.

Spock didn't think anyone saw him give the alien a small pat. He wondered if they made suitable pets for starship Captains. He could sense in this one's mind a fierce devotion, and the capacity to knock out a hunting *morgril.*

This one was Mori's. However, for another birthday . . .

Presently Kirk surrendered Mori to his grandparents and friend.

And then he turned on Uhura and his command crew, and the fire was back in his eye.

"Now Captain," Uhura said hastily. "It isn't *my* birthday."

"Consider it an unbirthday party," Kirk said, moving slowly toward her.

Spock took a step forward to her side and toward the Captain. It was not, of course, a threat.

In an instant McCoy flanked Uhura on the other side. The entire command crew moved slowly toward the Captain.

His eyes widened. "You—all of you. Bluffing."

They moved. He threw up his hands. "I'm not calling. For once, I know when I've been out-maneuvered." He started to break up, the laughter starting from his stomach. Then he made one very quick move, got through their guard, kissed Uhura quickly but very firmly—and then was more or less falling on their necks. "I ought to throw you all in the brig. Did somebody say something about a party?"

Eventually they were all a little numb, from shock or other causes. The party had spilled out into the corridors to include more of the crew—all of it, at one time or another, Spock thought. The grandparents had left with Mori and friend—and a promise of allegiance to the Federation.

Kirk was feeling mellow. Gifts had been presented. Cake had been consumed. Practically everyone had gone home. Spock abstracted Kirk from the remaining guests and they drifted into the chess alcove. Spock made the one move he had left to make, the only one possible.

Kirk saw it then. There had been no way out for Spock for the last several moves—provided that his opponent played faultlessly, brilliantly. No punches had been pulled. On the next move, Kirk would win with checkmate. Spock tipped over his king in acknowledgment of defeat.

He handed Kirk the package he had retrieved from his cabin. Kirk opened it. It was a gold medal, a grand master's award for a game of spectacular brilliance. Spock had sent the game record to the leading grand master for analysis, as if the game were already finished in the way he had known it would be. The medal was mounted on a cube which recorded the grand master's comments and citation for Kirk's game, and which would project a holographic display of the record of the game—the moves, occasionally their hands or faces. Spock had edited it.

Spock saw Uhura approaching them from the doorway, an approving glint in her eye, as if watching two little boys seriously at their play. She poured each of them a fresh drink. "A mother's work is never done," she purred over her shoulder as she started to leave.

Kirk looked back numbly at the gift, not quite taking it in. Spock touched the controls to show his projection of the last few moves, side-by-side with the actual ones, even the move which showed Uhura's hand. Her eye had been caught from the door and she saw the predicted moves and the real ones matching identically, as if Spock could read more than minds, at least where his Captain was concerned. The last holograms merged on Spock's hand tipping over his king. The grand master's citation flashed and hung suspended in the air.

Kirk only looked at the Vulcan.

"Surprise!" Spock said.

Editors' Introduction to "Snake Pit!"

The women who go "where no *man* has gone before" also have to be in the where-no-man, outside-the-square category, cast in no mold and stopped by no boundaries.

Star Trek recognized that with Romulan Commanders, Amazons, matriarchs and the like, but it remained for what we might call the second generation of *Star Trek* fiction to develop that kind of theme fully, particularly for Uhura and Christine Chapel. We have had many requests for stories featuring one or the other, or both, as they must really be.

Chapel, after all, is a doctor of research biology who trained as a nursing specialist in order to get into space to search for her lost fiancé Roger Corby. She found him, lost him, then found an outside-the-square love for a Vulcan—and a profound admiration for the starship Captain who saw her through the search for Roger Corby.

In this story, Chapel isn't going to let that Captain down, and she certainly is not going to go back to face a certain Vulcan without him . . .

Connie Faddis is also a woman who is stopped by no boundaries. A talented writer, she also does magnificent artwork, and is the editor and publisher of a beautiful, well-produced *Star Trek* fanzine, *Interphase*.

This marks her first professional publication, but obviously not her last—and it is by no accident that she is represented here by two stories, "Snake Pit" and "Marginal Existence."

SNAKE PIT!

by Connie Faddis

The belligerent heat of Vestalan stuck the brief skirt of her nurse's uniform to her legs with sweat, and Christine Chapel squirmed as decorously as possible while standing "at ease" beside Captain Kirk and in front of the head of the botanical collections station. Kirk had expertly prodded the Administrator into a defensive fury to test the man's honesty, and the crossfire became intense enough, finally, for Chapel to discreetly pull away the clinging fabric without anyone noticing. Her attention was focused more on her discomfort than on the argument. She already knew more about Vestalan and its problems than she cared to, anyway—this world held only sighs for her since Roger Corby had died. She was relieved that Dr. McCoy had decided he didn't need her in the station's infirmary. She preferred to leave this place. She'd have preferred not to return here at all, but a career on a starship precluded such choices: She went where duty dictated.

"No, for the tenth time, Kirk, my staff did nothing to offend the Hualans!" Gehres was sputtering, his voice cracking with unaccustomed shouting. He looked miserable in his wilting bureaucrat's tunic—the Hualans' crude sabotage of the station's air-coolers had been effective. "Nothing. They brought us the usual twenty *coatls* last month, we paid them the standard trade goods. Now, the *coatls* are gone, two of my people are dead, two missing, another injured, and the Federation sends you to torment me!"

"Mr. Gehres, I'm here to get at the facts and rectify the situation, if possible, and I can't do that if you're going to withhold information," Kirk accused.

Gehres was not a bureaucrat at heart, he was a

33

good chemist who'd been staked out to languish in the draining heat of administrative tension. The humid sweatbox of Vestalan's ocean-saturated biosphere did him as little good: He yanked open his tunic's fiendishly high collar and threw himself into the nearest chair, devil take protocol.

"I've told you everything I know. There's some kind of revival of an old cult—a *coatl* cult," he wheezed. "If the bigwigs at Starfleet hadn't cut back my staff, there'd be a sociologist on top of the problem. As things stand, we may have to abandon the whole station. Can't take *coatls* without 'express permission of the planet's inhabitants,' and the damned beasts don't seem to survive outside their biosphere. Can't make Derivative 249 without *coatl* venom. Can't treat pan-human neurotransmission disorders without D-249. Can't do a goddamned thing!"

"I'm aware of the significance of this project," Kirk said flatly. "My orders were quite explicit, Mr. Gehres: Find the cork and pull it."

Gehres squinted up at Kirk dismally. "Captain, please . . . I'm not your antagonist. And I'm not sitting on the cork."

Christine felt sorry for Gehres and not a little angry at Kirk's badgering. And she knew that if she didn't beam up to the ship's cool corridors soon, she might melt.

"Pardon me, sir," she interrupted, "but I know Lieutenant Commander Domberwicky, and I'm sure he'll reestablish his former rapport with the Hualans very quickly. May I suggest that we wait for his report?"

"Who's this Domberwicky?" Gehres snapped.

"One of my ship's socioanthropology staff," Kirk said. "He's had previous professional experience with the Hualans. I sent him out to appraise the situation this morning."

"Alone?"

"His professional opinion dictated it. I respect his judgment."

Gehres threw his hands up.

"They'll kill him! Didn't you see what happened to the last two emissaries I sent?"

Christine winced involuntarily, her mind drawn away on a tangent; she'd seen the Hualans' victims, gruesome sacrifices to some horrible ritual, their corpses contorted by the slow venom of Vestalan's priceless serpents. Only a few drops of the anti-venom would have saved those lives, but the station's supply had been stolen.

Ensign Chekov appeared at the doorway.

"Excuse me, Keptain, but it's almost sixteen-hundred. You're supposed to meet Commander Domberwicky. You asked me to remind you."

"Thank you, Ensign," Kirk answered. "How's Scotty coming on the damaged equipment?"

Chekov couldn't suppress a grin. "By hiss rate of cursink, sair, I don't think it's too serious."

The Captain turned back to Gehres. "All right, Mr. Gehres, I believe you—for the moment. I'll be back in an hour or so. Maintain tight security on the labs, and try to stay out of the way of the damage-repair parties, won't you?"

Chekov returned to his tasks, and Kirk gestured to Chapel, following her out of the stuffy office, down the long furnace of corridor, and out into the clearing. There, the heat was still oppressive, but at least there was the prevailing breeze up off the great global ocean that kept the archipelagos livable. Kirk stopped and leaned against one of the airy *'gav* trees to wipe his streaming face. He noticed, then, that Nurse Chapel was standing at a formal, full attention.

"Something bothering you, Nurse?" he asked politely.

"Yes, sir," she said earnestly, "I thought—if you'll pardon my opinion, Captain—that you were rather hard on Mr. Gehres, sir."

Kirk blinked at her in surprise. "As a matter of fact, I was a regular son of a bitch," he admitted wryly. "Part of the job, I'm afraid. Do you know Mr. Gehres, Miss Chapel?"

"No, sir, but I do know something about how

perplexing things can get on this planet. I know how complicated and tentative the trade arrangements with the Hualans are, and I appreciate how—illogical— their behavior often seems."

"And you said you know Domberwicky," Kirk added, intrigued. "Is there some connection I'm missing?"

Chapel flushed. "Irvin was the station sociologist when I was last here. His methods may seem eccentric, but he really does understand and get along with the Hualans."

"Commander Domberwicky's record is distinguished," the Captain agreed. "May I ask when you were on Vestalan before?"

The nurse hesitated. "Some years ago, I was a staff physician engaged in neurochemical research."

"Hmmmm. I didn't know you're a doctor!"

"It's a good background for becoming Head Nurse on a starship," she said, matching his smile.* She didn't add that this was where she'd worked as Roger Corby's assistant, where she'd fallen in love with him. Roger's work here, analyzing and improvising on the remarkable medical knowledge of the Hualans' long dead and lost civilizations, had made him famous. That fame, then, and his ideological zeal, had driven him to greater ambitions and, eventually, to his death.

Christine wanted to leave this place. It stirred feelings she'd rather not revive. "Request permission to beam back to the ship, now, sir," she asked.

"Sorry, Miss Chapel, but I think I want you along at the rendezvous with Domberwicky. Your opinions could be useful," Kirk said apologetically. "And we're late already."

Christine shook herself out of her dismay and trotted after Kirk. "Where are we going, sir?"

"There's an inlet at the bottom of the path," he said. "Domberwicky took a power-raft and went over

---

*This information is based on a statement made by Majel Barrett Roddenberry at the New York Star Trek Convention, February 1975.

to the big island. Didn't want to risk beaming down there."

Christine caught up to the Captain. The "path" they took was an obstacle course of razor-edged igneous extrusions and looping vines on an incline meant only for goats, but Vestalan's gravity was comparable to Luna's, and the humans moved in it lightly, leaping most of the obstacles. Still, some of the switchbacks were treacherous. Christine caught herself cursing Domberwicky for not reporting in by radio, until she remembered that the superstitious Hualans thought that the boxes that talked were bewitched.

Nearing the base of the mesa, Kirk and Chapel hopped the last rocks and ran down onto the black-grained beach. Several abandoned huts, raised on poles, sat in disrepair at the surf's edge, but no one was in sight. The *'gav* trees sighed in the wind and the waves sloshed the shore, but nowhere was there the sound of a power-raft.

"He's late," Kirk growled. "I *knew* he should have taken a communicator."

"Maybe he's around there," Christine suggested, pointing at an arm of the inlet that snaked out of sight behind the trees.

"We'll look."

Kirk led the way, staying on the packed sand at the water's edge. He ducked between the supporting poles of one of the huts.

With only the crackle of parting reeds, black-spotted ochre figures slipped down out of the rotting flooring and made a neat corral of bodies around Kirk and Chapel. Kirk spun around in momentary bewilderment and opened his mouth as if to say something, but he had no voice. Another Hualan blew a second dart into Kirk's torso, and the captain's legs collapsed under him, numbed.

Christine thought she was screaming and kicking for all she was worth, but her voice and limbs seemed to have a will of their own, or no will at all. She slumped face-down in the wet sand and watched minute shore-shrimps scurrying to merge into the grains before the next wave's spreading sheath sucked them back into the froth. Nature went on. After what seemed like hours, Christine felt remote sensations of being tied, and a mildewed fiber bag was pulled over her head, shutting out the light. She was carried and dumped on a hard, pitching floor that must have been an outrigger's deck, but her deadened nerves registered no discomfort. She could hear the Hualans' low, nasal voices around her, and recognized the characteristic *mechto* odor—the Hualans were drunk. Close by, someone was wheezing painfully, probably Captain Kirk.

The deck pitched more violently as the craft moved out of the cove and into the main currents. The Hualans began a soft chant with an obscure rhythm, and Christine noted with sleepy disinterest that whatever she'd been dosed with had heightened her nontactile senses acutely. But in her terror and anger, her central thought was: *Domberwicky told them where we'd be!*

Christine had never associated cold with Vestalan: some unexplained phenomenon had melted the polar ice cap millennia ago, drowning most of the planet and its beings while the little world sweltered in a perpetual heat wave. But the stone floor on which the nurse sat, her hands lashed to a post behind her, was as cold and damp as a freshly dug grave. Captain Kirk's body heat radiated across to her a little, but the upright pole between them obstructed the comfort of physical contact.

She'd never imagined thirst on Vestalan, either, where only the mightiest mountain fastness had escaped the great inundation, but now her throat scratched with dryness. At least her blindfold was gone, though night had come and the cramped stone chamber was plunged in inky shadows cut sharply by patches of brilliant moonlight peering through wide chinks in the roof. The room was musty with antiquity. Christine remembered that contemporary Hualans lived in simple shacks built over the surf; these ruins were used only for religious purposes.

One of those religious rites must be occurring somewhere near; drunken, clamorous voices and clattering rhythms, raucous music, drifted into the improvised brig with fluctuating intensity.

Behind her, Christine felt and heard the captain squirming against his bonds. His knuckles jabbed into the small of her back, but the restraining vines were smeared with a sap that stiffened and tightened them hopelessly. Kirk kept struggling until his lacerated wrists convinced him that it was no use. His panting subsided, and he was silent.

"Mr. Spock will have located us on the ship's sensors by now," Christine offered hopefully.

More silence.

"Maybe," Kirk said finally. "It takes time, though."

"He'll be worried."

"Frantic," Kirk admitted, "—for a Vulcan."

"He'll find us."

"Eventually. But it's not as simple to rescue us as it seems. This is a hands-off world: No force or forceful display to be used for any reason."

"Can't he just beam us up out of here?"

"Use of the transporter where the possibility exists of its being witnessed by the Hualans, would be considered a 'forceful display.' Spock's only legal option will be to try to trade for us, if there's time."

"Mister Spock has broken the rules before," Christine said, then added wistfully, "for you."

Kirk made no answer to that. He shifted his weight, trying to find some more tolerable position in which to sit.

"I wonder what's become of Domberwicky?" he mused.

"I think I'd rather not know, sir, if it's all the same to you."

"I should have let you beam up to the ship," Kirk berated himself. "I'm sorry, Christine."

She did not answer, and they said nothing for the length of time it took a single bright star to rise and set in an overhead aperture. The clamor from outside filtered in more loudly for a few moments, then subsided again into a dull background roar.

"Any idea of what's going on out there?" Kirk asked.

"I think it's a ritual. The Hualans only get drunk for religious purposes, if I remember correctly," Christine answered shakily. There'd been screams of pain among the screams of delight in that last outburst of voices. Her imagination was threatening to run away at full tilt.

So, apparently, was Kirk's. "Christine . . . what else do you know about the goings-on at these ceremonies?"

She had to swallow twice to find her voice. "Only what I read in the official anthropological reports," she breathed.

"Yes," the captain said softly, "I read those, too."

Footsteps crunched in the gravel-strewn terrace outside the room, and a torch was thrust through the portal, followed by dappled, pinto-skinned bodies. The Hualans, six of them, were armed with knives and sickle-shaped metal weapons unlike any of the usual Hualan artifacts. A woman, short, moon-faced and overweight, lowered the torch to illuminate Chapel's face and form. She fingered the uniform fabric at the nurse's sleeve, then leaned close as if inspecting Christine for possible ornaments or other souvenirs. Christine barely breathed. The odor of the Hualans' breath was strong enough to embalm a corpse, and there was a dangerous tone in the Hualans' amused conversation. But the woman pulled at the emblem on Chapel's uniform, and when it didn't tear away, she lost interest and walked around the post to gawk at Kirk.

The Hualan who'd inspected Christine ran her free hand over Kirk's body in an obscene manner, then made some suggestions that sent the others into an hysterical laughter which sounded, to Christine's hu-

man ears, more like severe hiccups. Kirk sat quietly
and endured the humiliation. But when the portly
Hualan reached for him a second time, he lashed out
with his feet, knocking her smartly onto her backside.

For that, he took a beating. When the Hualans
went back outside, Christine wriggled as far around the
center pole as she could, twisting to try to have a look
at the captain. He gasped with pain.

"Captain—Jim—lay your head back to slow the
bleeding," she said. "Are you hurt badly?"

Kirk sniffed, his nose still streaming blood.

"No . . . I'll be all right," he said soberly. "Don't
these people have *any* redeeming qualities?"

"I've never known them to be cruel before, except for the stories about cult rituals," she ventured.
"Domberwicky said the rites must have changed; he
said the Hualans are one of the gentlest, kindest peoples
he'd ever worked with."

Kirk shook his head. "What would make the
rituals change?"

"God knows. Maybe the yarrow sticks—or their
local analog—didn't fall right."

Further speculation was prevented by the return
of the Hualans. Kirk's tormentor was not among them.
One piebald-faced male crouched in front of Christine
and held his sickle-weapon at her throat. She got a
good look at it—it looked like beaten gold. A weapon
of gold would not keep an edge if used; such an im-
plement would likely be used only in a seasonal rite.
But it was sharp enough: the cold edge of it, touching
her skin, made her flesh creep.

They were untying Captain Kirk. He offered no
more resistance, but let them haul him up. They
lashed his arms tightly behind his back again with
fresh vines. Christine scrutinized him in the dancing
torchlight and was relieved to see that he was only
superficially damaged. For the moment.

The Hualans were talking excitedly, and they
prodded Kirk toward the exit.

"If you get a chance to run, do it, don't—"

The crunch of a bludgeon ended Kirk's orders.

He crashed to his knees, stunned, and the Hualans dragged him outside. Only then did Christine's guard withdraw the blade from her windpipe. He giggled drunkenly and followed the others. She could hear Kirk's scraping footsteps, as they hauled him down an apparent slope. The guards at the threshold resumed their places, and relative quiet returned.

The shaft of sunlight stabbed through her closed eyelids, and Christine awoke, her neck cramped painfully. She looked around muzzily for a moment and came to full consciousness with a jerking awareness. Daylight! And from the angle of the light streaming into her eyes through the open doorway, it was late in the morning. She pushed herself up straight against the post and wriggled her numbed fingers, stretched the muscles in her shoulders and back as best she could. She had a brow-beating headache and her nose was clogged. Her throat was stripped with dryness.

Then she noticed how quiet it was: there were voices, still, but the clamor of the previous night was gone. The relative silence was ominous, as ominous as the howls of glee and pain she'd heard in the darkness, but she feared this more: Her imagination could encompass what the noise might have entailed, but she had no idea at all what this dread quiet might mean. She strained her ears for some clue, and was rewarded with approaching footsteps. Many footsteps. She braced herself, for what she didn't know, gnawing the inside of her cheek with fright.

A brief flurry of voices erupted just outside, and a silhouette stepped through the sun-dazzled opening: Domberwicky! Alive, unhurt, and unrestrained. He knelt beside her and began to wrench free the knotted vines that held her.

"Are you all right?" he asked solicitously. His prim mouth, pale, squinting eyes and thin white hair made him seem the model of ineptitude.

"I think so," Christine blurted in relief. "When did you get here? Where's Captain Kirk? Why weren't you at the rendezvous—?"

Domberwicky put a hand to her mouth, a gentle yet authoritative gesture.

"There isn't much time. I've made an . . . arrangement . . . with the Hualans for your freedom. You're to go straight to the power-raft at the bottom of the mountain and go back to the station," he told her, and helped her to her feet.

Christine groaned as she straightened, and rubbed her wrists clumsily to stimulate the circulation. Her overtaxed mind was more than willing to obey Domberwicky's instructions, except that she couldn't help being worried about Captain Kirk. She resisted Domberwicky's coaxing assistance toward the door.

"Irvin—wait. Isn't Captain Kirk coming, too?"

The anthropologist's seamed face pulled down into a frown. "Yes, yes, he's fine," Domberwicky said quickly. "The captain's already back at the station. I'll explain everything later."

He was lying. Christine knew it instantly. One of Domberwicky's greatest assets as an anthropologist and intercultural contact with aliens was his transparency: the man abhorred lying and, as such, had simply never developed the skill. He was completely readable, and so was welcomed everywhere as a harmless envoy and an object of curiosity and amusement. His guilelessness made him appear somewhat of an eccentric among humans, but it was his unique brand of diplomacy among alien cultures, and for him it worked.

And Christine *knew* he was lying. The implications knotted her stomach. She spun and clasped Domberwicky's hands urgently. "Irvin, *where's Captain Kirk?!*"

Domberwicky winced. "He's at the station—"

Christine shook her head violently. "No, the truth!"

Undone, Domberwicky groaned. He couldn't lie convincingly to strangers; no use with Christine Chapel, then. "It doesn't matter, Christine, we can't help him. We're fortunate that they're willing to let *you* go. And you must go. *Now*. There may not be another chance."

Christine's mind whirled and threw out an image: Jim Kirk's comforting embrace. *Where?* Roger. Andrea and Roger dying in a blaze of phaser fire. And another image: what she knew now was Spock's first *pon farr*. She remembered Kirk's gray face, lifeless in the grip of the dangerous drug he'd risked to ensure Spock's life. She wasn't going to leave that man to the Hualans.

"Irvin," she growled, "I'm not budging until I know what's happened to Captain Kirk. I have to know."

Surprised at her vehemence, Domberwicky literally squirmed under her stormy gaze. The resolve in her eyes would permit no deception. It was almost a relief to tell her.

"There's a . . . ritual. It's like a game," he sighed, wrestling with words. "They love games. They even put bets on how long the sacrificial victim will last. How long he lives foretells, symbolically, how the tribe's fortunes will go in the next solar year.

"We can't help the Captain, Christine. He's in the snake pit. He's probably dead, believe me. You must take this chance and leave here, save your own life. They've been drunk for days now, and it brings out the worst in them. Go, now, before they change their minds," he pleaded.

Stunned, Christine could only mumble, "What about you?"

"Oh, I'll be fine here, I'm safe. I'm like one of the family, they put up with me," he said, herding her toward the door again.

Christine filled up with a sudden loathing that galvanized her. She threw down Domberwicky's hands in disgust.

"I won't go," she flared, "not without the Captain!"

"Impossible."

"I will not leave him here with those drunken animals," she vowed.

"Be reasonable, Christine," Domberwicky said desperately. "I think I'm close to working out the problem with the Hualans about the station. If you rock the boat now, we may lose our last chance at the galaxy's only source of D-249. Surely the many lives that depend on D-249 outweigh the scruples of your conscience or affections. In any case, the Captain's beyond our help by now."

The nurse, so agitated that her facial muscles cramped, nearly spat in his face. Fleetingly, she wondered how a man could possess such a deep appreciation for any other culture, yet have so little insight into the values of his own. He was genuinely, innocently oblivious to her loyalty to Kirk. His singleminded attentions were solidly fixed on his original goal, the treaty, and there could be no diversions, no delays.

Her bitterness armed her for autonomous action. "All right, maybe Captain Kirk is dead, but I want to see for myself. And if you don't take me there right away, I'm going to grab that guard's weapon and start a fight," she threatened, meaning every word.

"You can't do that!"

"I will do it."

"You'll get us both killed!"

"I'll take a few of the Captain's murderers with us," she said flatly.

"You're overwrought, Christine," the anthropologist groaned. He studied the nurse intently, weighing the alternatives. "All right," he gave in, "I'll see what I can do. I can't make any promises—they haven't let me see him either."

He strode to the doorway to talk to the guards outside.

"Irvin," she called after him, "either we see the Captain, or there will be trouble, and that *is* a promise."

Domberwicky hesitated, then went out, and Christine looked around the hewn-stone room, selecting the cleanest corner in which to sit. She was boneweary, as worn as she could ever remember. She questioned, for the first time, her compulsion to confirm Kirk's fate; Domberwicky was probably right, Kirk was surely dead. The thought wrung a quiet moan from her. But she could not leave this place until she was sure. She thought it was because she would not be able to face Mr. Spock, but she realized, now, that she would also not be able to live with herself.

Heat. Glare. Humidity. It was the litany of Vestalan from matins to vespers, every day. It had baked aspiration and civilization out of the Hualan culture. Now it went to work on Christine Chapel's resolve, broiling more of her compulsion out of her with every step under that noon sun. An impression of crowds around her made Christine force her squinting eyes open, and she realized there were Hualans all around where she walked, reclining on cloths or mats under impromptu ramadas of stacked tree fronds. The people laughed, shouted, pointed, sat up. They might have been on a picnic. *Maybe,* Christine thought, *they are.* There were many different ways to be devout.

Ahead of her loomed a very wide, circular pit lined with shaped stone. It was readily twice the diameter of the ship's bridge, and she immediately labeled it "the *kiva*," associating it with the Terran Anasazi cultural group, whose sacred places were similarly constructed, though usually roofed.

Christine walked toward the pit's edge, and the Hualans rolled out of her way cordially. She must have seemed like some goddess, or demon—blonde and tall and all of one pale skin tone, striding across the heath with a look of terrible sternness; but Christine was oblivious to the Hualans. Her eyes saw only into the *kiva*.

She stopped, gazing down the seven meters or so to the flagstone floor, and for that moment, she felt like she stood on the lip of hell. The *coatls* were there, maybe thirty of them. And Kirk was there. He was alive. He lay utterly still, on his side, with his arms bound in front of him, but he breathed. His skin was naked to the searing sun, and several *coatls* were coiled in the meager shade cast by his torso.

Every nerve in Christine demanded a scream. She

spun away, and Domberwicky was there to grasp her arms. He restrained her tightly, but not so tightly as she restrained her horror. She was in control, and she thought furiously.

"We'll go now, Christine," Domberwicky said firmly.

"No, we can't," she breathed. Then, with more vigor, "You told me these people can't resist a bet. Is that true?"

"It's true. Now, come on . . ."

"No. Wait. I want you to tell them that I'm going to make the bet of a lifetime, and they can share it . . . Go ahead, tell them!"

"Blast it, woman—"

"Tell them exactly what I said, or I'm going to start shoving the nearest ones into the pit," she warned. "And you'll be next."

"You've lost your mind!"

"Maybe I have. Now tell them!"

He told them something. It must have been close enough to her intent, because the Hualans glanced up at her with renewed interest.

"Well, they want to hear the rest of it," Domberwicky said sickly, the sound of a man with his neck in a guillotine.

"Tell them that I will wager my life for Captain Kirk's," Christine said hoarsely. "Tell them that I will go into the pit, with only a knife, and bring him out, without either of us being bitten."

Domberwicky blanched, and his eyes nearly bulged out of their sockets. He could barely make his tongue work words.

"You're completely insane!" he croaked. "You're a raving lunatic! You haven't a chance in hell down there!"

Calm, Christine waited out the reaction. She felt a unique *serenity*, having committed herself to this task. She didn't pretend that the risk wasn't titanic, but neither was it impossible. She listed her advantages quietly:

"I've handled *coatls* before; I respect them, Irvin,

but I'm not afraid of them," she said. "I'm strong, and I'm very quick, and the light gravity gives me an added advantage. Besides that, the snakes are hot—most of them will stay in the shadows around the edges of the pit. I believe, with luck, that I can get the Captain out, without being bitten."

The anthropologist's shock had spent itself; he had no more resources with which to cajole, argue, or insist. It was clear to him that Chapel was determined to suicide, and that he could do nothing, short of tackling her physically, to stop her. And, he admitted to himself, she could probably whip him if he tried that, too.

"You're sure you want to try this?" he sighed miserably. "You realize that Kirk's already been bitten."

"I saw the symptoms," she said. "There may still be time."

Several Hualans were tugging impatiently at Domberwicky's trouser legs, demanding attention. Domberwicky gave Christine one long, final look of resigned pain, and turned back to the Hualans. He would retrieve as much of the treaty as he could, whether Christine lived or died.

The response to Christine's proposal was a pandemonium of cheers, laughs, and frantic betting. Christine felt herself the object of a thousand eyes, being measured in every conceivable way. Some of the Hualans looked at her with visible approval, now: they had bet on her—a long shot—and stood to take big winnings if she survived. She almost laughed: she had every intention of surviving. She smiled back at the few faces that smiled at her.

Domberwicky finished parleying with a clutch of aged Hualans, and turned back to Christine with a battle of conflicting emotions on his round face. "They'll let you have a knife," he told her. "I got that much for you. But you'll have to strip nude; they don't want any margin of safety. If you get bitten, they want to know it. And if you do get bitten, they won't let either you or the Captain out of the pit alive."

She stared at him for a moment before her mind clicked back into gear.

"I agree," she acceded. She looked around at the sea of near-nude Hualans, shrugged mentally, and pulled her uniform off over her head. She stripped off the rest of her clothes, and strode back to the pit's edge. Someone eagerly handed up a chipped-stone knife, glassy black with a coral handle, and she hefted it. Her hand curled around it comfortably.

She began to walk the perimeter of the pit, choosing a place from which to leap down. The babble of voices died away, and the Hualans scrambled for sitting room near the edge.

Christine's skin cringed under Vestalan's ruthless sun, nearly overhead. As she'd predicted, most of the *coatls* in the *kiva* had slunk to the shadows near the east wall. Those shadows would disappear in another twenty minutes, and the nasty-tempered serpents would start roaming around, seeking other shade. But for now, they were out of her way. Most of them.

She stopped at the north wall and looked down. This was the best place. Only four *coatls* were between her and Kirk, here, and she might avoid a few of them, with luck. Two *coatls* still lay in Kirk's shadow, but she would have to deal with them as best she could, if she got that far.

Poised, she jumped.

She landed hardly a meter from the closest *coatl*. The slate-eyed creature eyed her suspiciously, coiling its long black body into lazy loops that could spring out in stinging death. Christine crouched where she'd landed, studying the beast and planning her strategy.

This isn't a game, she reminded herself coldly. *I could be dead soon. And this isn't a tranquilized, caged animal, either. There are no stunners here, and no wire loop restrainers. Only my stone knife.* Her stomach twisted with fear: good, healthy fear that would make her careful. But her hands and knees threatened to overreact—she felt suddenly weak, and shaky, dangerously shaky. Despite the heat, her skin prickled with chills. Some part of her was screaming for her *not to move,* to stay in that tiny space of safety and never move; to move was to die.

To stay is to die, she countered with her intellect. With mock steadiness, she stalked the nearest *coatl.*

The serpent flung itself at her before she'd calculated, but she reacted without thinking, twisting out of its path, with her free hand behind its ugly flared head, pressing the fleshy head against the flagstone, pinning it. The tail end looped up around her restraining hand, a full meter of powerful tail, and had the *coatl* been a Terran creature, it would have wrenched her arm from its head. But its muscles were accustomed to less gravity, and it lacked the strength of its Terran analog.

Christine held the writhing animal for a long, paralyzed moment of blanked mind before she realized what she'd done, and must do. Instinct alone had guided her, but now she took the knife and mechanically sliced off the *coatl*'s head, pitching it far away from her bare feet. The animal's brownish blood sprayed her legs. She tugged its still-lashing body from her arm.

Above her, the Hualans cheered and cursed, but she was already considering the next animal, a great-grandmother of a serpent, with a fleshy head the size of a duck's egg. It was, by far, the longest snake in the *kiva.* Christine began to crawl up on it, the professional part of her reluctant to destroy such a gigantic source of D-249. Her mind was obsessed with trivia, and she struggled to clear her thoughts for the contest. The whole situation seemed dreamlike, not quite real. She had to insist, over and over, that her full attention stay on what she was doing.

The *coatl* was huge, but its movements were sluggish. Probably, it had gotten too much sun in that exposed place, or it would have slithered into the diminishing shadows. *Coatls* were creatures of the twilight hours. Christine killed the big one almost casually.

She caught her breath and moved deliberately on the third serpent, when the air was suddenly filled with flying gravel: Threatened by her successes, the Hualans who had bet against Christine were pelting the *coatls* with stones. They drove several snakes back into the sun, toward the center of the pit.

Almost growling, Christine pinned the third coatl, but instead of beheading it, she flung it with all her might into the crowd. Screams exploded from above, but she couldn't see where she'd thrown the animal. After a few moments, the screams stopped. Someone had apparently dispatched the snake. But no more stones were thrown.

The fourth *coatl* obligingly snaked away when Christine approached, in no mood for a confrontation. Which left only the two animals still coiled by Kirk.

For the first time since she'd entered the *kiva*, Christine actually looked at Kirk. He lay as he'd lain, on his side, in a position nearly facing her. His eyes were open, but glazed, and he didn't seem aware of her. Where he wasn't sunburned, his flesh was gray, and his hair was matted with sweat. He was in pain, but he suffered in silence, barely breathing. She noticed his feet, then, and grimaced: the soles were punctured with thick thorns. It seemed the Hualans made sure their sacrificial oracles didn't run away.

The two *coatls* in Kirk's shadow presented an enormous problem; one was looped partly across Kirk's arm near his chest, the other lay in the shade by his hip. Coaxing them to coil and strike out, so near to him, was out of the question—there was no room to maneuver, and the slightest movement on Kirk's part could send the fangs into his helpless body.

There was no alternative. Christine knelt just out of range of the animals' farthest possible strike, and waited. The sun had slipped past the zenith, and the *coatls* in Kirk's shadow had lost that shadow. They must move soon. She hoped.

The sound of scales skithering across stone behind her startled Christine, and she turned her head sharply. She almost laughed in surprise and gratitude: the serpents which had hidden in the shade of the east wall in the morning were seeking new shadows, but all of them kept to the walls of the pit as they searched. After several long minutes, they discovered the meager shadows of the west wall. There was a brief series of snaky confrontations while the territorial pecking order was sorted out, then the animals settled down to sleep, each in its own little defined circumference of shade.

The smaller, darker of the two *coatls* near Kirk was stirring. Christine stayed still, watching it, waiting. Waiting. Then she realized that Kirk was looking at her, actually *seeing* her. He looked bewildered. At any moment, he might speak, or lift his head, or shift his legs. Instant death, though the dying would take its time.

"Captain, don't move!" Christine whispered. "Stay still, don't move a muscle. Our lives depend on it. Lie quietly and close your eyes."

He might not have understood her. He didn't close his eyes, but he didn't move, either. His breathing picked up a little. The darker *coatl* on his arm had had enough; it slid down onto the hot stones and slithered away toward the west wall.

The final *coatl* showed no sign of noticing that its spot against Kirk's thigh was becoming uncomfortable. But Kirk was. He moaned and shifted slightly. The *coatl* coiled up like a spring, agitated. Kirk, delirious, pulled his arms toward his chest, groaning. The *coatl* reared up, vibrating in the curious vanguard to its strike.

There could be no safety margin; Christine sprang at the snake, flicking the black-glass knife in an arc. Drawn to the broad motion, the *coatl* struck, catching the blade with its fangs and knocking it out of Christine's hand. She screamed but, in the same instant, instinctively caught the serpent behind the head to pin it. It was much more powerful than she'd expected, and it encircled her arms so that she could not throw it. She had no weapon. Its tail lashed and looped powerfully, and she had to cling to it with both hands, holding its fangs away from her. No way to kill it! Desperately, she pounded it down against the stone floor. Again, she smashed it down, and the snake thrashed wildly. Then, the third time, something gave. Blood and green venom splattered over her hands. She obliterated the remains of the animal's skull on the flagstone, and threw its squirming body as far as she could. Breathless, she dropped to her elbows, and stayed there, hunched over, gasping. It was done.

The Hualans had gone wild. Never had they seen such an entertainment; even the losers were jubilant, for no one was known who could handle *coatls* outside of the traps in which they were caught.

But to Christine, the celebration was remote noise. She was exhausted as she had never been. It was a supreme effort to push up. Somehow, she managed to get her arms under Kirk's torso and lift him, lighter in this gravity, onto her shoulder in a graceless "fireman's carry." She stumbled to the east wall of the *kiva,* which was clear of *coatls* now. As she lifted Kirk toward the reaching hands above, she glanced up—and into the apprehensive face of Mr. Spock. The Vulcan got a grip under Kirk's arms and pulled him up out of the pit. Other hands helped Christine out onto the sun-blasted heath.

McCoy was there, too, huddled with Spock over the Captain and surrounded by red-shirted security guards. Kirk's head lolled on Spock's knees. It would be close—they should get the man on life-support, get him to the ship, until a new batch of antivenom could be prepared. She wanted to say that, but the world of Vestalan was drowning her senses, full of frenzied, piebald faces and waving arms and colored cloths and dizzy black spots. Someone was wrapping a blanket around her. It was Domberwicky, grinning with a foolish, astonished smile.

"When'd Spock—?"

"Right after you went into the pit. He'd have gone in himself, but the noise would have thrown off your concentration. He had to wait it out with the rest of us. But, my God, woman, you did it!"

"I did it," she agreed numbly. Those black spots were spinning in on her, but at the center of the vortex she focused on Spock and McCoy, desperation embodied, so close, Kirk gray under his bruises, close, save him, I'm a nurse, no, a doctor, too, I can help, have to assist . . .

Domberwicky barely caught her as she collapsed.

Christine woke to coolness and antiseptic smells: home. She hummed to herself a little.

"She's coming around . . ." Dr. McCoy's voice was saying.

Who was coming around?

"Christine?"

"Um," she answered, and went back to sleep anyway.

"Well, I guess she deserves the rest," McCoy said reluctantly, turning to Mr. Spock. "Doesn't matter much when she finds out, does it?"

"Does what matter?" a weak voice demanded from the next bed.

"Now *you* really should be asleep!" McCoy grumbled, checking Kirk's overhead monitor-panel.

"Spock—what's happened?" Kirk insisted.

"Lieutenant Commander Domberwicky's new orders just came through from Star Fleet, sir, and his request for temporary assignment to Vestalan has been approved," the Vulcan reported.

"Let's hope he's successful," Kirk wished.

"It appears that he has the situation well in hand," Spock informed. "According to Domberwicky's report, the Hualan high priests are interpreting your unprecedented escape from the *coatl* ritual as an omen of perpetual good fortune for the tribe, provided they maintain friendly relations with the botanical collections station. A most logical deduction, under the circumstances."

"And Gehres has D-249 on the production line again," McCoy added. "Thanks to good old human stubbornness."

Spock cocked an eyebrow. "I would have phrased it, 'thanks to ingenuity and sound logic,' Doctor."

"You would."

"What's so important about this that you'd want to wake Miss Chapel to tell her?" Kirk interrupted.

"Starfleet is awarding Miss Chapel with a commendation for courage in the Vestalan affair, Captain," Spock told him. "An unusual honor."

"For an unusual woman," McCoy prodded.

Spock stared at McCoy inscrutably. "Indeed. A most extraordinary woman."

Editors' Introduction to
"The Patient Parasites"

You can't imagine how delighted we were to find in the very first boxful of *New Voyages* (1) mail a professional query letter from a man who was a professional writer of *Star Trek*—with his own stranger-than-fiction story to tell, from his own life, a *Star Trek* saga in itself.

We'll let him tell that as the best introduction to himself and his script. We thought you'd enjoy seeing an episode you never saw, in proper current-script form.

Bio-introductory Notes by Russell Bates

. . . I began to write while hospitalized in the US Air Force, and one of the very first things I wrote was a story using the ST universe and people. That one story did a lot, though it didn't sell and it wasn't very good.

Through it, I interested Dorothy Fontana in my writing, and she helped me enter the WGA Open Door classes for minority writers (I am a Kiowa Amerindian), and there I met Gene L. Coon. Soon I was working for him at Universal on *The Name of the Game,* and thereafter Ms. Fontana introduced me to Harlan Ellison, and the both of them browbeat me into going to the Clarion s-f workshop. There I met Robin Wilson and a veritable host of top-notch s-f writers. I improved my writing to the point that I began to sell to TV and to publishing markets, and . . .

. . . Ms. Fontana told me about the animated ST and that she wanted a script from me. I worked hard for two weeks and sent out the script that appears in this book. It came back, but *only* because it was too close to live film, lacking the scope that animation can bring. Six months later, I tried again, this time collaborating with a young filmmaker/animator to make sure the second script met all the special requirements. Apparently, we succeeded. "How Sharper Than A Serpent's Tooth" received top ratings for a children's show, got very favorable comments and mail, went to the International TV Film Festival at Monte Carlo, and was instrumental in the winning of an Emmy Award for the animated series. When the animated ST was nominated, "How Sharper Than A Serpent's Tooth" was the only credential presented to the judging committee.

But "The Patient Parasites" preceded it as the first attempt to do several things. 1, write ST in half-hour form and still be faithful to the show's original quality; 2, introduce an Amerindian character aboard the *Enterprise* (Dawson Walking Bear first appeared in this script; Dorothy Fontana sadly said that he was not very different from any other crewman; he was lifted out and later became pivotal to "Serpent's Tooth," which was an Amerindian myth-based story; thus it is that I have substituted Sulu for Walking Bear in this book); and, 3, finally write for ST as I set out to do back in the sixties.

"The Patient Parasites" was a story without a home. I did cherish Ms. Fontana's comment that, given greater length, it very easily could have been done on the original series. Then I saw the first volume of *Star Trek: The New Voyages* . . .

Briefly, a glossary of script terms for the needy: POV is Point of View; o.s. is off-stage or off-screen; b.g. is background; EXT is exterior ("outdoors"), INT is interior, etc. A script is written as though one has a small screen just in front of one's eyes and, I guess, should be read that way. But the greatest test is whether or not a story lives in among the shots and dialogue. *I* think a very good one lives here.

THE PATIENT PARASITES

by Russell Bates

CAST OF CHARACTERS

CAPTAIN JAMES T. KIRK
MR. SPOCK
DR. LEONARD MCCOY
SCOTT
SULU

FINDER VOICE

ACT ONE

FADE IN

EXT. SPACE—*Enterprise* in orbit around a red-brown planet; banded swirls of dark brown denote planet features. We see few clouds, no oceans, lakes, rivers.

> KIRK'S VOICE
> Captain's Log, Star Date 5459.4. The fifth planet in an uncharted and unin-habited star system has produced a mystery. Our sensor scan detected an intense energy source moving rapidly over the surface. But all efforts to identify it have failed.

EXT. PLANET SURFACE—DAY—Establishing an area of rocks in the midst of desert and desolation. Rocky hills fill the horizon under an orange-black sky. Gray-green vegetation is seen in scant patches in b.g. with grassy clumps closer in. Shimmer of transporter effect begins in clearing among rocks. Landing party of six persons begins to take shape.

KIRK'S VOICE
(*continuing*)

First Officer Spock has ordered up a
landing party to investigate.

Spock, Sulu, three other men, and a woman materialize
in clearing. All carry various shoulder-type instruments. They begin to move and look around. Spock
moves closer to us, checks his tricorder.

SPOCK

Take up positions of shelter. Monitoring will begin on my order. The energy source will pass this way in 1.9
minutes.

Others scatter out behind rocks, Sulu nearest to Spock.
Shot tightens on Spock in slow zoom. Spock takes out
communicator.

SPOCK

Spock to *Enterprise*. Mr. Scott, acknowledge.

SCOTT'S VOICE
(*filtered*)

Enterprise. Scott here.

SPOCK

Maintain Transporter lock on these
co-ordinates. We are well away from
the trajectory of the energy source.
This is only a precaution. Spock out.

Spock puts away communicator, turns and heads for
the rocks.

MEDIUM ANGLE—The landing party is hunkered
down behind rocks. Spock joins Sulu. All take up
their instruments and aim them outward.

SPOCK
(*loud*)

Begin monitoring now.

We hear tricorder hum mixed with low, strident tones
from other instruments. All personnel look intently toward horizon (o.s.).

THEIR POV—The horizon and a vast open plain dotted

with scattered rocky hills. Areas of vegetation are sparse. At edge of sky and plain begins a yellowish shimmer seen far off, coupled with a low rumbling. Shimmer grows, along with sound. Then a roiling mass of golden energy hurtles over horizon, rapidly growing in size and sound. Mass is an irregularly formed cloud, boiling, almost transparent. Dust is kicked up before and behind it, though it is airborne. *Very* obvious is its approach at angle away from our view and that it will pass some distance away. Sound continues to build.

BACK TO ANGLE—Spock raises himself to half-standing position, tricorder in hand.

> SPOCK
>
> Increase monitoring ranges and withhold reports until after it has passed.

Others remain crouching. Spock studies tricorder intently. He glances outward briefly, then looks back at tricorder.

> SPOCK
>
> Fascinating. The mass contains a spectrum of coherent energies. It should not exist at all.

Sulu tenses over his instrument, abruptly turns to Spock.

> SULU
> (*urgent*)
>
> Mr. Spock! It's changing course! Heading this way!

All react and quickly look outward.

THEIR POV—The energy mass is indeed swinging toward our view, growing larger, louder.

BACK TO ANGLE—Spock grabs out communicator, opens it. Others shrink back.

> SPOCK
> (*urgent*)
>
> Mr. Scott, energize!

A burst of static is his answer. He tunes it, but only gets more static. Rocks and landing party become tinged with yellow glow. Wind and dust blow past. Spock turns, waving others back.

SPOCK

Take cover!

ANGLE ON THE ENERGY MASS as it quickly fills shot, rumbling very loud. Then it explodes with tremendous sound and violent cascades of colors.

THE LANDING PARTY is struck by violent wavefront as they attempt to flee. They are knocked tumbling helplessly in a storm of dust and wind. Their instruments go flying. Our view shakes violently; rocks crumble around them. We hear a metallic screeching as explosion fades.

ANGLE ON THE ENERGY MASS which is now a stationary, pulsing yellow glow in midst of dust clouds and falling rocks. Screeching comes from within, growing.

CUT TO

EXT. SPACE—*Enterprise* briefly seen orbiting planet.

INT. TRANSPORTER ROOM—ANGLE ON DOOR as it opens to admit Kirk, McCoy, and four security men. Red alert indicator blinks; we hear alert signal sound. Kirk and McCoy head directly at us, while security men head in direction of Transporter Chamber (o.s.). McCoy wears medical tricorder.

WIDE ANGLE—EMPHASIZING TRANSPORTER CONSOLE manned by Scott and Transporter Chief. Kirk and McCoy hurry to front of console and stop. Security men are seen in b.g. near Transporter Chamber, watching Kirk and McCoy.

KIRK

(*urgent*)

Any contact with the landing party, Scotty?

SCOTT

None, sir! And I'm worried! Sensors show all six of them caught in a pool of energy!

Kirk and McCoy head for the Transporter Chamber on the run. Scott and Chief hurriedly program console.

Kirk and others enter chamber, stand on light panels, and face forward.

KIRK

Energize!

CUT TO

EXT. PLANET SURFACE—ROCKY AREA—Same as formerly occupied by the landing party. But no one is there. Dust still stands in the air. Transporter Effect begins, then Kirk and others materialize. McCoy points outward, shocked.

MCCOY

Jim! Look out there!

Others look, react in shock. Kirk takes a step forward.

THEIR POV—Establishing that the explosion site now contains a huge, intricate machine planted partway in the ground. It has no geometric or familiar design: *ALIEN*. Instead it is a convoluted mass of rounded shapes and extrusions, Picassoesque, with a roughly globular base, much like an upside-down frozen jellyfish. Frontmost portion of the base is flattened; this surface is alive with pulsing colors and convulsing amorphous shapes forming, disappearing, reforming. Accent here is machine-form but nothing recognizable in Earth terms. It emits tremulous low humming, gives off faint yellow glow. It is some distance away, far enough for us to see that the landing party is slowly walking toward it, roughly single-file, Spock and Sulu closest to our view. All six walk trance-like, their heads bathed in individual beams emanating from the center of the machine. Beams are filled with sliding, repeating bars of rainbow colors. People are quite close to the machine.

CLOSE ON KIRK AND MCCOY looking outward. McCoy uses medical tricorder. Kirk waves arms.

KIRK
(shouts)

Spock! Sulu! Everybody! Stay away from that thing!

McCoy turns to him, holding up his tricorder.

MCCOY

It's no use, Jim! It's got them in some
kind of trance!

Kirk looks outward a beat, then moves back. Angle
widens to include security men. Kirk draws phaser.
McCoy moves with him.

KIRK

Phasers to full effect! Put that thing
out of commission!

Others draw phasers, adjust them, move up to take
aim along with Kirk at machine (o.s.). McCoy quickly
steps back out of the way.

KIRK

Aim away from our people! *Fire!*

A fusillade of beams leaps forward, with scream of
energy.

ANGLE ON THE MACHINE—Full shot showing mes-
merized landing party now very close, Spock and
Sulu hindmost, a little removed from others. Beams
strike machine above and away from them. Instantly,
a silvery transparent bubble flicks into existence over
machine, blocking phaser beams and also sealing in the
four closest people under a hemisphere of energy.
Spock and Sulu are left outside the bubble; light
beams no longer hit them, being blocked by the bubble. They stand motionless. Phaser beams still strike
bubble, with no effect.

ROCKY AREA—Full shot Kirk and others continue firing
a beat.

KIRK

Cease fire!

They lower phasers. McCoy moves up, using his tricorder.

MCCOY

Spock and Sulu seem all right but the
others don't register! It's like they're
not there!

Kirk turns first to McCoy, then to security men.

KIRK

Then we're going out there! (to men)
Cover us! Give us supporting fire if we
need it!

Kirk and McCoy run out of shot. Security men aim
phasers.

ANGLE ON SPOCK AND SULU including portion of
transparent bubble nearest to them. Visible are one or
two of the captive personnel, light beams still on their
heads. Spock and Sulu recover a bit, shaking their
heads. Then they see the bubble and react.

KIRK'S VOICE

Spock! Sulu!

They both turn and head away from machine, stum-
blingly, dazedly.

ANGLE ON ROCKY AREA—FULL SHOT—Security men are
seen in b.g., phasers aimed. Kirk and McCoy are running toward us to meet Spock and Sulu, who stumble
into shot. Kirk and McCoy reach them and lead them
toward the rocks.

ANOTHER ANGLE—CLOSER as Kirk and McCoy reach
rocks with their dazed charges. Kirk looks back at
machine (o.s.) momentarily, then at security men.

KIRK

Weapons standby. But keep an eye on
that thing.

Security men lower phasers, still looking outward.
Kirk and McCoy lean Spock and Sulu against rocks.
McCoy aims Feinberger at Sulu.

ANGLE ON THEM—EMPHASIZING KIRK AND SPOCK—
Spock is slumped; Kirk grips his shoulders, gently
shakes him.

KIRK

(concerned)

Spock! Come out of it! Are you all
right?

Spock straightens, as though he has just been awakened.

SPOCK

Captain. I—
> (*shakes head*)

Yes, Captain. I am undamaged. The
explosion . . .

Spock abruptly tries to stand. McCoy steps over to
them and urges him back, then uses Feinberger on
him. Sulu watches them.

SPOCK
> (*offended*)

Doctor, I am perfectly fine. If I were
not, I would know it.

McCOY
> (*gruffly*)

Logic makes a poor doctor, Spock.
Hold still.

McCoy finishes, glances at Feinberger, turns to Kirk.

McCOY

They both seem okay, Jim. Just a little
disoriented.

KIRK

Spock, what happened?

Spock stands away from rock, now completely recovered.

SPOCK

We were monitoring the energy source,
Captain. It veered in our direction
and somehow jammed my communicator. My last memory is of an explosion.

Kirk turns to look at machine (o.s.). Others look also.

KIRK

That thing is what came at you?

THEIR POV—BUBBLE AND MACHINE—Machine is
clearly visible in bubble; captives are still bathed by
beams of light. Shot tightens in slow zoom.

SPOCK'S VOICE

No, Captain. It was a mass of seething

energy. Obviously, it has taken on physical form.

The light beams abruptly begin to fade.

> MCCOY'S VOICE
> (*alarmed*)
> Jim, something's happening!

Light beams suddenly flick off; captives collapse to the ground. Bubble and machine appear much as before.

BACK TO ANGLE—Kirk, McCoy and Sulu are alarmed. Spock looks quizzical. Then Kirk moves quickly toward the security men.

> KIRK
> Let's get them out of there!

NEW ANGLE—FULL SHOT—Spock, McCoy and Sulu follow Kirk to security men. All form up into a line, facing us, quickly drawing phasers.

> KIRK
> All phasers to full effect! Aim for
> the upper portion of that bubble! On
> my order, continuous fire!

All aim phasers directly toward us.

> KIRK
> *Fire!*

Beams converge toward us, washing out our view. Energy screams.

ANGLE ON BUBBLE as beams strike upper portion. At first, no effect; then bubble darkens, obscuring machine, until bubble is like a solid metal dome. Beams have no further effect, washing off uselessly.

BACK TO KIRK AND OTHERS

> KIRK
> Cease fire!

All stop firing. Kirk and McCoy look outward, dismayed. Spock stoops, picks up tricorder, aims it outward and begins to scan. Kirk and McCoy watch him. Then Spock looks up from tricorder. Tricorder sound is continuous.

SPOCK

Interesting. A force field of coherent
energy. Not only is it impenetrable, it
appears to be self-sustaining, using all
environmental energies.

THEIR POV—THE BUBBLE—It begins to shift from
silvery solid toward transparency. Shot tightens in slow
zoom. Tricorder sound drops out.

MCCOY'S VOICE

Could you translate that, Spock?

SPOCK'S VOICE

The perfect defense, Doctor. It uses
sunlight and energy from the planet
itself. Our attack only gave more
power to the field.

Bubble is now transparent again. We see machine and
captives.

ANGLE ON KIRK, SPOCK AND MCCOY—Kirk and Mc-
Coy look at machine (o.s.). Spock studies tricorder.

KIRK

Spock, what are we up against? What
is that thing?

Spock lowers tricorder and turns to Kirk.

SPOCK

A machine, Captain. Alien to us and
to this planet. No technological race
exists here or anywhere near this system.

(*looks outward*)

Beyond that, I am stymied. The tricorder cannot pierce the field.

McCoy moves closer to Spock, looking upset.

MCCOY

What does that mean to our people
in there? Are we helpless?

Spock raises an eyebrow; Kirk regards McCoy closely.

SPOCK

No, Doctor. It merely means that di-

rect attack is useless. This matter requires further study.

McCoy is angered. He gestures outward at the machine (o.s.).

> MCCOY
> *Study?* Spock, those people could be
> dying!

Spock regards McCoy with aplomb; Kirk touches
McCoy's arm.

> KIRK
> (*not unkindly*)
> Bones, he's right. Impulse got us
> nowhere. We'll get them out. But we'll
> need patience.

At that, a reverberating voice speaks: Finder, the
machine (o.s.).

> FINDER'S VOICE
> Patience. Indeed, that quality is the
> key to the cosmos.

All three quickly look outward, surprised. Spock uses
tricorder.

CLOSE ON BUBBLE AND FINDER—Pulsing colors and
crawling shapes on the flattened surface are slowing,
changing, finally solidifying into a revolving moire
pattern (doubled, preferably). Lines within moire appear to retreat into infinity. View through bubble has
silvery tinges.

BACK TO ANGLE—Kirk steps forward, camera moving
with him. Spock continues tricorder scan; McCoy looks
on intently. Kirk then halts.

> KIRK
> It spoke. Then it isn't just a machine.

CLOSE ON BUBBLE AND FINDER—Random sparkles flit
over Finder's surface, in time to voice. Silver tinges
also shift. Moire is steady in motion and position.

> FINDER
> I am but a machine. You judge too
> quickly. You know patience but do not
> understand it.

CLOSE ON KIRK

> KIRK
>
> Who—What are you? Why do you hold my people prisoner?

HIS POV—FINDER INSIDE BUBBLE

> FINDER
>
> I am Finder. My masters have sent my kind among the stars to find. Your people have that which my masters desire.

CLOSE ON KIRK AND SPOCK as Spock joins Kirk, tricorder operating. Kirk turns to him and Spock lowers tricorder.

> SPOCK
>
> The voice is produced by force field vibrations, Captain. And while it was speaking, I was able to probe for information.

Angle widens and McCoy joins them.

> MCCOY
>
> What about our people, Spock?

> SPOCK
>
> Merely comatose, Doctor. At this point, they are alive.

Kirk and McCoy are relieved.

> KIRK
>
> Then whatever Finder's game is, we've got to play it. Spock, anything else?

> SPOCK
>
> Nothing on Finder itself, Captain. However, our people show no brain wave activity. Please speak with Finder again.

Kirk looks outward, as does McCoy. Spock raises tricorder; its sound is continuous.

> KIRK
>
> Finder, who are your masters?

CLOSE ON FINDER

FINDER

That, I may not tell you. Suffice it to know their civilization is vast, though confined to a single star. They are a patient people, to whom patience is supreme.

CLOSE ON KIRK who clearly shows irritation.

KIRK

Patience. That's fast becoming an ugly word.

(*pause*)

Finder, what do your masters want?

KIRK'S POV—Shot tightens in slow zoom on bubble and Finder.

FINDER

Knowledge. And the wisdom for its use. Long ago, my masters found that knowledge destroys without wisdom. Now we Finders bring them knowledge with wisdom. Thus do my masters remain safe from destruction.

ANGLE ON KIRK, SPOCK AND MCCOY—McCoy is appalled; he grabs Kirk's arm. Spock watches them.

MCCOY

Jim, they're parasites! They steal technology and never have to develop it for themselves!

KIRK

(*nods; sharply*)

You didn't answer my question, Finder! What do they want?

CLOSE ON FINDER as an aerial-like probe rises from within its central mass.

FINDER

Their want is simple. They wish your knowledge that propels a vessel faster than light.

CLOSE ON KIRK AND SPOCK as Spock looks up from tricorder, almost in alarm.

SPOCK

Captain, I detect a powerful transporter-like system. I believe Finder has removed our people's minds and is preparing to transport them to its masters.

Angle widens to include McCoy, who is shocked.

MCCOY

Jim, they'll die!

KIRK
(*angry*)

You speak so lovingly of patience! Are your masters now so patient that life means nothing to them?

CLOSE ON FINDER—At first, it appears the same. Then it glows with a slow, green-tinged pulsing, with a rising hum. Top of probe glows brightest.

KIRK

Those host bodies will expire painlessly. I am the instrument of my masters. Their concerns are my concerns. Their primary concern here is knowledge.

With this, pulsing accelerates and humming grows very loud.

ANGLE ON KIRK, SPOCK AND MCCOY—Their faces are tinged by green glow. Kirk draws phaser, starts to rush at Finder (o.s.). Spock and McCoy quickly restrain him. Kirk struggles, but they manage to hold him back.

SPOCK

Captain, this is illogical.

MCCOY

Jim, there's nothing you can do!

Kirk looks at phaser, then out toward Finder (o.s.).

KIRK
(*shouts*)

Stop it, Finder! I won't let you kill my people!

ANGLE ON THE BUBBLE—We see the pulsing speed up, its light casting shadows from the inert captives. Yellow blobs of light begin to move up probe, faster and faster. Sound is loudest of all.

THREE SHOT—KIRK, SPOCK AND MCCOY as they watch helplessly. Camera zooms in to close on Kirk, who is aghast. Hold on him for

FADE OUT

ACT TWO

FADE IN

CLOSE ON KIRK as we saw him at the end of Act One: anxious, face tinged by green pulsing. Humming rises higher in pitch. Camera pulls back to reveal Spock and McCoy also watching anxiously.

CLOSE ON FINDER—Green pulsing and rising yellow blobs are now almost solid hues.

BACK TO KIRK as he shakes free and steps closer, gesturing desperately.

> KIRK
> (shouts)
> Finder, your masters are wrong! You
> said their concerns are your concerns!
> If they're wrong, you're wrong!

Angle widens to include Spock and McCoy. They all stare at Finder (o.s.). Then Kirk and McCoy look puzzled; Spock raises eyebrow.

THEIR POV—BUBBLE AND FINDER as the green pulsing and rising yellow blobs slow down; the hum falls in pitch. Effects continue to slow, then quickly cease. Probe is withdrawn and Finder appears much as before.

> FINDER
> A challenge? Very well. I am allowed
> to consider such. My masters have
> often entertained opposition. Patience
> demands it.

CLOSE ON KIRK, SPOCK AND McCOY—Kirk and McCoy are relieved. Spock studies tricorder.

KIRK

Spock, is it telling the truth?

SPOCK

Machine truth, but truth nonetheless, Captain. My analysis is incomplete. However, its memory banks reveal that no Finder has ever been successfully opposed. I surmise the masters only wish to test its defenses.

McCoy regards Finder (o.s.) suspiciously.

MCCOY

So, we've got a reprieve. But what it didn't say is how long.

KIRK

You'll be challenged, Finder, with every resource I command. But what's my time limit, if you know what I mean by time?

THEIR POV—BUBBLE AND FINDER

FINDER

I have access to repositories that contain your concepts. Challenge will be entertained until Star Date 5459.7.

BACK TO KIRK, SPOCK AND McCOY—Spock looks on placidly. But Kirk and McCoy are angered.

KIRK

Agreed.

Kirk turns and heads back toward rocky area with Spock and McCoy.

TRAVELING SHOT—KIRK, SPOCK AND McCOY—They walk briskly, at a near running pace.

SPOCK

Precisely five standard hours, Captain.

MCCOY

Five hours.

(*glances up*)

That's just about when this planet's sun

wiil set. Finder is certainly taking no
chances with its power sources.

KIRK
(*sharply*)
It'll be time enough, Bones. It has to
be.

ROCKY AREA—WIDE ANGLE as Kirk, Spock and McCoy
walk quickly into shot. Sulu and security men move
forward to meet them.

KIRK
(*briskly*)
Sulu, you're coming with us. You men
will remain here on watch. Report the
slightest change immediately.

Kirk, Spock and McCoy hurry past them, with Sulu
quickly joining them. Security men watch them go, then
all look outward.

MEDIUM ANGLE—ANOTHER CLEARING not too much
different from rocky area. Kirk, Spock, McCoy and Sulu
come to a halt. Kirk takes out communicator, opens it.

KIRK
Kirk to *Enterprise*. Mr. Scott, acknowledge.

SCOTT'S VOICE
(*filtered*)
Enterprise. Scott here.

KIRK
Scotty, notify department heads to
assemble for emergency meeting Four
to beam up. Stand by.

He closes communicator but keeps it at hand. He
turns to others.

KIRK
Five hours, gentlemen. The best minds
on the *Enterprise* should be able to
challenge Finder. But I want your
impressions now, while they're still
fresh.

Others look thoughtful, McCoy and Sulu just a bit uncomfortable.

> SULU
>
> Captain, I know machines. They're only as good as their power sources. Finder just can't be invincible.

> KIRK
>
> All well and good, Lieutenant. But this machine has some good sources.

Sulu nods. McCoy turns to Kirk

> MCCOY
>
> I'm a doctor, Jim, not a strategist. But I say those four lives are worth any cost. Couldn't we trade with Finder, exchange our people for what it wants?

> KIRK
> (*morosely*)
>
> No, Bones. We would only set a precedent with far-reaching consequences for the Federation.

> SPOCK
>
> I concur, Captain. We must prevent Finder from achieving its purpose, perhaps even at the cost of our people's lives.

Kirk and Sulu are shocked, but McCoy is angered. He quickly moves to confront Spock, gesturing angrily.

> MCCOY
> (*loud*)
>
> You sound like that machine out there! But maybe I'm being unfair! Finder's probably showing more compassion than any Vulcan who ever lived!

Spock regards McCoy calmly, though he raises an eyebrow. Kirk touches McCoy on the shoulder. Sulu looks on interestedly.

KIRK
(*firmly*)

Bones!

McCoy looks at Kirk, then falls silent, though still very angry.

KIRK

Mr. Spock, explain yourself!

SPOCK

Captain, two considerations here are unavoidable. The masters are parasitic and therefore extremely dangerous. They cannot be allowed to obtain our Warp drive.

Kirk blinks, then nods, a little unwillingly. Sulu also nods. McCoy mulls it over and looks less angry.

MCCOY
(*abrasive*)

All right, Spock. That much makes sense. What's your other point?

SPOCK

Simply that if we fail in our challenges, there is but one course left by which we may stop Finder.

All look at him expectantly.

CLOSE ON SPOCK

SPOCK

Captain, you will have to destroy this entire planet.

ANGLE—ALL

Others are shocked. But Kirk nods. He takes up communicator.

KIRK

Energize, Mr. Scott.

Angle widens, Transporter effect shimmers on them; they vanish.

EXT. SPACE—*Enterprise* in orbit as we have seen it before.

KIRK'S VOICE

Captain's Log, Star Date 5459.6. Despite careful and exhaustive analysis, our challenges for Finder remain dangerously few.

INT. BRIEFING ROOM—CLOSE ON KIRK—BEGINNING PAN OF TABLE past Spock, McCoy, two men, Sulu, Scott, and three other men seated around table in deep discussion. Determination and grimness is evident on all faces. As camera passes table's viewing screen, we see tiny color view of bubble and Finder.

KIRK'S VOICE
(*continuing*)

With most of our time gone, I have reluctantly ordered five planet-wrecker missiles placed on standby, with my First Officer's concurrence. But I refuse to accept Finder's invulnerability.

PAN ENDS on Kirk and holds. Kirk suddenly brightens.

KIRK

What about logic, Spock? Could we conceivably argue Finder into releasing our people?

CLOSE ON SPOCK who looks thoughtful, then shakes his head briefly.

SPOCK

I think not, Captain. Finder has displayed a finely logical awareness. But it is after all only a machine. Its concepts are not its own and therefore it may not change them.

Angle widens to include McCoy, who leans toward Spock.

MCCOY

Spock, is there something in the universe immune to logic?

Spock turns to him, looking almost annoyed.

SPOCK

It is logic, Doctor, that reveals Finder
not to be immune at all. It may not be
able to change its concepts. But given
proper new information, possibly it
would react differently within the
bounds of those concepts.

ANGLE ON KIRK AND SPOCK—Kirk appears hopeful.
Spock turns to him when he speaks.

KIRK

What proper new information, Spock?

SPOCK

Impossible to know, Captain, without
further data on Finder and its masters.

WIDE ANGLE—ALL

MCCOY

Like the old saying, Spock. It takes
money to make money.

SPOCK
(nods)
Anachronistically stated, but essentially correct, Doctor.

KIRK

Gentlemen, please. Let's stay on the
subject.

SCOTT

Captain, the young lieutenant here
would like to earn his keep.
(nudges Sulu)
Go on, lad. Tell them what you told me.

CLOSE ON SULU who looks dismayed.

SULU

Well, Captain, I . . . It's just that . . .

KIRK'S VOICE
(sharply)
Mr. Sulu, if you have something to say,
I want to hear it loud and clear!

Sulu straightens.

SULU

Aye, aye, sir! I mentioned this before.
If Finder takes power from the environment, couldn't we somehow shut
off its sources?

CLOSE ON KIRK AND SPOCK who both think a beat,
then look doubtful.

KIRK

Lieutenant, that would mean dis-
rupting the planet, and we couldn't
do that short of destroying it.

Angle widens to include McCoy, who shakes his head
briefly.

MCCOY

Furthermore, our time limit is too
much ahead of sunset for *even that* to
be useful.

Both of Spock's eyebrows go up and he leans forward.

SPOCK

Captain, something still bothers me
about the energy mass. Perhaps we
should hear him out.

CLOSE ON SULU who sits forward, crossing his arms on
the table.

SULU

Captain, maybe we can't disrupt
gravity or the planet's electrical charge.
But what about sunlight?

ANGLE ON KIRK AND SPOCK—Kirk looks thoughtful.
Spock turns to him.

SPOCK

Now it is clear, Captain. The mass
contained a spectrum of coherent
energies. Quite likely it was in motion
to remain ahead of planetary rotation.
Finder must be highly dependent upon
sunlight.

Kirk suddenly brightens and slaps table with palm of
his hand.

                        KIRK
        Then what we need is an eclipse,
        Spock! An artificial eclipse!

Spock raises an eyebrow, then he nods.

WIDE ANGLE—ALL

Kirk quickly gets to his feet.

                        KIRK
        Scotty, the young lieutenant not only
        has earned his keep, he's got shore
        leave at our next four ports!
                    (a beat)
        Posts, gentlemen! Spock, I want that
        proper new information. Run what
        you have through computer a hundred
        times if necessary. Mr. Scott, we'll work
        Transporter and tractor beam attacks
        first. Mr. Sulu, I want that eclipse.

Others file out quickly, leaving Kirk and McCoy alone.

CLOSER ON THEM as McCoy steps up to Kirk, shaking
his head.

                        MCCOY
        I must be getting old, Jim. I just
        couldn't see the obvious.

                        KIRK
        Bones, the day you stop thinking like
        my medical officer, that's when I'll
        turn you over to Scotty.
                    (a beat)
        Come on. We're beaming down to the
        planet.

They start out.

EXT. PLANET SURFACE—DAY—ROCKY AREA

Kirk and McCoy are in foreground, crouched down behind rocks. In b.g., we see the security men also
crouched. All look outward. Kirk flips open communicator.

                        KIRK
        Scotty, begin tractor beam sequence.
        We're safely out of your way.

SCOTT'S VOICE
(*filtered*)

Aye, sir. Beginning now.

ANGLE ON BUBBLE—FULL SHOT as a faint white outline of tractor beam shimmers around it. A dim rumbling is heard, followed by dust rising along the outline. Bubble vibrates slightly and bulges upward somewhat, but remains intact. Rumbling grows louder, dust flying upward grows thicker, rocks break free of the ground to fly upward. Bubble then begins to darken slightly, as it did under phaser attack.

CLOSE ON KIRK—Dust blows past him in direction of bubble; wind whips his hair and clothing. He shields his eyes and tries to look upward. Then communicator beeps and he opens it.

SCOTT'S VOICE
(*filtered*)

No good, Captain! Finder's soaking up our beam like it was so much water! Shutting down tractor beam now!

BACK TO BUBBLE—FULL SHOT as the white outline vanishes and rumbling ceases. It resumes regular dome shape; dust and rocks fall on it, ricocheting off. Darkening slowly fades and we see it much as before.

ANGLE ON KIRK AND MCCOY—Kirk wipes dust from his face; McCoy coughs, brushes off dust.

MCCOY

I wish I could remember why the desert's supposed to be healthy!

Kirk ignores him, speaks into communicator.

KIRK

Phase two, Scotty! Transporter to full power!

CLOSE ON BUBBLE as shimmer of Transporter effect begins *inside* bubble, low to the ground around the four inert forms, continuous.

CLOSE ON KIRK

> SCOTT'S VOICE
> (*filtered*)
> Captain, we've locked on!

> KIRK
> (*surprised*)
> Pull them in, Scotty!

BACK TO BUBBLE as shimmer grows brighter, then fades away. But we still see the four inert captives within the bubble much as before.

CLOSE ON KIRK AND MCCOY who only stare helplessly. Then Kirk takes up communicator.

> MCCOY
> But he said he locked on.

> KIRK
> Scotty, what happened?

> SCOTT'S VOICE
> (*filtered*)
> We got through, Captain. But only because that blasted machine let us! We pulled in phasers, communicators, and a bunch of instruments! It's playing with us, sir!
> (*pause*)
> Captain, Mr. Spock has something to report.

Kirk and McCoy exchange glances. A beat, then Spock comes on, sounding very grave.

> SPOCK'S VOICE
> (*filtered*)
> Spock here, Captain. If my researches are correct, it has become even more imperative that Finder be stopped.

Kirk looks puzzled; McCoy looks on, frowning.

> KIRK
> Spock, explain. What is it?

> SPOCK'S VOICE
> (*filtered*)
> Computer search indicates that Finder's masters may have been Tullvans,

a fossil culture once located in the
Zeta Geminorum system. Their demise took place 1,809.3 Earth years
ago.

Kirk and McCoy are shocked. They stare outward at
Finder (o.s.).

KIRK

Spock, Finder's masters are *extinct?*

SPOCK'S VOICE
(*filtered*)

Entirely possible, Captain. If Finder
Transports our people's minds, there
may be no one on the receiving end.
They will be lost to us forever.

Kirk and McCoy stand up slowly, looking outward in
disbelief.

THEIR POV—BUBBLE AND FINDER glistening in the
sunlight of what is now late afternoon. Hold for

FADE OUT

ACT THREE

FADE IN

EXT. PLANET SURFACE—DAY—WIDE ANGLE showing
the rocky area, the bubble and Finder, and the flat,
open expanse between them. Shadows are long from
the rocks and from the bubble. Between them is seen
the planet's sun, now quite low in the sky (Note: but
not so low that sunset appears imminent in only a
few minutes), very big, orange-red.

CLOSE ON KIRK AND MCCOY—They still look outward,
anxious and upset. Kirk takes a step forward and
speaks into communicator.

KIRK

Verify, Spock. You're positive that
these extinct Tullvans and Finder's
masters are the same.

SPOCK'S VOICE
(*filtered*)

No, Captain. But my correlations have an 83 percent probability of being correct.

Kirk glances at McCoy, who shrugs.

KIRK

Spock, this may be a weapon in itself. Give me some facts.

ANGLE ON BUBBLE—FULL SHOT—We see well-defined shadows from it across the ground. Shot slowly tightens in slow zoom.

SPOCK'S VOICE
(*filtered*)

Certainly, Captain. Finder's alloys compare favorably with specimens of Tullvan origin. The nature of the Tullvan demise is unknown, but it was decidedly cataclysmic. Surviving records indicate that patience was central to their philosophies.

TWO SHOT—KIRK AND McCOY—Both look hopeful.

KIRK

That convinces me, Spock. But will it convince Finder?

SPOCK'S VOICE
(*filtered*)

I think not, Captain. Logically, Finder would consider it suspect.

Kirk and McCoy register disappointment. McCoy looks outward.

KIRK

Then go to phase three, Spock. The eclipse. Status report.

SPOCK'S VOICE
(*filtered*)

Mr. Scott and Mr. Sulu recommend placing an ionization cloud in high orbit. I concur.

KIRK

Then proceed at once. The sun is
already low in the sky.

He pauses and McCoy turns to him.

KIRK

Spock, record your Tullvan data and
bring it down when you return. It still
may be useful.

SPOCK'S VOICE
(*filtered*)
Order unnecessary, Captain. I have already done so.

Kirk looks surprised. McCoy smiles. Kirk glances at
McCoy.

KIRK
(*slow, ironic*)
You've already done so.
(*a beat*)
Very well, Mr. Spock. We'll be waiting.
Kirk out.

EXT. SPACE—*Enterprise* breaking orbit and heading
away from the planet.

INT. BRIDGE—ANGLE ON COMMAND POSITIONS

Spock is in command chair, Uhura is seen at her
console, and an ensign mans the library-computer.
Angle widens to include the Navigation-Helm console.
Sulu is at Helm, Scott stands nearby.

SPOCK

Mr. Sulu, assume orbit at 37,800
kilometers.

SULU

Aye, aye, sir. Orbit in twenty seconds.

Sulu leans back toward Scott without looking at him.

SULU

My ancestors wouldn't approve, Mr.
Scott. They thought eclipses were
omens of coming misfortune.

SPOCK

As did mine, Lieutenant. Usually,
they were right.

Scott glances at Spock in surprise, then looks forward
again.

SULU

Orbit achieved, sir.

SPOCK

Ready carrier missile, Mr. Sulu. Fire
on my order. Fire.

Sulu presses buttons; we hear electronic tones. Then a
burst of sound follows, not unlike photon torpedo effect.

SULU

Missile away, sir.

THEIR POV—MAIN VIEWING SCREEN—We see a point
of light speeding away across background of stars,
leaving a vaporous trail that quickly fades.

CLOSE ON SPOCK

SPOCK

Lock phasers on missile and fire on my
order. Fire.

EXT. SPACE—*Enterprise* firing double beams of phaser
energy, with energy scream.

CLOSE ON MAIN VIEWING SCREEN—We see a brief
explosion against background of stars. A green-black
blot, scintillating with sparkles of light, begins to
spread, blanking out view of stars as it slowly grows.

ANGLE ON SPOCK, SCOTT AND SULU—Scott points
forward very briefly; Sulu nods, looking serious.

SPOCK

Take us in, Mr. Sulu. Resume standard
orbit.

Spock rises quickly.

SPOCK
(*continuing*)

Take the con, Mr. Scott. I shall be in
the transporter room.

Spock crosses toward the turboelevator. Scott quickly slips into the command chair.

EXT. PLANET SURFACE—ROCKY AREA—WIDE ANGLE showing *Enterprise* contingent, Kirk and McCoy closest to us. Shadows are now even longer, sun is lower in the sky, and scene has taken on a ruddy cast.

CLOSE ON KIRK AND MCCOY—Kirk looks outward. McCoy looks upward at sun (o.s.), shading his eyes. Suddenly, McCoy points upward.

> MCCOY
> Jim, look! The eclipse!

Angle widens to include security men. Kirk and others look up.

THEIR POV—THE SUN

A definite blotch covers one edge, much like a *thin,* irregular bite. It does not increase while we look at it. (Note: *none* of the eclipsing cloud should be visible except for the portion covering sun's disk.)

CLOSE ON KIRK AND MCCOY—Kirk looks outward again. McCoy looks upward a beat longer, shading his eyes. There is a hint that sunlight is decreasing. McCoy turns when Kirk speaks.

> KIRK
> Well, there goes Finder's main power
> source. Now we'll see if it can do with-
> out it.

Communicator beeps. Kirk takes it out, opens it.

> KIRK
> Kirk here.

> SCOTT'S VOICE
> (*filtered*)
> Scott here, Captain. One eclipse, to
> order. Mr. Spock is beaming down now.

> KIRK
> Acknowledged, Scotty. Kirk out.

Kirk puts away communicator. Lighting is definitely decreasing. Transporter sound comes in from behind them; they turn to look. Sound dies, angle widens,

Spock enters shot to join them. Then Spock unlimbers his tricorder. All look outward together.

ANGLE ON BUBBLE AND FINDER—INCLUDING SUN showing sun to be half-covered and the land area growing darker. No changes are evident in either bubble or Finder.

ANGLE ON KIRK, SPOCK AND McCOY as they watch in growing darkness. Spock operates tricorder.

> KIRKS
> (*anxiously*)
> Any changes, Spock?

> SPOCK
> None, Captain. Perhaps ...

He raises an eyebrow as he pauses; Kirk and McCoy look at him.

> KIRK
> Yes, Mr. Spock?

> SPOCK
> I almost recommended that you have more patience, Captain. But it is most inappropriate.

Kirk and McCoy exchange ironic glances, then look outward again.

ANGLE ON BUBBLE AND FINDER— INCLUDING SUN showing last vestiges of sun's disk disappearing behind irregular black outline seen *only* over disk. Sky goes black and becomes filled with stars. Bubble glows vaguely; green energy glints shimmer randomly over it. Within, Finder glows dully red, slowly pulsing brighter and dimmer. Moire glows brightly. Sparkles of light still flit randomly over Finder's surface. On ground, the unmoving captives are vague outlines lighted by moire and pulsing glow. Darkness becomes complete; sun is gone. Shot tightens.

> KIRK'S VOICE
> Still no change.

> MCCOY'S VOICE
> What are we looking for, Spock?

SPOCK'S VOICE
It must be changing, Doctor. However,
such changes need not be visible ones.

CLOSE ON KIRK AND MCCOY who are seen in
bluish light; faces, clothing, and surroundings retain
colors but only dimly under bluish tinge. They watch
Finder. McCoy turns to Spock, who operates tricorder.

MCCOY
Well, is it or isn't it changing, Spock?

SPOCK
(*looks up*)
It is, Doctor. The force field is far less
dense than before. It is still impenetrable. But it is steadily weakening.

Kirk looks at him hopefully.

KIRK
We have just under an hour, Spock.
How weak is it?

SPOCK
Difficult to tell, Captain. I know its
power utilization curve. But I am
unable to measure the power Finder
continues to obtain.

Angle widens and Kirk takes a step forward.

KIRK
Then I'm going out. It wanted a challenge. Now it's got one.

Kirk starts away. But Spock takes out small cube,
follows him.

SPOCK
Wait, Captain. The Tullvan data are in
in this cryomemory cube.

KIRK
(*takes it*)
Thank you, Mr. Spock.

MCCOY
Be careful, Jim. If Finder's in a corner, it may do anything.

KIRK

I'll watch for snakes, Bones.

Kirk heads away out of shot. Spock and McCoy watch intently.

THE BUBBLE—WIDE ANGLE—Finder glows as before. But bubble wavers a bit; green glints are fewer, more brief. Kirk enters shot, stops well away.

KIRK

Finder, have you considered my challenge?

No response. Kirk frowns and steps closer.

KIRK
(louder)

Finder, you asked for challenge. Now I have asked you a question. Will you give me an answer?

Finder's voice is slower, with less volume. But its pulsing glow, the moire, and the random sparkles are much as before.

FINDER

I am considering. If this is your challenge, it is worthy. But I must also consider natural coincidence or my own error.

Kirk is exasperated. He gestures angrily.

KIRK

You're playing for time! I want my people released! Now!

CLOSE ON FINDER as the aerial-like probe ominously rises again from the central mass. Pulsing speeds; humming begins, rising in pitch.

FINDER

I still function. And I have found a new power source.

With that, a yellow beam lances upward with a buzzing howl.

CLOSE ON KIRK who is surprised. He looks upward, then back at Finder (o.s.). He is lighted by flickering yellow glow. Buzzing is loud.

KIRK
What is this? What are you . . . ?

Communicator beeps. Kirk grabs it out, opens it.

KIRK
Kirk here.

SCOTT'S VOICE
(*filtered; urgent*)
Captain! Something's stopped us dead
in our tracks! I'm trying Warp power,
but we can't budge!

EXT. SPACE—*Enterprise* caught in a faint yellow beam
and indeed held motionless above the planet. It vibrates, then drifts in toward the planet. It corrects its
position but vibrates and drifts inward even more.

CLOSE ON KIRK—He is shocked. Yellow lights his face
even brighter. Buzzing howl is loudest of all.

SCOTT'S VOICE
(*filtered; urgent*)
It's all I can do to maintain our
position!

Kirk looks at Finder, then looks upward.

KIRK
Scotty! Cut power! Shut her down
completely! Now!

SCOTT'S VOICE
(*filtered; shocked*)
But we'll hit atmosphere for sure, Captain! It's suicide!

KIRK
(*shouts*)
That's an order, Mr. Scott! Cut all
power!

SCOTT'S VOICE
(*filtered*)
Aye, sir! Shutting down!

Kirk looks at Finder (o.s.).

HIS POV—BUBBLE AND FINDER as yellow beam and
buzzing falter, then slowly fade out. The bubble

wavers violently. Finder's pulsing slows, as do all other effects.

CLOSE ON KIRK as he quickly speaks into communicator.

> KIRK
>
> Scotty, full impulse power! Break orbit and get out of range!

> SCOTT'S VOICE
> (*filtered; relief*)
> Aye, Captain! Underway!

Kirk puts away communicator and regards Finder (o.s.). Glow on him now barely dilutes bluish light tinging him.

KIRK AND FINDER—WIDE ANGLE—Kirk steps closer. Bubble is now faint, almost nonexistent; glow is faint; moire is very dark, slowing; pulsing has ceased.

> KIRK
>
> You're through, Finder!

He takes out cube, hefts it, then looks at Finder.

> KIRK
>
> But I'm not! Here's one more challenge! Consider this!

He throws cube at Finder. Surprisingly, it penetrates bubble in a splash of yellow sparks and lands near the central mass.

CLOSE ON KIRK

> KIRK
>
> You're an artifact, Finder! You serve no one! For all their stolen knowledge and wisdom, your masters still were destroyed!

CLOSE ON FINDER

> FINDER
> (*slow, whispering*)
> It is so. They are no more. What could have happened?

CLOSE ON KIRK—His anger fades. He is calmer, his voice level in tone.

KIRK

Not even their patience could have
saved them, Finder. They took and
gave nothing back. You can't live
without sharing.

KIRK AND FINDER—WIDE ANGLE—Scene is quiet for
a beat. Then bubble vanishes. Stabs of light from
Finder touch each of the captives in rapid succession.
They begin to stir, then slowly try to sit up. Kirk
moves closer.

FINDER

Take your people. Leave here. My
course is clear. My masters were destroyed. So must I be. I have been
patient too long.

Kirk rushes in to help the dazed people. Finder's glow
increases, while other effects cease. Kirk helps the
woman to her feet, then looks toward rocky area (o.s.).
Finder emits rising whistle tone.

KIRK

Spock! Bones! Help us! It's going to
self-destruct!

Spock, McCoy and two security men run into shot to
assist Kirk. All four released captives are quickly gotten
to their feet. Then everyone hustles quickly out of
shot. Finder glows even brighter and brighter; whistling grows louder. Then Finder is swallowed up in
the brightness of a star itself; whistling is loudest of
all. Glow fills shot and washes out all details until
shot is solidly fiery red. Hold a few beats.

EXT. SPACE—*Enterprise* in orbit as seen in Act One.
INT. BRIDGE—WIDE ANGLE—Kirk is in command
chair, Spock to his right. McCoy and Scott stand to his
left. Uhura and Sulu and all other Bridge personnel
look forward intently at Main Viewing Screen (o.s.).
THEIR POV—MAIN VIEWING SCREEN showing magni-
fied view of planet, its horizon visible in one edge of
screen. Central to view is intensely bright red patch,
like a volcanic eruption in very slow motion. It remains bright for a few beats, then begins to fade.

ANGLE ON KIRK, SPOCK, MCCOY AND SCOTT—All look forward; Kirk has one hand to chin; he turns to Spock.

KIRK

Observations, Mr. Spock?

Spock turns to him, looking thoughtful. Others watch.

SPOCK

Probability dictates that more Finders will be encountered, Captain. But the information we sent to Star Fleet renders them no longer dangerous.

Kirk crosses his arms. McCoy looks at Spock, smiling.

MCCOY

Spock, suppose that Finder's masters hadn't been destroyed?

KIRK

(smiles)

Yes. Consider for a moment that they did get our starship drive.

Spock raises an eyebrow.

SPOCK

Logically, we would have sent out our own finders, Captain, to find the masters. Purely in self-defense, of course.

Kirk nods, smiling even broader. Others exchange smiles.

MCCOY

Then they would send finders out looking for us. And we'd send finders out after their finders.

Spock appears puzzled. Kirk, McCoy and Scott are enjoying this.

SPOCK

Doctor, that does not follow.

KIRK

Spock, there was an old lady who swallowed a fly, and then a spider to catch

the fly, and then a bird to catch the
spider, and then a cat . . .

SCOTT

Yes, Mr. Spock. 'Cause it wriggled
and jiggled and giggled inside her.

Spock looks at them stonily, then quickly turns to go.

SPOCK

Excuse me, gentlemen. I have my
duties.

They watch him go; all are smiling broadly. Then Kirk
turns to McCoy and Scott, as Spock goes off out of shot.

KIRK

Well, you two. No duties?

McCoy and Scott quickly head their various ways. Shot
tightens on Kirk, who smiles and shakes his head.

KIRK

Mr. Sulu, take us out of orbit. Lay in
a course for Starbase Six.

EXT. SPACE—*Enterprise* leaving orbit and heading outward from the planet. Hold for

FADE OUT

Editors' Introduction to "In the Maze"

The excellence of certain *Star Trek* fanzine publications can be seen in stories like "In the Maze"—published here essentially as it appeared in *T-NEGATIVE,* which is scrupulously edited by Ruth Berman, a writer and editor with a Ph.D. in English, whose work appeared, twice, in *New Voyages* (1).

In *New Voyages* (1), of course, we acknowledged in the introduction our profound debt to *Star Trek* fan fiction, to the fanzines which published it, and to the writers, including many professionals, who wrote it. We want to continue to acknowledge that debt. This time only three of our ten items were published in fanzines before being submitted for *New Voyages 2,* and one since. But this volume of *New Voyages* continues to include both previously published professionals and those whose first professional publication is in *New Voyages*.

Jennifer Guttridge is now both. Her first professional publication was "The Winged Dreamers" in *New Voyages* (1)—which drew extremely high praise from readers.

Here she appears with a second publication in *New Voyages 2*.

Jennifer, a close long-distance friend for many years, lives with her husband and two daughters in the English countryside. The power of her writing argues a brilliant future—more forcefully each time. She is, among other things, a very physical writer with a tough grasp of the tough-universe aspects of physical reality —and a deep understanding of love.

Here in "In the Maze" is another hard-hitting, sometimes gut-wrenching story of the bonds which can bind men together in the face of a tough universe. It is perhaps those very bonds of love which can be the basis of a bond of understanding with very different life-forms—even when they are not remotely like us.

Or—*are* they . . . ?

IN THE MAZE

by Jennifer Guttridge

Uhura looked up from the communications console. She had a tired, worried frown on her face. "There's still nothing, sir," she said. "No word from the landing party at all, and I can't trace them."

Kirk sighed and turned away, the weariness in his face mirroring hers. "It's been twelve hours," he said fretfully. "Something's gone badly wrong. They must need help."

Spock turned in his seat. "Captain, our orders from Star Fleet specifically forbid—"

"Bull," said Kirk. He went back to pacing the bridge balcony. In any circumstances the loss of the six-man landing party would be a matter of grave concern, but this case was exceptional. The planet seemed normal enough—a feudal society, based on agriculture, and closed to visitors from space so that it could develop without interference. But then an automated probe had discovered a building which could not have been constructed by the natives, perched on a high hill just outside one of the most populous areas. Star Fleet had ordered *Enterprise* to carry out a discreet investigation. When sensor readings failed to give any indication of who had constructed the building or for what purpose, Kirk sent down a landing party on his own initiative.

Spock had objected: "Captain, in view of the possibility of cultural contamination, it is unwise to—"

"But we're getting nowhere from up here."

"We have not yet exhausted all the possible tests which can be performed from the ship, sir. Until we do, a landing party is quite illogical."

Kirk's lips tightened. "Nevertheless, I'm going to

see what a team on the spot can do. Objections, Mr. Spock?"

"I have stated my objections already, Captain. With your permission, I will enter them in the log."

Kirk stiffened. "Go ahead," he said, and turned away.

Spock had not said "I told you so" when Wardoff failed to report, but Kirk could read the thought in his face. The two did not speak to each other, except to carry out ship's business.

Kirk paused in his pacing and looked at the screen. *Enterprise* hung in orbit high above the night side of the planet, and the dark globe filled a third of the screen. It turned slowly against the distant haze of stars. Black seas glinted through the heavy cloud cover, and the land masses were a dead black. The towns were invisible, the sparse fires of hearth and torch being too small to register on that scale.

Kirk paced back round the balcony, his mind made up. "Mr. Spock, equip a landing party. We'll beam down and try to locate Wardoff's team."

Spock looked doubtful. "Captain, if the original landing party has been apprehended, the arrival of a further contingent could only compound the risk to this society."

Kirk slapped his palm against the balcony rail. "We're going, Mr. Spock. Get ready." He turned on his heel and strode to the turbo-lift doors. "Lieutenant Uhura," he said in passing, "have Dr. McCoy join us in the transporter room in fifteen minutes." The turbo-lift doors closed on him. Spock sighed a silent sigh and turned once more to his computer.

The landscape was dark and wet, and the ground underfoot decidedly soggy. As the drone of the transport beam faded away, a drifting rain splattered coldly into the faces of the landing party. All six wore the usual dress of the native people: slack trousers, laced knee-length tunics, and head-dresses fastened to a band round the forehead and draped back over the head and down to cover the neck and shoulder. Spock had pulled his forward to cover his ears, and the result resembled something midway between an Arab sheik and a sophisticated red-Indian.

Kirk studied the black ground. There were clumps of long, rain-flattened grass, an occasional gleam of surface water, and vast tracts of mud. They stood in the middle of a low-lying water-meadow bordered on one side by a wide river and on the other by a dark, humped hill. The meadow was emptied of its grazing daytime occupants, and the starship crew had it to themselves. There was no other living being to be seen.

"Are these the exact co-ordinates Wardoff used?" Kirk asked.

Spock looked up from his tricorder. "Affirmative. There is the structure on the hill."

Kirk looked up, and by squinting his eyes against the rain he could distinguish an angular shape against the skyline. He wiped some of the water off his face. "I see. Their last report was that they had reached it and were investigating." No one bothered to point out that it was then they had lost contact with the landing party. "Keep together, keep low, and keep quiet." Kirk began to slosh through the mud and water toward the hill.

The hillside was closed in shrubbery, and they soon found out why no fences were needed to keep the beasts in the field. The bushes had gnarled, twisted roots that wriggled across the surface of the ground; in the darkness they were unseen stumbling blocks. The leaves were upright and broad, and razor-sharp at the edges. Several cut fingers quickly taught the landing party not to hold on to the bushes to pull themselves along.

Halfway up, Kirk paused for breath and waited for his men to catch up with him: McCoy, three security guards, and Spock.

McCoy looked at the Captain with irritation. "How much further is it?" he said, as quietly as he could and be heard over the wind.

Kirk glanced upward. "Not far."

"Nobody said anything about an assault course in a monsoon!"

Kirk grimaced in sympathy and resumed the ascent.

To a local observer they would have appeared no more than a bedraggled line of commoners making their way through the rain, except that on that planet hardly anyone went out at night, and no one at all went toward that hill.

The rain became heavier, driving downhill on the wind and rattling among the foliage. The headcloths whipped round their faces, and the cold rainwater ran steadily down their backs; by the time they reached the side of the building they were glad to rest in its shelter and attempt to wring some of the water from their clothing.

"Life forms, Mr. Spock?"

Spock raised his eyes from the tricorder and looked noncommittal. "Vague readings, Captain. Nothing definite."

"What's behind these walls?"

"Impossible to say. The substance seems to be resistant to scanning. I get vague indications of life low down on the scale. Location indeterminate, shifting."

"Rats," McCoy said.

Spock raised an eyebrow. "Doctor?"

"You're picking up the local equivalent of rats. Every place like this has rats."

"If it's responsible for the disappearance of our landing party, that's not all it has," Kirk said. "Spock, can you see any sign of a way in?"

Spock looked both ways along the wall. "Negative, Captain."

"Let's try this way," Kirk said, and started for the nearest corner.

The building was a block, a perfect cube forty feet on a side, half buried in the hillside. The substance of the walls looked like pebble-dashed concrete, but it registered as an integral substance, not an amalgamate. There was no sign of a door or window. Moss and the green slime of constant damp, together with an occasional climbing vine, found purchase, but the walls were not cracked.

The landing party climbed up along the line where the side wall vanished into the hillside, along the top where the flat roof sloped back into the ground, and down the other side. Nowhere did they see an entrance.

"Comment, Mr. Spock?" Kirk said when they were within one corner of their starting point.

"Interesting," Spock said without interest. By now he was too wet and cold to be "fascinated" by anything.

"The landing party disappeared at this point. They must have gone—or been taken—inside."

"It is logical to assume so."

"If we're going to follow we'll have to make our own way in." Kirk turned to the security team. "Mr. Sheckley, Mr. Lopez, set your phasers on full; blast a hole through this wall." He stepped aside, and the two men stood shoulder to shoulder and fired in unison. The rain turned into steam, the moss and slime blackened, and the surface of the wall brightened through red to white, but the wall remained intact. "Probe- and phaser-resistant," Kirk said. "What the devil is that stuff?"

"Captain," Spock called.

Kirk turned and went over. Spock was investigating a place where the sharp-leaved vegetation grew right up to the wall, and the ground sloped steeply upward.

"There seems to be a sort of doorway, Captain. I can't reach it."

Kirk gestured to the security guards. "Burn these plants down."

The men's phasers made short work of reducing the vegetation to ashes, revealing a low, wide arch in the wall, and in the arch an old but very solid-looking door.

"The landing party didn't go through there," Kirk said at once. "That door hasn't been opened in years."

"But it is a way in, Captain."

Kirk nodded, frowning, and Spock reached for the catch . . .

. . . The door swung slowly inward. It opened without a sound to reveal an impenetrable blackness beyond. Kirk called Wardoff's name into the opening. His voice seemed to bounce flatly back. No one answered.

They looked at each other.

"Do we go in?" McCoy whispered.

"Not yet." Kirk stepped back from the doorway. "These walls are phaser-resistant and impervious to the tricorder. The chances are that the ship's sensors can't penetrate them, either—the transporter won't be able to reach us. We'll be on our own." He pulled the communicator from under his tunic, shook it dry, and flicked open the lid. "*Enterprise*. Kirk here."

"Scott here, sir."

"We've found a way into this structure down here. It may put us out of touch for a while, but track us with the sensors if you find you can."

"Aye, sir. How long shall I give ye before I send down a search party?"

Kirk met Spock's eyes over the communicator, and saw that his First Officer agreed with him. "No search party, Mr. Scott. Kirk out."

"Jim, we don't know what's in there," McCoy said, as Kirk put the communicator away.

"No." Kirk eyed the doorway. "We don't. And it obviously isn't going to come out and show itself." He leaned on the arch and squinted into the blackness. "I can't see anything," he said. "Spock, you'd better follow me at a discreet distance."

Spock nodded and watched as Kirk pulled out his phaser and stepped into the doorway. Kirk bent low to pass beneath the arch and . . . vanished.

"Captain!" Spock stepped to the doorway, his phaser aimed and ready. There was no target. "Captain! Jim!" No answer came.

McCoy joined Spock in the doorway. "What happened to him?"

Spock shook his head. "I do not know, Doctor."

"Then what are we going to do?"

"My orders were explicit," Spock said, checking the charge of his phaser and studying once more the internal blackness.

"What about us?"

Spock raised an eyebrow. "What about you, Doctor?"

"Are you going to leave us standing out here?"

"If you wish to return to the ship you have my consent, Dr. McCoy," Spock said without looking at him.

"And leave Jim in trouble and you walking into the same mess? Not likely! And if you tell me I'm being illogical—!"

Spock considered him for a moment, then looked at the guards. "Keep watch until daybreak. If we are not back then, return to the ship. Shall we go, Doctor?"

McCoy nodded warily, and together he and Spock stepped through the archway.

They dropped into a black vortex. There was a strong, cold blast of air that stung their eyes until tears came. The sensation was one of movement, not exactly of falling, but a displacement. McCoy stretched out a hand, feeling for the touch of Spock's sleeve. There was nothing. He drew breath to call the Vulcan's name, but the wind whipped away the words before he could utter them. He felt a surge of panic, and then even that was driven from him as he landed on a hard floor. Something inside his chest gave, and he gasped at the sharp pain. A sudden redness flooded into his brain, and he lost consciousness.

Still dazed, Spock rolled over onto his back. The drop had been a long one and the landing heavy. He was essentially undamaged, but he could feel numerous bruises, and he was winded. He lay sprawled on a gray stone plinth in the center of a gray stone room. There was a generalized gray light, a flow of cool air, and utter silence. His own breathing sounded harsh and unnatural, and he could hear the hissing sigh of his blood. His eyes drifted across the featureless gray slab of the ceiling and down the wall. Then he blinked and made an attempt to focus, and sat up. He could see no way out. He got up, put a hand to an especially painful muscle in his back, and limped over to where McCoy lay.

The doctor was sprawled over the edge of the plinth, half on it and half off, his eyes closed and his breathing shallow. Spock made a quick examination. The doctor's skin was cold and damp, and his heartbeat rapid. There was a dark, spongy bruise on his left side that Spock didn't like the look of at all. There was nothing he could do for McCoy while he was still unconscious. He made his position as comfortable as he could and went to examine the walls.

They were made of the same substance that formed the walls of the cube: a coarse, lumpy material that felt rough to the fingertips but showed no seams. There was no sign that any segment had been constructed to move aside. Spock stood still and looked slowly round, his mind pondering the problem. He conjectured that there must be a portal concealed somewhere. But there were no furnishings at all; the gray floor was bare, and its only feature was the central circular plinth. He could find no source for the dim light that filled the room. Spock walked back and inspected the plinth. It was of the same gray material, and it seemed to be of one piece with the floor.

McCoy stirred and groaned. Spock crouched down beside him and held him still. "Try not to move, Doctor."

The blue eyes opened and gazed up at him icily. "What d'you mean, don't move? Where'n hell did you vanish to? And who stuck the knife in my ribs?" He insisted on sitting up, so Spock helped him settle on the edge of the plinth.

"I have been nowhere, Dr. McCoy. Indeed, I can find no means of leaving this place. No one has knifed you. I believe you have broken a rib."

McCoy probed the bruise beneath his tunic and winced. "You're right," he agreed grudgingly. "Where are we? Where's Jim? And for God's sake take that headdress off! The color's running down your neck."

Spock pulled the cloth from the headband and looked at it. "Wherever the Captain is, he is not here, Doctor. And I do not know where 'here' is."

"You don't. . . . But we must be inside that block-shaped thing . . ."

"I think not." Spock got up and began to prowl round the cell.

"We stepped through the arch, Spock," McCoy grated. "Where can we be except on the other side—unless you think it's a transporter of some sort?"

"Possibly."

"Oh. Well, we came here to find the Captain. If he's not here, we'd better start looking."

"You're in no condition to move, Doctor."

"Nonsense, I—" McCoy stopped. He reached for his medical kit, slowly drew it out, and opened it. "Here." He handed Spock a tube of foam-bandage. "Tape me up." He gritted his teeth while Spock opened his leather tunic and sprayed the foam over his side. It hardened as it hit, and he relaxed a little. "That'll hold it a while. Now let's—" He stopped again, and looked around. "No doors."

Spock shrugged and went back to his pacing, testing the walls for any hint of a break.

McCoy watched him helplessly. The Vulcan favored his left leg as he walked, and McCoy, forgetting his own injury, struggled to his feet. The room swayed, but he waited until it steadied and went over to Spock. "You're limping."

"A pulled muscle, Doctor."

"Are you sure?" He tried to hold Spock still for examination, but found himself leaning on the Vulcan for support as another wave of faintness swept through him.

Spock stood with his legs braced and supported McCoy until the weakness passed.

"I'm sorry, Spock," McCoy said. "I didn't mean to—"

"Quite all right, Doctor," Spock said in a dis-

tracted voice, staring over McCoy's head, back toward
the plinth.

McCoy turned around carefully. In the air above
the plinth there hung a translucent curtain of silver.
"What's that?"

"Unknown, Doctor. Possibly the entrance—or the
exit." Spock took a tentative step forward.

McCoy grabbed his arm. "We can't risk being
separated."

Spock nodded, and they went slowly toward the
plinth. The silver curtain hung from almost the ceiling
to almost the floor. They could see the far wall through
it, but Spock was quite certain that if they stepped
through it they would not find themselves on the other
side of the room. The curtain shivered as if it were a
fine fabric in an air current.

"Do you think Jim could be on the other side of
that?" McCoy asked in a whisper.

"Possibly."

"Then what are we waiting for?"

Spock held him back. "We have no idea what lies
on the other side of that curtain. Some entity constructed this place. We may be on the verge of meeting
him."

"Someone, or something. Is that what you're saying, Spock? Are you afraid to go through there?"

Spock looked at him sideways. "Not afraid, Doctor. I am merely weighing the possibilities."

"You didn't wait to follow Jim through that first
arch. Come on!"

"You were not injured at that time, Doctor. I now
have a responsibility—"

McCoy tore himself away from the Vulcan's support. "You're not responsible for me, Spock. We've got
to find the Captain."

Spock stared at him, startled by his vehemence.
"Doctor—"

"I'm going through, anyway, with you or without
you." McCoy stepped forward, then swayed and had
to wait.

Spock steadied him and looked again at the silver

curtain. "Very well, Doctor." They stepped up onto the plinth, and Spock reached out a hand toward the silveriness. He felt nothing, but it parted at the touch of his fingers as if it were made of a million strings of minute silver beads. Beyond it was a flat, black void.

"Here we go again," said McCoy.

The two men locked their hands about each other's wrists, and McCoy tucked his elbow in tightly against his injured side. They stepped through the curtain.

They stepped down into a dark, narrow passage with a high ceiling. Water ran freely down walls coated with black patches of slime.

"Well, now where in hell are we?" McCoy growled.

Spock raised an eyebrow at him and started to ask on what grounds McCoy concluded that they were in a mythological domain. Then he thought better of it and remained silent, looking up and down the passage.

"Spock? You're in command here. Which way do we go?"

Spock shook his head as if slightly bewildered, and then he turned abruptly. "This way, Doctor," he said and began to stride along the passage.

McCoy pulled a face at what looked like a purely arbitrary decision, and began to follow more slowly.

Spock looked back and saw that the Doctor was falling behind. He slowed his pace and waited for him to catch up. Then he started on ahead again impatiently. Mentally, McCoy cursed all Vulcans, gritted his teeth, and pressed on as fast as he could.

Kirk tested the crystal bars of his cage, trying his best to break one. Beyond the cage the being ignored him. It swayed along almost fluidly on a dozen or more multi-jointed leg-like appendages, moving from one item of complex electronic equipment to the next to make fine adjustments with its almost human, black shelled hands. Kirk had recovered from the first shock of horror at its ugliness: the insectlike scuttling, the soft, pallid flesh of the body, the neckless head with the face of a corpse eight days drowned. Hidden in the bloated white rolls of skin were two large, round yellow eyes. Somewhere amidst that damp tissue there might also be a mouth, but Kirk had seen no sign of one. The creature clicked like an excited radiation counter; sometimes fast, sometimes more slowly, but always with a purposeful intensity. Kirk tried to interpret the clicks as a language. He clicked back, trying to mimic it, then talked at it, shouted at it. He only barely refrained from stamping his feet in frustration when it failed to do more than stare at him with apparent startlement out of its unblinking eyes, and then scuttled off crabwise back to its ranked equipment. He told himself firmly that intelligence came in many shapes and sizes, and the packages were not always beautiful. However, communication with the thing seemed impossible.

In his years in space, Kirk had seen a great many alien installations, but he found the equipment around him unfathomable. There were dials and screens alive with shifting, colored shadows; mirror-bright silver panels with complex patterns of controls; tubes and bulbs and cylinders of colored gasses, blue and green and pinkish gray. Beyond these were vague presences, hard even to concentrate on; colored curtains pulsed and faded, patches of light drifted, courseless and directionless, sounds wavered on the edge of audibility. . . .

There were no walls. Beyond the point where the floor ended, a pink-lit gray mist hung suspended, flaring occasionally as if a firework display were being held somewhere behind the fog. The air was cool . . . Kirk shivered.

He decided to try once more to communicate with the being. He gripped the bars hard and pushed his face between them. "Where is this place?" he said. "Where are my men?"

The being turned toward the raised platform where the cage stood. The yellow eyes protruded and looked at him.

"Where's my landing party?" Kirk said. "Where are my officers?"

The soft flesh of the being's back rippled as if the soundwaves of Kirk's voice were hitting it. It clicked thoughtfully and then returned to its devices. Kirk scowled, and rammed the palms of his hands against the bars that shut him in. Then his attention was drawn away from himself.

On one of the larger screens, the colored shadows were clearing. A small patch appeared in the center and enlarged into a picture that filled the screen. Kirk saw Spock and McCoy walking in a confined passage. They moved slowly, as if swimming in a thick fluid. The being clicked and did something to one of the silver panels, and the movements of the two men became normal. Kirk watched transfixed.

The place was an interminable warren of narrow, gray passages, damp-stained stairwells, and misleading cul-de-sacs. Already it seemed to McCoy that they had been exploring the tunnels for half of eternity: retracing their steps from the blind alleys, choosing and then choosing again where many passageways converged, pausing frequently for McCoy to lean against a wall and rest, panting.

It was during one of those rest periods that McCoy put the idea into words. Spock was making use of the time, exploring for a short way down each of two adjoining passages, examining every inch of the rough walls, investigating every corner, and constantly pausing to listen to the dripping silence, his head on one side like an intent bird. "Spock, what if Jim isn't in these passages at all?"

For a moment Spock continued to look back down the passage the way they'd come; then he raised his eyes, turning his head slightly toward McCoy as he did so. McCoy could see that the same thought had occurred to Spock a long time ago. He must have kept silent about it for McCoy's sake.

McCoy straightened stiffly, aware that the ache in his side had suddenly become almost crippling in its intensity. "Any idea what our next course of action is?"

"We can do one of three things, Doctor. Go on, go back, or stay here."

McCoy looked sour. "They all sound pointless."

"No. If we go on, we may find the Captain." Spock eyed the passageway. "I believe he is being used as . . . bait, to encourage us to go on."

"Like rats in a maze?" McCoy said skeptically. Then he looked around again. "Yes, I see what you mean. But—"

"I suggest," Spock interrupted, "that you refrain from further discussion, and rest, Dr. McCoy."

McCoy glared at him, making no impression on Spock. McCoy sighed, then obediently lowered himself to the floor, resting his back against the wall. He wrapped his arms round his chest. The wall was cold and damp, and the moisture got inside the leather jerkin and ran down his back. But McCoy was very tired, and pain had exhausted him. His eyes closed, flickered open, and closed again. His head fell forward. Soon his breathing steadied, and he slept.

For a while Spock continued to prowl the passage. Then he crouched at the Doctor's side and felt for his pulse. It was rapid but strong. McCoy shifted uneasily but continued to sleep. Spock left him and sat down against the opposite wall, drawing his knees up into his chest and wrapping his arms round them. He watched McCoy for a time and then closed his own eyes, leaning forward so that his forehead rested on his knees, and allowed his metabolism to slow. He was not asleep, but his body relaxed and rested, and after a time a part of his mind switched itself off.

The screen clouded again, and as the picture faded Kirk found himself lonelier than before. He unlocked his clenched fists from around the bars; his fingers were stiff. He stepped back and looked down at the being with growing dislike. "Where are they?" he asked. "What are you doing to them? and why?"

The being ignored him. It was still busy about its equipment and seemed to be switching most of it off; screens and dials darkened, and lights went out. Kirk sat down on the floor and watched, feeling helpless and drained. Beyond the boundaries of the laboratory the pink mist still hung unmoving, but beyond it the aural displays had brightened and intensified. The being finished what it was doing and came toward him, clicking slowly. In its hands it held a tray bearing a small quantity of pale brown powder. It pushed this into the cage through the narrow gap between the bottom of the bars and the platform top. For a long moment it gazed at its captive with that bright, brassy stare; and Kirk looked back at it hopelessly. Then the being turned and scuttled away between the ranks of equipment to the clear space beyond. It stepped into the folds of a red curtain and vanished, and after it the curtain vanished, too.

At once the lighting dimmed and went out, as if without its owner it knew there were no need for it. The laboratory was lit only by the flaring colors from beyond the mist, and they danced eerily across the floor, casting weird reflections in the silver faces of the machines. Kirk noticed that even in the darkness the crystal bars of the cage seemed to gleam with inner light.

He dipped a finger into the pile of brown powder. It seemed to be intended as nourishment, although it was tasteless and dry. He ate some of it and then returned to the side of the cage. He sat down with his back to the bars and watched the flow of light across the floor, and soon he, too, slept.

Spock roused himself. Time had passed, measured by the watchful portion of his mind, and he knew that the time had come to move on. All was as it had been before: the gray light and the damp passages. McCoy still slept, humped awkwardly against the wall. His mouth was open, and his breathing harsh. His face had become gray. Carefully, aware that his body temperature was too low for rapid movement, Spock stretched each muscle in turn and flexed himself. He felt a pang of hunger and frowned at it. He himself could set it aside almost indefinitely, but McCoy, in his weakened condition, would not be able to ignore hunger so easily. Spock stood up slowly and on stiff legs went over to McCoy. The Doctor's ashen face was cold to the touch and damp with a thin film of sweat, but he started awake and stared at Spock.

"What is it? Is it time to go? How . . . how long have we been here?"

"Several hours. Move slowly, Doctor."

McCoy tried to sit up and grunted with the pain of cramp. "I see what you mean, Spock."

Spock put a hand under McCoy's armpit and the other arm round his back, and almost lifted him onto his feet. McCoy's face contorted, and he remained doubled over for a long minute, leaning heavily on the Vulcan before he was able to straighten his back. He was hungry, but realized, as Spock had, that there was nothing they could do about it and so said nothing. He composed his face and looked at Spock. "I'm not going to get far like this. You'll stand a better chance of finding Jim on your own."

A slight smile flickered for a fraction of a second around Spock's lips. "And what about you, Doctor?" he asked.

"I'll be all right here till you get back. Besides, if something has arranged all this, it'll take me out of here once I've stopped performing tricks for it."

"What do you do with laboratory animals once their usefulness is curtailed, Doctor?"

McCoy met the almost amused black eyes and swallowed hard. "All right, if we can't stay here, we'd better get moving."

Spock's look became anxious, and he eyed the medical kit on the Doctor's belt. "I could give you a pain-killing injection—"

"I'm quite capable of seeing to my own injections!" McCoy snapped. "If I'd wanted one I'd have taken one before. How far do you think I'd get filled with dope? We both need clear heads."

"But a light dosage would—"

"Yes, I know," McCoy interrupted. "But you're not a doctor, and I don't trust me to prescribe it. I'm . . . not an objective physician with this patient."

Spock nodded, still with a frown of worry between

his eyes, and stood back, although he kept one hand under the Doctor's arm, in support. More slowly than before, the two men started to limp along the passage.

For Kirk it was a relief to see them. No matter how far they were from him, at least he knew that they still lived. Both he and the being stood quite still, watching, he inside the cage and the other out.

The next flight of steps sloped steeply and unevenly downward into a circular stairwell. The walls were wet, and water dripped from step to step with steady plops. From out of the well came a slow stream of dank, damp air. McCoy deposited himself against the wall and looked down, wheezing painfully. "Do we really have to go down there, Spock?" he asked.

Spock, on his haunches studying the steps, nodded distractedly. "Yes, Doctor. However . . ." He looked up at McCoy with doubt. "You may rest first if you wish."

"No, I don't wish. What I mean is, do we have to go that way? Can't we find some other way around?"

"Negative. We have explored the other passages already. If we are to find the Captain, our way lies ahead. And he may be in need of our help."

"You still think we're going to find him?"

"I intend to find him, Doctor."

McCoy saw the grim lines of determination in his profile. "You didn't want to be on this landing party at all, did you, Spock?" he asked, with sudden insight.

Spock thought for long seconds before he replied. "In my opinion, none of us should have come here."

McCoy eyed him narrowly. "Did you quarrel with Jim about that?"

"I obey my instructions, Doctor, as you do."

"That doesn't mean you approve?" McCoy allowed the statement to end in a question. Spock did not reply. "Well, maybe you were right. But . . . whatever this is, it's interfering with the normal development of this planet's culture. Jim has a duty to stop it, if he can."

For a moment Spock was silent. Then he looked

around at the stained walls. "However, it is possible that our presence here could be even more . . . disruptive."

"How?" McCoy asked, his back tingling at the tone of the Vulcan's voice.

"The entity has been experimenting with a primitive native culture. In these clothes we resemble them closely enough, but if it should discover—as it must if its experiments continue—that we possess a higher level of sophistication, it might consider us a threat. The result could be war."

McCoy stared at him in horror. "Yes," he said softly. "I suppose it could."

Spock turned. "Shall we go, Doctor?"

Kirk looked from the screen to the creature, and suddenly was afraid for his friends. If the maze was a test of intelligence, then surely the tests would grow progressively more difficult—and dangerous? "Go back, Spock," he groaned. "Don't come."

Spock and McCoy continued unhearing down the steps, but the being turned and looked at him with interest.

The crude steps twisted down in a shallow spiral, and as Spock and McCoy descended, the light gradually faded into darkness. At the bottom the stairway straightened and ended in a large, dark chamber. The only illumination spilled from the stairwell, and in it they could see that the floor sloped down to a pool of still black water that covered more than two thirds of the room.

McCoy scowled at the oily surface. "Is that what we've come all this way to see?" he asked. "Jim isn't here."

Spock began to explore the wall with his fingertips. McCoy watched him a moment and then began investigating the wall on the other side of the entrance, looking for some sort of opening, he presumed. Gradually they both moved away from the single source of light.

Behind Spock the surface of the black water broke without a ripple, and something began to inch its way up the sloping floor.

McCoy's foot struck something in the darkness, something that moved with a grating sound on the floor. He bent down and groped for it. It was a phaser. As he picked it up he noted automatically that its power level was at zero. He turned with it in his hand. "Spock. . . . Spock!"

The Vulcan turned, but at the same moment that he raised the alarm the black, whip-like tentacle wrapped itself round the calf of Spock's leg and jerked tight. Spock overbalanced and went down with a crash that drove the breath out of him. The tentacle, stretched straight from the water's edge, began to retract, dragging him with it. Spock's hands scratched for a purchase on the rough floor and found none. He kicked hard, trying to shake the thing loose, and failed. Its grip was strong and very tight; his foot started to ache from blood starvation. He arched his back, struggling, and a wildly flying hand struck something hard: a cold, metal ring solidly imbedded in the floor. Both Spock's hands locked on to it, and Vulcan muscles knotted with effort. The remorseless drag toward the water's edge ceased, but the tentacle continued to retract.

McCoy knelt at his side, the empty phaser and the mystery it posed forgotten. Desperately he fought to unwind the hard coils from the Vulcan's leg, but it was impossible. He pulled out his phaser and sent a beam lancing toward the tentacle. It glanced harmlessly off the armored black rope of muscle and dissipated. He fired again.

"No, Doctor," Spock gasped. "The energy of our phasers has no power in this environment."

That explained the empty phaser, and looking toward the black water McCoy realized what had happened to its owner. Again he tried frantically to free Spock's leg. The Vulcan's body was stretched out as if on the rack. His breath came in agonized gasps, and there were beads of sweat on his face, something

McCoy had rarely seen before. His hands were white, knotted about the ring.

McCoy wrenched open his medical kit and snatched out the largest scalpel it contained, cutting himself in his haste to remove the guard from the blade. He slashed at the tentacle, pressing as hard as he could. His hands became covered with thick, black blood, but the cuts were shallow, and the scalpel quickly became blunted on the iron-hard flesh.

Spock looked over his shoulder, trembling in spite of himself. "The leg, Doctor. You'll have to . . ."

"No! Hold on just a minute longer—"

"I can't." The white hands were slipping.

McCoy put his hand on the leg, and raised the scalpel. "I can't." He chewed his lip and tightened his hold on the scalpel, then threw it down and rummaged again in the medical kit.

The hands came free of the metal ring. The tentacle began to drag Spock once more toward the water.

McCoy pulled out a hypo, fumbled with a capsule, punched it into the end, and pushed the whole of the contents into the wound he'd made. Then he put Spock's arm around his neck and braced all his weight against the force pulling the Vulcan back. Their progress slowed, but they were still dragged inexorably down to the water's edge. McCoy arched himself up and cried out in pain as movement of the broken rib tore at his lungs. He felt the coldness in his feet as his boots touched the surface of the water and went under. He cursed, wondering first how sluggish the monster's circulation could be and then if the drug had any effect on it at all.

The tentacle heaved, and both men slid deep into the water. McCoy gasped and fought to keep their heads above the surface. He slipped, foundered, and took down a great gulp of the foul liquid. Then he realized that they'd stopped moving. He pulled back, but Spock was still held fast.

McCoy coughed, spat out water and blood, and ducked under, reaching toward the trapped leg. The tentacle was still wound about it, and it resisted his efforts, but he mustered all the strength he had left and loosened it enough to drag Spock's foot through the coils. He dragged the Vulcan back up the slope and half out of the water, where for a long time he lay half sprawled across him, both unconscious.

Kirk dropped back from the crystal bars of the cage. His face was ridged with the marks of the bars. He looked at the being, his eyes blazing with hatred. "You tried to kill them! What sort of bloody evil monstrosity are you?"

The being gazed at him out of the large, golden eyes. He could not read expression on the alien features. Its face was still, but the soft white flesh of its body was rippling beneath its skin, and it was clicking rapidly.

Kirk seized the glowing crystal bars in his fists and tried to heave them apart.

The pattern of rippling flesh on the being's body changed. It shifted uncertainly from one set of legs to another, studying Kirk intently. Then, abruptly, as if it had reached an important decision, it turned and scuttled to the silver consoles.

McCoy stirred and sat up shakily. He coughed a little and swallowed blood. Spock lay quite still beside him, with his feet in the water. That alarmed McCoy. With a grunt he got to his knees and wedged his hands under the Vulcan's arms. Inch by inch he dragged him up the slope to the entrance of the chamber and the stairway beyond. The effort exhausted him. He sat down on the bottom step and watched the black water, searching for the quiver or flick of a tentacle. All he wanted was to get as far from that dark pool as he could, but he was scarcely able to move himself, let alone carry Spock.

He looked down at Spock and saw that the leather jerkin was contracting across his chest as it dried. He unlaced it, thought for a moment, and then removed it. Shaking the water out of the medical scanner, he passed it over Spock's chest. There were distinct indications of water in each of his lung sacs. Clearly, he'd come very close to drowning. And now there would be the possibility of pneumonia.

McCoy took Spock's arm and heaved him over onto his belly. Then he leaned on his back, pumping. Spock's breathing rasped, and then he retched and vomited, bringing up black water. McCoy sighed with relief, and then turned sharply. Something had moved. The tip of a tentacle was visible at the water's edge, exploring upward.

He shook Spock. "Wake up! We've got to get out of here."

Spock was only just conscious, but something of McCoy's urgency communicated itself to him. He fought to get onto his knees. McCoy took his arm around his shoulders and stood up. Spock staggered onto his feet. The injured leg promptly collapsed under him, and they both fell.

McCoy looked up and stared. At the first turn of the stairway, a silver curtain hung across the steps. McCoy tightened his grip round Spock's back and started upward. Mindlessly, Spock followed his urging, crawling up the steps on hands and knees. McCoy pulled the tenuous strands of the curtain apart, and they tumbled into the void beyond.

The screen clouded. "Where have you put them?" Kirk demanded, glaring at his captor.

The being's back rippled and flowed, but it ignored Kirk. Its eyes had vanished into the folds of flesh, and its hands were moving rapidly over the controls. There was a flash and a flow of light over a hump in the floor. The being scurried away in that direction and stood clicking excitedly. The outline of the two men appeared on the top of the hump, shimmered silver, and slowly solidified. Spock lay quite still, sprawled face down. McCoy sat up slowly. He shook his head groggily and then looked at his surroundings with bewilderment. His eyes then fell on the being, and Kirk saw his face register the same alarm and disgust he had experienced himself at first sight of it. Then McCoy saw the circle of tall crystal bars that formed Kirk's cage. "Jim!"

"I'm all right," said Kirk. "What about Spock?" He tried frantically to free himself from his prison, but the bars moved not one fraction of a centimeter.

The being turned toward him and studied him again. Then it seemed almost to shrug, and it scuttled sideways, back to the silver consoles. It did something to the controls, and a section of the bars flicked out of existence. Kirk forgot about wanting to throttle the creature, and raced to the top of the hump. The being followed, clicking. Kirk dropped to his knees beside McCoy.

"Bones, is he—"

"I think he's all right. There was a thing—"

"I know. I saw what happened."

McCoy adjusted a hypo and pumped a dose into Spock's shoulder. "He should come round in a minute or two. Jim, where are we? And . . ." He stared at the being. "What . . is . . that . . thing?"

The creature stood still, clicking slowly.

"I don't know what it is. I can't communicate with it," Kirk said. "I don't think there's any way. We're . . . more than worlds apart."

Spock groaned, and his eyes opened and focused on McCoy's face. "Dr. McCoy," he said. "My leg. I can't feel it. Did you . . . ?"

"No. The leg's numb, but it's still there," McCoy said.

Spock's eyes bored into his as if for a moment he didn't believe him, and then he nodded slightly, and the lines of his face relaxed. Briefly, his eyes closed. Then he opened them and started trying to get up. For a few moments McCoy tried to discourage him, then let it go and waved Kirk to help Spock sit up.

McCoy checked him with the scanner and grunted with satisfaction. "Constitution of a slime-devil. He'll be all right."

Spock's eyes turned toward him, formal once more. "That is obvious, Doctor."

"Well, you were worried enough about that leg for

a while there," McCoy growled, but Spock was no longer listening. His eyes roamed about the laboratory with intense interest. Kirk had the feeling that Spock's hands were itching to explore the possibilities of the silver consoles, if only his legs would carry him there.

Spock's restless eyes settled on the alien being. "Fascinating," he murmured. "Quite fascinating."

The skin on the being's back rippled. Spock drew a sharp breath and put a hand to his head.

"What's wrong, Spock?" said McCoy. "Does it hurt?"

"No. A . . . mixture of sensations."

The being took three slow steps sideways toward them, and its skin rippled again.

"It is inquiring . . . if we are harmed," Spock said.

"Harmed?" McCoy glared at him, then at the being. "Why, that cold-blooded—"

"Doctor." Kirk silenced him with an upraised hand. "Spock, is it telepathic?"

"A little. Not exactly." Spock's eyes were vacant, his mind concentrated on the foreign sensations. "It did not realize that beings with such a paucity of manipulative limbs could have developed intelligence, until your reactions to the screened image of our actions, Captain, made it realize you were capable of analyzing a set of visual cues and responding compassionately to the peril of others." Spock suddenly gave them a startled look. "It does not distinguish between the concepts of compassion and intelligence," he said. "It communicates chiefly by the radiation and reception of emotions. Fascinating!"

McCoy's face lit up, but Kirk shook his head. "Ask it about Mr. Wardoff's party," Kirk said.

"It regrets . . . two are dead," Spock said. "The others are well and will be returned."

"Then it means to let us go?"

Spock nodded. He seemed slightly surprised himself. "Indeed. And it assures me that its experiments will cease forthwith. It considers it unethical to interfere with developing intelligences. Such as ours." He looked at Kirk with ironic amusement.

"Well, just tell it to be a little more careful whose intelligence it picks on next time," McCoy said.

"There will be no next time," said Spock. "If it performs any further experiments it will be most careful to check first for potential intelligence."

Kirk was silent for a moment. Then he said, "Ask it the way home, Mr. Spock."

"Unnecessary, Captain. Your desire has communicated itself."

The being had already turned to a console, and in a few seconds a shimmering silver curtain materialized beside them.

Kirk looked at the Vulcan. "Can you stand?"

"I can try."

Kirk held out his hand, and Spock gripped his forearm. The Vulcan lurched onto his feet, swayed a moment, and steadied.

"Bones?"

McCoy sighed. "Give me a hand, Jim."

Kirk stretched out his free hand and helped McCoy to his feet.

Spock gazed wistfully at the pink-lit mist.

"One universe at a time, Spock," Kirk said softly He started forward, supporting his two officers.

The being watched the three men step through the curtain. Its bright yellow eyes vanished into the flesh of its face. It clicked what could have been farewell, and then it turned to its equipment. Its flesh moved slowly beneath its skin, displaying regret, perhaps, or sorrow, or maybe it was loneliness . . .

The water meadow was lightening with the first streaks of a watery dawn. It was the long, cold hour when everything was still and colorless. Even the rain had for the moment stopped falling, and the gray river flowed placidly. The flattened grass was gray, and the hill where the cube stood was silhouetted against a gray sky.

The rest of their landing party was there, and so were Wardoff and the remains of his group, looking bewildered and slightly ridiculous in their native head-

cloths. Wardoff stared at Kirk, and then shook his
head, spreading his hands helplessly. "Sir? How did
we get here? We were looking for a way into that building, and then—"

"We'll explain it to you later, Mr. Wardoff,"said
Kirk. "Just as soon as we finish figuring it out." He
flipped open his communicator. *"Enterprise.* Kirk here."

"Scott here, sir. Did ye find them, then?"

"No, they were . . . returned to us. There are ten
to beam up, Mr. Scott. You may take us in any order
that's convenient."

"Captain," Scott said, with a note of urgency in his
voice, "sensors report somethin' odd down there. On
the hill."

All eyes turned toward the gray tor. The square
outline of the cube was shimmering, and as they
watched, the entire structure faded away. Nothing remained but a patch of dry earth beginning to turn to
mud as the rain started again.

"It's all right, Scotty. Just . . . an ethical scientist
closing up shop and going home." He glanced at Spock
and McCoy. "Have a medical team on hand. Prepare
to beam us up, Mr. Scott."

Kirk grinned at the Vulcan, settled somewhat unwillingly in a sickbay bed. "You don't have to apolo-
gize, Mr. Spock," he said. "Your objections had merit.
I don't expect you to agree with me all the time—just
most of it."

Spock's eyebrows climbed toward the top of his
forehead. "I was not apologizing, Captain. I still consider your sending two landing parties down illogical."

McCoy could not snort with his ribs tightly bound
up, but he grinned, and Kirk shook his head ruefully.
"Well, it worked," he said mildly.

Scott tactfully changed the subject. "What I canna
understand, sir, is how all that laboratory fitted into
that wee block, let alone the maze Mr. Spock an' the
doctor reported."

"Well, they weren't exactly there . . . you see,"
said McCoy.

Scott didn't see. "Then . . . where were they?"

Kirk shrugged. "Elsewhere on the planet? Another planet? Another dimension?"

"Our phasers had no effect there," Spock pointed out. "Your third suggestion is, in all probability, the most logical."

Kirk winced. "Thank you, Mr. Spock." He flicked on the intercom. "Mr. Sulu, take us out of orbit. Ahead warp factor two."

Editors' Introduction to "Cave-in"

"Cave-in" is an interesting little item—it's hard to know what to call it: story? poem? dialogue?—which embodies what Leonard Nimoy calls "open texture."

He means that the artist leaves room for the viewer, reader, or audience to use imagination and to read into the work or performance things which even the artist may not have fully intended.

Try reading this with that in mind, and let us know what you think. Who goes here? And what goes on?

We suspect we'll get as many answers as letters. It should be, in a word, "fascinating."

Jane Peyton, by the way, is fully capable of writing a narrative poem in which it is absolutely and heartbreakingly clear what is going on. She is the author of the brilliant, painful "Lament for the Unsung Dead" which is discussed in *Star Trek Lives!*. But the events of that poem happened only in some alternate universe, or some nightmare—not in the real universe where the *Enterprise* still flies with all hands alive and well.

Jane Peyton has a gift for evoking drama and profound emotion in a remarkably small space and in novel forms of writing. This is her first professional publication—not, we trust, her last.

CAVE-IN

by Jane Peyton

It's very hot in here.

Not hot enough.

Oh. I forgot.

Understandable.

No, I should remember.

Why? You owe me
nothing.

I should remember:
Your world is hotter.
I owe you that, at least.

Niceties will not change
the way things are.

No?
Perhaps they are *all* that
will:
The little things.

Minutiae.
Indeed.
You see aspects of me
well.

I know your weaknesses
and your strengths.
They appear to be the
same.

That is illogical.

Perhaps,
But true, nonetheless.

You are like the rest,
Attempting to tell me
that my humanity is my
strength.
It is not.

125

Spock, can't you see?

See what?
What is there to see that
I do not already
perceive?
You and your kind credit
me with little more
intellect than a rotifer.
Disgusting.

"Disgusting."
A term of emotion.

Naturally.
I am using your language.

You're annoyed.

I am incapable of being
annoyed.

Do you know what I
think?

Do you think?

You're an experiment.

I beg your pardon.

You are a hybrid: the
son of an ambassador.
The Ambassador of all
Vulcan was allowed to
have a son like you.
Is that not odd?

I might express the same
incredulity over your
conception.

They hoped you would be
like you are: Partially
emotional.
Guided by logic,
but yet susceptible to
emotion.

Flatly illogical.

Oh?
To what one factor does
your father attribute

his greatest margin of
error?

> The . . . emotionality of
> those with whom he deals.

And is that not because he
   cannot completely
   comprehend such
   emotionality?

> I will concede as much.
> So?

You are a *better* model.
You can comprehend.

> No.

You *refuse* to see the logic
   of what I've said.

> There is no logic to see.

True enough;
They probably didn't
   expect you'd be so
   maladjusted.

> I am not maladjusted.

Understandable, of course.
Simply that margin of
   error taking its toll.

> I am not an experiment.
> It would not be allowed.

No?
Haven't you ever
   wondered why you were
   allowed to be born?
Do you think they didn't
   know you'd be part
   human?

> My human factors are
>   simply random chance.

Are they?
Then why were you reared
   by your Earth mother?
Why was she allowed to
   "contaminate" you?

Do you think Sarek did
   not know his own wife?
He *knew* she'd try to make
   you human.
They *wanted* it that way.

        You are fantasizing.

You are evading the issue
   by resorting to labels.

        The mind instinctively
           categorizes.
        I evade nothing.

But yet it's never occurred
   to you why you're part
   human.
Haven't you avoided
   asking yourself that
   question?

        I do not question what
           already is.

You don't question
   "fate," eh?
This wasn't fate.
It was planned.

        I concede planning.
        I do not, however,
           concede purposeful ego
           destruction.

*Con*struction, Spock.
Not *de*struction.
They hoped you would be
   a more viable specimen.

        Vulcans are extremely
           viable.
        I see no logic to your
           proposal.

You are a stubborn man.

        Admittedly.

I'm sorry we're in this
   mess.

        It is equally my fault.

No. *I* fouled the system.
If I hadn't,
   we wouldn't have
   beamed down here,
   wouldn't have got
   caught in this cave-in,
   and we wouldn't be
   wasting our air arguing.

        They will find us.

I concede the possibility.

        There are always
           possibilities.

I *am* sorry you dislike me.
Poor company doesn't
   enhance equally poor
   situations.

        I do not dislike you.
        However . . . I *will*
           concede a certain
           amount of friction.

I would've been
   disappointed if you
   hadn't noticed.

        I am not surprised.

I've conceded error and
   personal deficiency to
   you.
What else do I have to do?

        Remain silent.

Just making small talk.
Sorry if I made you think.

        Thinking is one thing no
           one can prevent me
           from indulging in.
        You, least of all.

Well.
Back to safe subjects.

        If you insist.

Hot in here, isn't it?

        Hotter than you know.

Editors' Introduction to "Marginal Existence"

"Marginal Existence," another story first published in *T-NEGATIVE*, raises some rather chilling questions about fixed purposes which can get out of hand, pleasures which can turn into pain, and savagery which can rise out of the marginal remains of a once-flourishing civilization.

It is, hopefully, a road not to be taken.

But it is one which would be available to us, even now. Drugs, life-support systems, automatic maintenance machinery—none too bright, but designed to perform a function . . .

No worries, no troubles, no worlds to conquer, no working for a living, no sweat, no end to pleasure . . .

Anything wrong with that?

Well . . .

One of the functions of science fiction—and of the *Enterprise*—is to explore roads not to be taken.

And the enterprise can be hazardous to your health—especially if you are a starship Captain.

MARGINAL EXISTENCE

by Connie Faddis

A happily engrossed Doctor McCoy was up to his elbows in dusty antique medical equipment when his communicator bleeped impertinently. Grumbling, he gently set down the interesting instrument he'd been examining, and hauled out his "squawk box."

"McCoy here," he answered in a long-suffering voice.

"Doctor, we found one! A live one!" the radio crackled.

"Found one what? Gorshim, is that you?"

"Yes, sir, it's me, Gorshim. We found a live being in one of the sleeper-units. It really is alive. Elva's in there with it now. It looks almost exactly like a—"

A muffled shriek erupted through the communicator. "Elva!" Gorshim's voice shouted.

"Gorshim, what was that? Horst?"

There was a clatter over the radio, then only static, but the channel was open.

"Now what the devil?" McCoy yelled. "Lieutenant, what's going on there!"

He shouted worriedly into the little box for several minutes, then gave up and grabbed his tricorder. Determining the coordinates of the voiceless transmission, he hurried out of the empty building and into the vine- and brush-overgrown city streets. He couldn't begin to imagine what possible trouble there could be. This city had been deserted for at least six hundred years, standard. He knew each towering building or domed dwelling he passed contained only the dead, the crumbling bones in the rusting sleeper units, hung with clogged plastic intravenous tubes and impregnated with traces of unknown drugs.

But a *live* being? It was incredible. Even if the

units had actually been designed for hibernation, a six-hundred-year survivor was an astonishing discovery.

McCoy crossed bootprints in the undisturbed dust of the windless streets. Centuries of dust. *Dust thou art . . .* If Gorshim wasn't hallucinating, McCoy reflected, then the little exploration-survey team could well have uncovered more than a rich archeological find, but perhaps a greater medical find. Six hundred years!

The bootprints crisscrossed each other in scuffled profusion in front of one particularly well-kept building. McCoy glanced around, noticing that all the buildings in the neighborhood looked better-kept than where he had been. Then he spotted Gorshim's communicator, lying open in a doorway as though it had been dropped, not placed there deliberately.

McCoy didn't move. Nervously, he surveyed the silent street. Silence, silence, not even the sigh of a breeze at his ears. He checked the chronometer on the tricorder: Only two hours until all of them had to be aboard the shuttlecraft to leave; only four hours more until rendezvous with the *Enterprise*. Damn. Not enough time to extract a tooth properly, let alone make a half-decent survey of all the findings. And where in the hell had the others gone off to?

"Gorshim!" he called. "Vigeland?"

His voice bounced back hollowly from the canyons of glass and steel.

"Horst, are you here?" he tried again.

Only the echoes answered.

He hesitated before entering the building; anyone who made surveys of unknown places learned to hate entering enclosures. He picked up Gorshim's communicator and tucked it onto his belt. Then, drawing his phaser, he set it for heavy stun and slipped into the hallway, treading softly so as to make no sound. The long corridor led to a dimly lit chamber. When McCoy's eyes were sure of the changed light, he peered in at the row of undamaged sleeper-units inside, and his stomach tightened sharply. He rushed across the room to the nearest one, automatically trading his phaser for his medical tricorder.

Horst Gorshim and the geologist, Elva Vigeland, lay on their backs in two of the units, their limbs strung with a web of intravenous tubes. The connecting computer-contraption above the glass lids of the units seemed to be activated. Beside the two humans, in the other occupied sleeper-unit, was the living body of a beautiful male humanoid, similar in appearance to *homo andoriens* but a paler blue than any Andorian could ever be, even in death.

Silence hung in curtains, but the sleepers were not still. Eyes closed, they twisted as though in the grip of a dreadful nightmare. McCoy checked sensor readings and swallowed drily: The pain levels for all three sleepers were off the scale. He made an immediate decision and worked the catch on Vigeland's glass coffin until it opened. Shoving the counterweighted lid aside, the doctor began gingerly to withdraw the needles from Vigeland's arteries and veins.

Her life readings dipped. McCoy dug out his hypospray and injected a stimulant. The woman rolled her head, moaning. McCoy yanked the last of the ugly needles out of her, and put an arm under her neck, lifting her slightly.

"Come out of it, girl," McCoy called, slapping her cheek gently. "Lieutenant, wake up!"

The sound of his voice sliced across the intense silence of the metal-lined room. There was a reflection off the walls: metal gleaming on metal gripped McCoy and pinned him, howling but helpless, into a vacant sleeper, among the dust of a former occupant. *Dust thou art!*

McCoy shrieked and fought back.

Stinging, then. And glass. And then the pain . . .

Spock was reluctant to go with the search party. The *Enterprise* was on its way, with its consignment of astrophysicists from Starbase Six and all their intriguing new instruments, to measure and record that rarity among celestial events: a supernova. Even a Klingon ship was racing to the safety-perimeter to observe the phenomenon, though the general opinion was that the Klingons' motives were probably less than wholly scientific.

Spock had considered himself particularly fortunate to be in the proper place and time to witness the extraordinary occurrence, but now his skills might be required elsewhere. Captain Kirk had not ordered him along on the search party, had left the decision to him. But Chief Engineer Scott had all but volunteered to assume command of the ship's mission, which was still essentially routine and not beyond the scope of Scott's capabilities. And Kirk was awaiting an answer.

Spock experienced a long moment of frustrating indecision: the mission or the search team? Dr. McCoy, whatever else Spock might think of him, was an efficient officer. He had never yet missed a rendezvous, and Lieutenant Uhura could not raise the survey shuttlecraft on any channel. The probability was high that the survey team had encountered a serious problem, but the *Enterprise* herself was committed to monitoring the nova, and a rescue shuttlecraft was being readied.

It was a difficult decision until the Vulcan perceived the tension in Kirk's tightly folded hands, and read the worry in Kirk's eyes from across the briefing-room table.

Scott took command of the *Enterprise,* and Spock accompanied the search team. Perhaps the lost landing party could be quickly located, and all could return to the ship in time yet to join the astrophysicists. Perhaps.

The city must have been beautiful at one time, but now much of the metal had lost its gleam and taken on the dulled brown of barbed wire on ancient battlefields. The glass was rippled and dust-caked, and the jungle had invaded everywhere, the roots crumbling the concrete into soil. The silence was startling. Only a few insect buzzes disturbed it. Captain Kirk slapped at a hungry bug on his arm, and Chekov, next to him, nearly jumped into orbit.

"Steady there, Ensign," Kirk said. "Spock, find anything?"

Spock pulled his head out from under the engineering panel of the *Discovery*, a mildly perturbed look on his face. The survey shuttle had been easy to find, as its recognition beam had been left on automatic transmission, as per standard procedure. But there had been no sign of its occupants. The interlock, too, was gone—standard procedure to prevent theft.

"I am unable to ascertain any mechanical failures which might explain why the *Discovery* did not make rendezvous," Spock reported. "We must assume that the survey team encountered difficulties which prevented their return to the shuttlecraft."

"I did a full scanner sweep, Captain," Chekov said, "and the survey team is not within range."

"Where could they be?" Christine Chapel whispered. It seemed oddly improper to speak in a normal voice, to break the pervasive quiet. She inched inconspicuously closer to the men.

Kirk gazed around the broad, vine-choked plaza, shading his eyes with his hand.

"There is no guarantee that they are here in the city," Spock said. "They could, given the four days they have been here on foot, be anywhere within a radius of a hundred and thirty kilometers, possibly more."

The Captain nodded thoughtfully. The brilliance of the noon sun was dazzling, and cut stark shadows in the canyons of the streets. Light like death; shadows like death. Kirk gave his orders.

"Spock and Miss Chapel, follow this street south. Mr. Chekov and I will head east at the intersection. Take it a 'block' at a time, setting scanners for human readings, and keep in contact by communicator."

Both groups found the shattered glass coffins as they explored. There were, it seemed, at least several of the units in every building, all containing remnants of disintegrated corpses. Kirk discussed it with Spock via communicator.

"Six hundred years old?" he said with awe.

"Six hundred and fifteen point eight years, standard, Captain," Spock's voice corrected. "That is the age of the oldest mortal remains I have scanned. Other corpses have not been deceased quite that long. It is my hypothesis that the units were designed for life support in suspended animation."

"Like the supermen we found on the *Botany Bay*," Kirk murmured. He fingered one of the plastic tubes hanging down from the machine overhead where he stood. It was sticky with age and adhered to his fingers. "It looks like medical equipment, all right. It *could* have been intended for life support during some sort of cataclysm—maybe a plague. Spock, could this city have been some sort of hospital complex?"

"Possibly," Spock answered. "The equipment in the structure in which I am situated appears to have terminated its functioning somewhat more recently than those I scanned earlier and, indeed, the general condition of the machinery has been improving as Miss Chapel and I continue southward. Have you noticed, however, that each of the units appears to have been deliberately damaged in some way?"

"Yes, I have. Any conjecture, Spock?"

"No, sir. Insufficient data at this time."

"And no sign of Bones or the others?"

"Not so far."

Kirk grimaced and dragged a sleeve across his damp forehead. It was close in the dusty buildings. It was just as hot in the streets, and intolerable out in the sun. And it was quiet. Quiet as a tomb . . .

"All right, carry on, Spock. We have a lot of ground to cover."

It was just about then, as Kirk was closing his communicator, that Christine Chapel found the footprints—and their owner.

The powder-blue youth cowered in the blind alley where Spock and Chapel had confined him, and Kirk gaped at him in amazement. The youth looked very much like an Andorian, except that he lacked the antennae and his "hair" was deep blue. He could not have been more than half grown, but his musculature was that of a mature, hard-working adult. The pale eyes that peered out from the unkempt hair were more the eyes of a cunning animal than those of an intelligent humanoid.

"He hasn't made a sound since I first saw him," Chapel reported. "I'm not sure he can."

"Indeed, any vocalization appears to frighten him immeasurably," Spock added. "He was armed with a metal bar which he uses quite capably as a club, and I believe that he would have seriously damaged me had not Miss Chapel's cries immobilized him."

"Where did he come from?" Kirk said. His words wrung a soundless snarl from the wild man, who backed farther into his corner.

"He may know something about the survey team," Chekov suggested. "He may even have killed them."

Kirk spun to glare at the ensign. "We don't know that anyone has been killed, Mister. Spock, what do you make of the alien?"

"Fascinating. When the being attacked me, his attentions were decidedly murderous, yet Miss Chapel's voice incapacitated him with terror. I strongly doubt that he had ever heard a humanoid voice before. Observe him now as we converse." The wild man cringed against the metal walls behind him each time someone spoke. "Mr. Chekov, I do not believe that we need fear that this creature could have murdered the survey team. I have never known Dr. McCoy to refrain from speech for more than a few minutes at a time, and it is therefore doubtful that this being has had any contact with him."

Kirk snorted, and everyone relaxed.

"Your observations, Mr. Spock, are, as usual, meticulously logical," the Captain said. "All right. I don't see any reason to keep the boy captive. He can't be interrogated by ordinary means, and probably doesn't know anything anyway. From now on, though, we'll all stay together for protection. And keep your phasers handy. Spock. How long until dark, do you think?"

"Considering the planetary rotation and the current angle of the sun, we have approximately 5.62 hours, standard, of usable light remaining."

"Good. We'll spend the next four searching, and if we don't find anything, we'll head back and spend the night in the shuttlecraft."

Another two hours of sweltering searching yielded an eventual reward: They intersected another of the endless alleys, and in that one, there were bootprints in the settled dust. Breaking into a trot, the search team followed the prints to the well-kept building, then into the metal-lined room where the survey team were stretched out like carefully tended corpses in some bizarre funeral parlor.

Kirk blanched as he recognized McCoy's writhing body, and he charged over to tug at the glass cover. "Good God, what is this? Bones!"

The robot was a fitted section of the metal wall. At the sound of Kirk's cry it disengaged itself from its storage place and extended its dozen jointed arms. Moving swiftly, it entangled the Captain, shoving him bodily into a vacant sleeper unit, and began to insert thin hypodermic needles into his flesh before anyone could clearly comprehend what was happening.

Spock recovered first. "Jim!" he shouted, and the metal robot turned away from Kirk and started after Spock. Chapel screamed, and the mechanism hesitated, confused, turned toward the nurse—and dissolved into a glowing, melted heap as Chekov's phaser beam found its mark.

Kirk shoved himself up dizzily, and Spock was at his elbow instantly.

"Captain, are you injured?"

"I don't think so," Kirk gasped. "What *was* that thing?"

Spock's answer was cut off by Chapel's call.

"Mr. Spock, I need your help with Lieutenant Vigeland!"

The Vulcan, trained in first aid, did what he could to assist the nurse. Under her direction, they managed to stabilize the life-functions of Vigeland and McCoy. There was nothing they could do for Gorshim; the man had been dead for hours.

Kirk and Chekov, meanwhile, examined the pearl-pale alien in the other unit. The being was of the same species as the wild man had been, but this creature was emaciated, and restless in his coma, the tendons of his arms straining against the restraining bands. Kirk reached to unlatch the unit's cover, then hesitated, glancing over to Chapel.

"I don't think you should open it, sir," she said.

"What's wrong with them, Chapel? What's this thing pumping into them?"

"I'm afraid I don't know. They're all in considerable pain, and their life readings are dangerously low. I'd like to try administering sedations but I don't dare try anything else at this time, not even disconnecting them from the unit. We don't know what it could do; it might kill them."

Kirk stared down at Lieutenant Vigeland's sweated form, then beyond her to McCoy. Agony was written in every crease in their faces.

"There must be something we can do. If we can analyze the drugs being pumped into them, maybe we'll get a lead on an antidote. Spock, can we bring the survey-shuttle here, land it in the street outside?"

"Yes . . . of course. The *Discovery* is equipped with extensive analytic instrumentation. Landing it here should not be a problem. However, I doubt that we can safely return to the shuttlecraft before dark. The sun is about to set."

"We'd be an easy mark for an ambush by the natives," Chekov added.

"What about—" Kirk stopped, his eyes widening. The blue-skinned youth they had met earlier stood poised and armed in the doorway. Behind him, seven or eight others appeared in the gloom, both male and female, all carrying metal bars or clubs.

Kirk drew his phaser smoothly but soundlessly, setting it for heavy stun, and the others did the same. They waited, not sure what to expect, as the natives filed into the room cautiously, crouching, ready to fight or run. The first youth stepped in a wary semi-circle around Spock until he could see into the vacant section of wall from which the robot had come, then kicked at the partly melted remains of the thing. He glanced up again at Spock, then at the comatose alien in the glass unit before him.

Without warning, the native brought his metal bar down on the lid and smashed the skull of the sleeping humanoid. He aimed next at Vigeland's unconscious body, but found Spock suddenly in his way.

The two groups threw themselves at each other. Kirk managed to stun two of the attackers before his phaser was knocked from his hand, and a woman's strangling fingers gouged into his throat. He remembered to yell, and as soon as he could peel the powerful fingers away, he did. She bit his hand and ran. Kirk staggered slightly and looked around. The room was still again. Three of the natives were unconscious on the floor, the others were gone. Chekov was sagging against a wall, and Christine Chapel went to examine him.

Spock returned through the doorway. "They did not exhibit signs of turning or regrouping. I do not believe that they will return for some time."

"Mr. Chekov's wrist is broken," Chapel reported. She was already rigging a temporary splint. "We'll have to wait until we get back to the shuttle tomorrow to mend it."

"He yelled when I hit him," said Chekov, a little dazed. "He said 'ouch'—I mean—the equivalent. Clear as Antares cymbals. He spoke."

"I, too, heard the native's voice," Spock said, eyebrows on the rise. "This alters my theory significantly. It is now logical to assume that at least a portion of the more recently deceased sleepers in the damaged units were murdered during similar native forays. It is imperative that we find and awaken another live sleeper and attempt to communicate with him. More than two lives depend on our solving this enigma."

Chekov and Chapel stayed with the delirious sleepers and guarded the bound natives. Chekov resourcefully improvised fortifications around the room's only egress, and electrified them after Kirk and Spock departed. Then he covered the corpses of the murdered alien and Lieutenant Gorshim with wilted plastic sheeting scavenged from an adjacent room.

"It is an hour past sundown," Chekov complained as he paced the gloomy chamber. "I wish the Captain and Mr. Spock had waited until daylight to go out."

Chapel unclamped her stiff fingers from McCoy's damp ones and stood up wearily to check the tricorder readings. "No change," she sighed and dabbed the moisture from her patients' brows. Vigeland mumbled fretfully, and Chapel leaned close, but the Lieutenant's words made no sense.

"I wish they could tell us what happened," the nurse said. "I wish there were something we could do besides wait."

Chekov shrugged miserably and went over to the bound prisoners, sitting down on his heels in front of the nearest. "You know what this is all about," he said to them, "but you won't tell us. Maybe you don't have language. I wonder how you communicate with each other? Maybe . . . maybe you are touch-telepaths, like Vulcans." He pressed his good hand to the native's head, but the man only shrank back, staring with obvious horror at Chekov's lips. "They're not touch-telepaths," Chekov announced.

"I saw the one that killed the alien use very fast hand-signals when he was looking for the robot in the wall," Chapel said.

"Hand-signs," Chekov mused. "And the first thing they did, even before they bothered with us, was to check for the robot. I wonder . . . the robot . . ."

"The robot?" Kirk said incredulously.

"Exactly. I believe that the robots are the reason that the natives do not use their voices. I cannot deduce their motives," Spock said, "but it would appear that the local primitives have been murdering the occupants of the sleeper-units for approximately six centuries. The anthropological implications are intriguing, as it would seem—"

"What *about* the robots?" Kirk interrupted.

"The robots would appear to be the guardians —or possibly the jailers—of the sleepers. They respond only to the sounds of the humanoid voice, so far as we are able to discern. The robot we encountered did not attack you until it scanned your exclamation upon discovering Dr. McCoy, and it directed its actions against only you until it was distracted by my call."

"And the natives have learned they're safe from the robot as long as they don't use their voices. I see. But why in the blazes are they killing the sleepers? It doesn't make sense."

"Their motives may not be comprehensible to us, even were we to discover them. What we must secure now is the cooperation of one of the sleepers. They may know, or at least be able to direct us to, information on the drugs injected by the units."

"What if they can't?"

Spock lowered his eyes as he walked. "The medical facilities aboard the *Enterprise* should be at our disposal in 4.91 days."

"Spock, you saw the tricorder readings on our people. You know they won't last four days."

"It is my hope that there may already be an antidote formula built into the reservoirs of the individual chemical dispensing units, and that it will be possible to program the monitor-computers to inject such an antidote. Jim, at this moment we do not have enough data to attempt anything other than what I have suggested."

"That's Bones back there in that thing," Kirk said softly. "And a geologist who's not much more than a girl."

To that, Spock had no reply. They walked in the still darkness, guided only by the illumination of their phaserlights. Kirk wiped the trickle of sweat from the back of his neck.

"It sounds like we're going to have to contend with another robot, then," he sighed. "And you'll want to examine it." He squared off his shoulders. "I'll be the bait, and you phaser it. Then we'll see what we can do to rouse one of the sleepers."

They found another occupied room almost immediately. Apparently the natives had murdered methodically over the centuries, and this area was on the fringe of the most recent activity.

Kirk squinted around the dark room, following the cone of his phaserlight until he located the fitted section of wall that was the storage space for the robot. There were two sleeper-units in the room, both occupied. There was one robot. Kirk pushed the insistant memory of what had happened before out of his mind, and stepped quietly into the center of the hushed room, but did not draw his phaser. Facing Spock, who crouched by the doorway, he said loudly, "Ready or not, Spock, here it comes."

It came. It launched itself at the Captain, even though he backed away from it frantically. It followed him and reached him. It was cold; it was all around him, with fingers of steel ice, and it lifted him and put him down on top of someone. Needles again—and shooting pain—and a blaze of light. Then darkness.

He came back to consciousness as though waking from a restless doze, and Spock was kneeling among stacks of micro-circuits, wires, resistors, capacitors, and other antique electronic paraphernalia. The Vulcan glanced over at him. "I trust you are recovered, Captain."

Kirk closed his eyes, still groggy. The robot reared up behind them and—he opened his eyes, shuddering, and found that he'd been arranged on some sort of cot, and that the electronic components heaped around Spock were all that remained of the machine.

"That was too close," Kirk commented drily.

"My apologies, Jim, but the machine moved too quickly to prevent your being caught by the nimbus of my phaser charge."

"I'll live, I guess," Kirk said, and poked at a micro-chip. "Find anything new?"

"We have uncovered a number of new possibilities. There is a high order of probability that the robots were designed to confine an awakened sleeper, not necessarily to prevent intruders. Also, the robots are not programmed to monitor the life-support units themselves; this mechanism attempted to place you into a unit which was already occupied by a living being."

"You mean it thought that I was the sleeper who had somehow awakened?"

"So it would seem, and an awakened sleeper's vocalizations are its cue to initiate action."

Kirk lurched to his feet and studied the comatose aliens under the glass. "What could be the purpose of this? The sleepers, the drugs, all this sophisticated gadgetry?"

"The 'gadgets' are not truly sophisticated," Spock said. "The robot is no more than a single-purpose device with a strictly limited capacity for decision-making. It is definitely a servant for some central directive mechanism, probably an elementary-level computer. The robot itself is only semi-solid-state, and the computer which controls it cannot be more sophisticated than a ferrite-core device."

"Like the old IBM 360's, or your ancient Vulcan A'YOR'IK."

"Precisely. And such a device should be easily reprogrammable. If we can find the central computer, the reprogramming should be all that is necessary to release the remainder of the sleepers."

"That may work for the aliens, but McCoy and Vigeland are human. We need an antidote, Spock, one that will work on our people."

"Once we determine the formulae to awaken the sleepers, we should be capable of making appropriate chemical alterations for humans. The chemical data are likely contained in the data banks of the central computer. It would expedite the translation of that data if I were to learn something of the language of these beings. And we must, in any case, determine whether the aliens can safely be awakened without an antidote."

"Do you want to try to wake one now?"

Spock rose and cleaned his oily hands on a scrap of cloth he'd scrounged. "If you deem such an action appropriate, Captain. A strict interpretation of the Prime Directive might indicate otherwise."

Kirk contemplated the nearly translucent forms under the glass covers. The beings writhed. Their sleep was not a sleep of peace, they were shackled in a chemical Gehenna. And so were Bones and that young woman.

"If Miss Chapel is right, we may well kill them. But we can't ethically leave them here like this, either, for the others to murder. I think we have to risk waking one of these people."

Spock glanced up at Kirk. "The mental contortions by which you arrive at logical decisions never cease to amaze me, Captain."

Kirk met the smiling eyes and grinned. "So I'm a rational acrobat," he said. He raised the cover over one of the aliens, a female.

Spock took a reading with his tricorder. "It is astonishing that these beings have survived six centuries at such an active metabolic rate. The drugs being administered to them may have interesting age-retardant properties."

As he spoke, he began to remove the needles and tubes. There were thirty-six in all. The puncture wounds each bled one pale azure droplet and no more.

There was no immediate reaction. Spock touched the artery at her throat. The pulse had quickened. The woman's eyes fluttered open, and two orange irises struggled to adjust to the dim light. Then she took a long, shuddering breath and began to howl in a rasping voice. Her screams resounded through the halls. Kirk lifted her, instinctively pressing her to his shoulder to comfort. "Wake up, wake up, you're safe now, safe . . ."

If she could understand his tone, it was not reaching her. Her mind was trapped in the nightmare dimension of six drugged centuries, and it would not give her up. Then Spock stepped close and wrapped one large hand around her thin wrist, and arranged his other at her temple. Kirk opened his mouth to protest, but stepped back instead to watch.

The Vulcan's eyes had widened, and now they went blank. The woman's eyes, too, lost focus. She stopped screaming, abruptly, and both of the faces faded to gray ash. An endless minute passed, and they breathed more harshly at each breath. Then Spock's mouth contorted, and the two of them began to choke. The woman's color went to chalky white.

Spock's lips twisted, and he strained to speak. "J-jim," he wheezed.

Not sure what else to do, Kirk wrenched Spock's cold hands from the dying alien, and lowered his friend to the floor. Spock was a dead weight in his arms. Kirk shook him frantically, but Spock snapped into a fetal pose and lay rigid, not breathing at all. "Spock!" Kirk cried. He shook the Vulcan again, then slapped him sharply. "For God's sake, break the link!"

Spock made no response. His lungs drew no air. Desperate, Kirk did the only thing he could think of; he unclenched the icy fists and forced the fingers to his own temples. "Find my mind," he pleaded. "Borrow my strength . . . my mind is clear . . ."

A single flame traced a searing path through every nerve. Kirk stiffened, gasped—and collapsed.

When the Captain next dared to open his eyes, Ensign Chekov's face floated over him fuzzily.

"Captain? Miss Chapel, the Captain is conscious!"

Someone was helping Kirk to sit up. His stomach did a flip-flop, and he had a headache like a chisel through his skull. "This hasn't . . . been my day," he groaned, and forced his vision into focus, realizing he was back in the chamber with the others.

"Spock," Kirk demanded. "Where's Spock? What am I doing here?"

"Mr. Spock carried you here, sir," Chapel answered, running her medical tricorder over him. "He said to tell you that he was in good health, and that he was going to find some kind of computer, then bring the *Discovery* here. It's almost midday outside. What happened to you, sir? Both you and Mr. Spock looked like death warmed over."

"We got," Kirk said wearily, "a proxy dose of what the sleepers are getting." He shoved his way to his feet and stood woozily while the nurse pressed a hypo to his arm. Some of his energy flowed back, and he stood straighter. He managed to walk on his own power over to McCoy and Vigeland. "They both look a lot better," he said.

"They began to improve a few hours ago. The unit started dosing them with a new drug. There were some problems with side-effects at first, but I've been compensating with injections of other drugs. I have no idea what's happening, though."

Kirk's face brightened with triumph. "Spock found the computer."

"Captain!" Chekov's voice called from the hallway. He ran in behind them. "The *Discovery* is setting down outside."

Kirk, swaying a little as he moved, began wrestling McCoy free of the sleeper-unit. Chapel hurried to assist him, and Kirk nodded to Chekov to release Vigeland.

"What do we do with our prisoners?" Chekov asked.

Kirk glanced over at them. They seemed to have gotten over their fear and glared back at him malevolently. "Leave them here. Their friends will find them."

Spock arrived, and between the four of them they carried McCoy and Vigeland and the sheet-wrapped body of Gorshim into the street. Chekov gazed up at the sky through the tangle of overgrowth. The white sun blazed down at them. Its noon brilliance plunged the shadows of the artificial chasm into inpenetrable darkness. The shadows were inky coldness; the sunlight was broiling. One shadow molded itself into a staggering figure, trailing wires and tubes from a splintered-glass door as it swayed into the stark light. It laughed insanely, joyously, hopelessly. It collapsed into a quiet heap by a curb. Inside, its robot/keeper remained wallbound and ignorant, in the shadows and the dust. There were more sounds. They were in praise of death —and of freedom.

The offworlders stumbled hurriedly across the pavement and into the waiting shuttlecraft.

"They had been in agony for the better part of six centuries," Spock said, as the solar system fell away behind them. "Too much pleasure became an intolerable torture."

"Pleasure?" Kirk said. "Do you mean to say that those people *put themselves* into the sleeper units?"

"Affirmative, if I have interpreted the information in the central computer correctly." His tone denied the possibility of error.

Doctor McCoy was sitting up, nearly recovered, in one of the shuttle's seats. "What it all adds up to is that an entire civilization retired—or escaped—from their way of life and its problems by retreating into drugged pleasure," he said. "In time, though, the nerve tissue became exhausted, and the sensations became sheer agony. And the sleepers couldn't escape—they'd designed their safety devices too well."

"Pleasure," Kirk repeated. "You didn't seem to like it, Bones."

"A moderate difference in body chemistries," Spock explained.

"Moderate?" McCoy said shakily. He met Spock's eyes briefly, then looked away.

"The natives," Spock went on, "were either escapees from the units, or, more likely, were descended from those who refused to take part in the initial retreat. Those original nonconformists not only disposed of language for their own safety, but formed the ritual murdering of the sleepers. It is possible that the homicide we witnessed was no more than a tribal rite of passage for the youth who performed it."

"But that's ended now," Kirk said. "You reprogrammed the central computer."

"Precisely. The sleepers are now free."

"And dying, most of them," added McCoy. "The physiological shock is too much for an adjustment." He and Vigeland were themselves both pale.

"At least the primitives are free to develop, if they can, without the danger of the robots," Kirk said, and the memory of the cold metal grasp returned to him. He shrugged it off and gazed out through the forward window. The second shuttle, piloted by Chekov, was ahead of them. And beyond it were a million points of light in the darkness. One of the lights was the *Enterprise*.

Editors' Introduction to
"The Procrustean Petard"

You'll have to let us know what you think of this one.

And we don't doubt that you will . . .

Meanwhile we'll say only that this is an example of what may prove to be a vanishingly rare species: a short story by us.

Shall we admit that our *Star Trek* novel, *The Price of the Phoenix,* started as a *short story* for *New Voyages* (1)?

You should only see what happens when we *set out* to write a novel . . .

This one could handily have turned into a novel, and threatened to, but we exercised monumental restraint. It could easily have gotten a little too hot to handle. And if you wonder what happened off camera —we aren't talking. Maybe we'll write a sequel . . .

THE PROCRUSTEAN PETARD

by Sondra Marshak and Myrna Culbreath

Kirk bombed out the door of the "pleasure palace" into the circular plaza of the dead alien city.

"Maybe I should have had myself lashed to the mast," he said sourly.

Uhura winced, and almost ran to keep up. "You don't mean that the signal was a siren song, Captain?"

"Wasn't it?" Kirk fumed. "A sophisticated one, meant to lure sophisticated interstellar travelers. Hints of vast scientific knowledge, medicine." He looked at the Vulcan science officer and at Dr. McCoy. "Arts, new means of communication." He looked back at Uhura. "These sirens scratched the plain bump of curiosity—guaranteed to get any starship captain. And all they've really got to show for a dead civilization are—pleasures and palaces."

He turned a rueful look on Uhura and on Laura Breen of security. "Some of what we've seen here has been pretty—exotic. I'm sorry you had to see it."

Uhura sighed and traded a look with the stolid Breen, confirming that the men had been far more embarrassed than either of the women. One step forward, two steps back. "Captain," she said, softening it a little with a look of mischief, "the theory is that we are officers, if not gentlemen."

He had the grace to look embarrassed.

"Captain," Spock cut in urgently, "an unknown force-field has snapped on around the planet." The Vulcan was working over his tricorder. "We have lost communications. I am picking up a life-form reading—"

Kirk's hands reached for communicator and phaser.

151

Uhura felt a stun effect and saw him falling even as she fell and blackness closed over her.

Kirk snapped awake—and knew.

There was no mistaking the one overwhelming fact: He was in the body of a woman.

It—he—was laid out on a bench in a black, sleeveless coverall, showing bare, slender arms, slim hands which shot up to his smooth face . . .

Dear God. The others . . .

He was alone in a bare cubicle. He heaved himself off the bench and lurched to the door. The whole sensation of movement was different, wrong. His slender hands—look at them!—fumbled at the door, and shook.

Don't think about it. Move.

He was out into the corridor.

The door opposite opened and a woman came out.

Then Kirk knew everything in one long, slow take.

"Bones," he said with certainty.

"Jim," the blue-eyed woman answered with equal conviction.

There was no mistaking Bones McCoy. Everything was different, and everything was the same. Kirk knew beyond question that this was the woman Leonard McCoy would have been if he had been born a woman.

He made a handsome woman, slim, almost willowy, yet with the strength of his experience still written in the woman's face, his quizzical, ironic eyebrows a little finer, black hair a little longer, skin softer. But he was still—Bones.

"My God, Jim," McCoy burst out in contralto. "You look beau—" He broke off.

Kirk tried a command frown. "All right, Bones, let's get on it." His own voice was impossible in his mouth, incredible in his ears.

McCoy gathered himself and nodded. Good man, Kirk thought, and almost choked on the thought.

Two doors down they found Uhura, looking like

some magnificent black warrior carved in living flesh, as handsome as she had been beautiful.

She was standing carefully, suppressing the shock of movement, suppressing the shock at seeing them, searching their faces and focusing on Kirk's. "Yes, sir," she said solidly, her eyes widening at the new baritone.

Kirk nodded and allowed himself a small smile of approval. She had always had the heart of a warrior. "We'll think about it—later," he said. "Let's go."

"Spock," McCoy said, voicing the dread Kirk knew they must all be feeling. Why did it seem so much worse for the Vulcan? Worse for them to see it happen to him? Kirk knew only that it did.

The thought was driving them down the line of doors. They came to a cross-corridor. "Split up," he said, pointing the others down the cross-hall. "Find Spock. Find Breen and Collins."

He shot down the opposite hall, opening doors. Finally—

He leaned against the doorframe, suddenly weak with relief.

The Vulcan was there—in his familiar male body.

But he was in a black coverall, unconscious, looking fevered.

Kirk stepped to the head of the bench, out of the Vulcan's first sight. "Spock!" he whispered and, when there was no response, felt the hot forehead. Yes, he thought, it was above even the Vulcan's normal high temperature.

"Jim?" The Vulcan's eyes had not opened.

"One moment," Kirk whispered, "before you look. A change—"

"In you?" Spock said, keeping the eyes closed.

"In me," Kirk stepped around where he could be seen. "All right."

The Vulcan's eyes opened and widened, but the Vulcan mask—almost—held.

Spock sat up, his lip drawing suddenly against his teeth as if the movement were agony. But he ignored it to look at Kirk. "Fascinating," he said through his teeth. "The change would appear to be genetic. And the others?"

Kirk nodded. "You're hurt. I'll get McCoy."

"I am—functional," Spock said. "Although why I should be an exception—"

"The poor machinery couldn't figure out your crazy Vulcan genes," McCoy said from the doorway.

"A distinct possibility, Doctor," Spock raised an eyebrow and inspected McCoy, but didn't rise to the bait.

"Check him, Bones," Kirk said. "He must be sick if he can't keep up the famous quarrel."

"Right," McCoy said, already falling back on fundamental medicine, hands checking in place of scanners—incredibly slender hands. He shook his head. "Temperature, pulse, pain—you're a wreck, Mr. Spock."

Spock stood up suddenly, looking furious. "Poking, prying! Doctor, you will *cease*—"

"Mr. Spock," Kirk snapped.

But the Vulcan was already catching himself, looking astonished at himself. "My apologies, Doctor," he said with the familiar control.

"It's all right, Spock," McCoy said, "they must have put you through a meat-grinder."

They heard a sudden scream and were off running, without even time to consider the strangeness of the running.

At the cross-hall they converged with Uhura and a big, raw-boned man who could only be Laura Breen.

Then they saw a diminutive blonde woman being carried by a handling robot into a mirrored room.

The little blonde had to be security man Brad Collins. He screamed again.

Kirk moved, but Breen was already down the hall. She snatched Collins out of the metal arms and toppled the robot with a shoulder block. It smashed a mirror -and fell heavily and was still.

Breen put Collins down, and suddenly they saw themselves in the mirrors and stood transfixed.

Kirk made the mistake of looking and was caught by it, too, in spite of himself.

He saw—himself. It *was* himself. Herself? No. It was—a face that was and was not his own. He had seen the same transformation in the others, and never quite thought how it would apply to him. The smallness, the shape, the face—and if Uhura was a handsome man and McCoy an attractive woman, this woman in the mirror was—

Kirk cut it off. He wouldn't say the word, either.

"Out," he said. "We can't think in here." He strode into the hall, managing not to run.

He whirled on the others. "All right. Spock, that force-field, the life-form reading you picked up—?"

"Klingon," Spock said.

"Klingon?" Kirk echoed. "But—this has to be —what? a kind of pleasure palace? This—as a *pleasure?* And why would the Klingons spring it on us? Just under the general heading of dirty tricks?"

"Not entirely, Miss Kirk." a cool voice said behind him and he whirled to see Kang stepping out of the open door to the mirrored room, a disruptor in his hand. "Although it is a most amusing trick and you did look quite precious seeing yourself in the mirror. In fact, you look quite precious. Ravishing."

The big Klingon ran an appreciative eye over Kirk, and Kirk jolted forward involuntarily with the idea of belting him in the chops. A near-knockout slap like the one Kang had knocked him down with once, or the crisp punch he had delivered in payment—

But he remembered. And stopped. Something tied into knots in the strange body.

"I am still Kirk," he said. "State your business."

Kang nodded more soberly. "Once, Kirk, we did not fight in a burning house. Now the Organians do not permit us to fight at all. I have had a great sufficiency of alien interference in a perfectly good war. The Organians, however, do not control all means of war. I prefer a more forthright approach. However, this will have to do. There are certain planets in your sector which are properly ours and which we will claim while you look the other way. This will be just between you and me, Kirk."

"You know better than that, Kang," Kirk said.

"Do I?" Kang smiled. "The force-field will be beyond your technology to cope with. You will try. You will get certain unpleasant surprises. Then, Kirk, you will come to me. You will find a way to come, and you will come alone." Kang grinned wolfishly. "Consider it your—maiden voyage."

"You can still go to the devil," Kirk said.

"We still have no devil," Kang answered. He rose on the balls of his feet. "Now, I must take my leave and join my people. Momentarily, you will be transported to the *Enterprise,* although your transporter will not work."

"Why let us go if you want us—me—back?" Kirk asked.

"Dear Miss Kirk," Kang said. "I want you back on your own hook. And knowing the problem. Let us say I merely want you to come to me, Kirk. Perhaps I want to show you—the pleasures and palaces."

Spock stepped around Kirk. "If anyone comes, it will be me—to take you apart."

Kang backed up a pace and laughed. "So it has warmed your Vulcan ice, Mr. Spock. You will find out a most amusing secret about that. No, I will deal with no one but Miss Kirk. I am entitled to that—a certain poetic justice."

Kang laughed and loped around the corner of the intersection.

There was a transporter whine.

They emerged directly on the bridge of the *Enterprise*.

There was a gasp from communications and Scott turned from the engineering board. Sulu craned his neck.

There was a Klingon battle cruiser showing on the viewscreen.

"Bishop to Queen's level two," Scott said levelly.

Bless him. "Rook takes bishop," Kirk answered, seeing the shock of his voice strike the unflappable Scot, and knowing that Scotty was convinced even beyond need of the chess code. "Report."

"Aye—sir," the chief engineer said, swallowing and coming to attention. "The Klingon ship must have been using the cloaking device. It popped out big as life when the force-field came on. We're stuck in the field like a fly in honey. The Klingons won't answer a hail—not that we have any communications or sensors to speak of. Our weapons won't fire. When we lost contact with you, we tried to send a shuttlecraft, but it was rocked by severe turbulence, barely made it back. We hit the same turbulence effect with the ship if we try to move, and it rocks us sometimes even if we don't. I'm putting heavy power to the stabilizers, but it won't compensate. We're not goin' anywhere."

Spock spoke from his station. "Accurate, Captain. It is like nothing we have ever encountered."

Uhura had displaced Ann Aronsen at communications. Kirk nodded to Uhura. "Clear deck seven around sickbay. I don't want the ship tied in a knot about this until we know more. Bones, take Breen and Collins. Get me some answers."

He plumped down in the command chair. His feet wouldn't reach the floor.

They went through the numbers on trying to figure out the force-field. "Tell me what it's *not*." They got nowhere.

The Vulcan was irritable, but severely controlled. Everybody else clung to routine and tried not to die of shock or curiosity.

McCoy called from sickbay. "I want to see you, Jim. And I want a tissue sample from Spock."

"On my way," Kirk said. "Spock, five minutes." He started to bomb up the steps to the turbo-lift, pulled up and moved a little more sedately. He escaped into the lift like a haven, and fought down the impulse to detour to the haven of his quarters—stop, take a breath, change clothes—nothing would fit—look in the mirror . . .

Some instinct told him to keep moving. When something tampered with a man's fundamental identity ... Man's? He caught himself on the word. But he *was* a man. There was nothing which was more fundamental to his identity, at least as the foundation of it. He had had his identity tampered with and challenged before, in more ways than he cared to remember—and he had forgotten nothing. But none of it helped on this one.

There was nothing more fundamental in the universe than the difference—whatever it was—if any—between male and female. But there *was* some difference—spanning entities as different as the Companion, The Horta: a cloud, a living rock, but female.

And what was *he?* What his body said? Or what his mind said?

He was the woman he might have been. But he was the man he *had* been.

This was worse than being trapped in someone else's body. This was his own body. Even the others knew it instinctively. And he knew that he felt responsible for this body, involved with it, affected by what it was and how people responded to it. This was James Kirk as woman.

Should the difference make so much difference? It did.

He stalked out into deck seven corridor—knowing that the walk was all wrong for a woman. It was *his* walk. He caught the startled double take of a crewman. Somebody must have slipped on clearing the corridor. The crewman started the beginnings of an appreciative once-over for an unexpected stranger; then Kirk saw startled recognition, rejection of the idea, slowly dawning belief—red-faced and total confusion.

"As you were, Mr. Adams," Kirk murmured with a certain sympathy—and the feeling that his new face was as red.

Adams gulped. "Yes—*sir*? Sir." He tried to move on with the look of discipline.

"Into sickbay, Adams," Kirk added. "Someone will brief you. No scuttlebutt." Adams nodded and plunged through the doors.

Kirk did not quite plunge, but he moved smartly into McCoy's office, as if it were refuge. McCoy glommed him without a word and took samples, handed them to a wide-eyed Christine Chapel.

"My God, sir," she said, "you're love—" She broke off, straightened and dived through the connecting door.

McCoy shoved a brandy into Kirk's hand, plunked him unceremoniously into a chair, and sank down gloomily into his own chair at the desk. "You'd start a first-class riot in any spaceport from here to the barrier."

Kirk felt his mouth fall open. "Can it, Bones," he said. "Report."

"I *am*," McCoy said. "That's a key aspect of the problem," he sighed. "Okay, Spock's first guess was on the nose. It *is* genetic. It involves manipulation of the X and Y chromosomes, the DNA, RNA, the genetic code—just those factors that specifically affect sex. We are perfectly normal males and females. We are— *us*. But we've been taken apart cell by cell and put back together. Don't ask me how."

"How?"

McCoy shrugged. "Ask Spock. It's basically an information-coding problem. I'm just your good old country doctor. But I'll tell you this: we can't do it. Our only chance is on that planet. You'd better bury the broadsword with Kang again, and fast."

"How, Bones? It's straight blackmail."

"Right," McCoy said. "So—you pay. Or, you call the cops. Or—you kill the blackmailer."

"Brother! What's got into *you?*" Kirk said incredulously.

"*Sister*," McCoy said pointedly. "I don't see an Organian cop handy. We can't dent the Klingons. So—"

"Solve it on our own hook," Kirk said. "Or— live with it."

McCoy shook his head. "The chromosome and gene alteration is just not in the state of the art—not by a couple of orders of magnitude. As for living with it—" He shook his head again. "I might be able to do *my* job. Do you really think that you could do *yours?*"

Kirk felt his jaw set. "No law says I can't. Law says I can."

"Law is law, and fact is fact," McCoy snorted. "Say you tried to brazen it out. Want me to show you what's wrong with *that?*"

He picked a mirror up from the desk and aimed it at Kirk.

Kirk forced himself not to look away. And he knew that McCoy was absolutely right. The doors whooshed open and Spock came in. Kirk met his eyes in the mirror, then McCoy's over it. "So?" he said.

McCoy grimaced. He hadn't wanted to have to say this in front of the Vulcan. But his blue eyes didn't waver. "So—you've never exactly cracked mirrors. But *now*—I tell you, you can't walk down a street, let alone into a face-off with Romulans, Klingons, miscellaneous aliens. *Think* of some of the men we've met."

Kirk took a breath. "Still *me* here, Bones."

"You think that'll *help?*" McCoy exploded painfully. "If they knew that in *that* package was a starship Captain—*the* Captain Kirk?" He slammed his fist down on the desk—and recoiled from the blow in surprise. "Blazes—*tell* him, Spock."

"I concur with the Doctor," Spock said flatly.

Kirk swung around to look up at him. "You, too, Spock?"

"Kang said as much," Spock said stonily. "And—he knows."

Kirk stood up. "You two," he said, "are *not* going to start treating me as—Miss Kirk."

"Face it, Jim," McCoy said. "However we treat you, it's never going to be the same. You and I are still going on momentum, still acting like men. That would have to—change. The crew's still going on momentum. You know where they'd follow you. But what happens when they really begin to see you? What happens when they have to protect you from things they never had to worry about before? What happens when there's a crunch where you need muscle?"

"I can take care—"

"Hogwash," McCoy said. "Maybe if you'd come up through the ranks as a woman—even looking like *that*. *Especially* looking like *that*. Maybe you'd be hell on wheels in unarmed combat. You'd have to be—with exotic techniques designed for no muscle."

"I'll learn."

"Lifetime disciplines. You were good, as men go. But there's no way you can take a good man, now. Let alone some of the aliens. Vulcanoids—"

"I—never could," Kirk said glumly. "However—" He straightened his shoulders against the new weight.

"However," Spock said, "you always behaved as if you could, and there is a certain tendency to take a man at face value. There is, unfortunately, also a certain tendency to—take a woman at value of face."

Kirk found himself breathing hard. "What's got into you, Spock?" he said harshly. "Even if some of this is true, it doesn't cut any ice at the moment. We haven't admitted to being stuck with this yet. You are the last one I would expect—"

"To remind you of logic?" Spock said.

"To—quit," Kirk said bitterly.

Spock remained carved in stone. "Kang gives you one hour to come to him, alone."

Kirk adjusted the strange body to stand very straight. "Or else—?"

"He does not specify. He says we will know within the hour why you must come."

"How?" McCoy said fiercely. "By flying carpet?"

"He says we boast of Federation technology—are we willing to concede that we cannot send one shuttlecraft—or that our Captain is afraid to come?"

"All right," Kirk said, "get on the shuttlecraft problem."

"Jim—you're not thinking of *going?*" McCoy burst out.

"You said it yourself, Bones. The Klingons have a lock on the situation. Therefore, go to the Klingons."

"Jim," Spock said. "You have nothing to prove. *I* will go."

Kirk smiled. "Thank you, Spock. But how does that help me? He won't deal with you. And he can hold you as hostage."

"Do you not understand that he can hold *you?*" Spock said.

Kirk nodded. "I do."

"Then——"

"I am the Captain," Kirk said. "I go where I have to go, do what I have to do—or I *am* unfit to command." He looked up at the Vulcan. "We're going to have to find out."

Spock didn't answer.

Kirk felt his jaw set. "Mr. Spock, give the doctor a sample. Then join me on the bridge."

He left before Spock could answer.

It occurred to him that Spock had not called him "Captain," not since this happened.

Uhura worked the controls with hands which were too big. But they still worked by her mind, and what she could not do with this board could not be done.

At least the Captain would know that, even if they still had no communications and could not identify the nature of the alien Transmitter Kang had used to deliver his ultimatum.

She swore silently for the umpteenth time. Scotty had forgotten himself and swore over the force-field and the ultimatum, impartially, and in half a dozen languages he would not have used if it had fully registered with him that there was still a woman on the bridge.

Was there?

Uhura grimaced. There *were* some advantages. Minor and major. Scott could swear, and she—

Let *her* go down and take on Kang now.

The ship bucked slightly and Scott said, "Increase power to stabilizers—"

The doors whooshed and Kirk bombed onto the bridge.

"—now," Scott finished.

Sulu punched it in. The ship heaved.

Uhura was thrown up out of her chair, against the rail, against Kirk.

But this time Uhura caught *him*.

She snagged him with one arm, and the rail with her other hand, and held them both against the tilt.

She felt the ease and power of doing it, felt her incredible strength and his small astonishment in her arms.

He clung to her for a moment in simple reflex, and then the mind of the captain reasserted itself.

He levered himself out of her arms as the ship righted, catching her arm for an instant in a touch of gratitude, even in his shock. "Report, Scotty. Uhura, damage control."

But she was already turning to her post.

"The force-field," Scott said, "I increased power to the stabilizers, but it only rocked us more."

"It rocked the Klingon ship, too, Captain," Sulu said from the helm.

"When we put power to the stabilizers?" Kirk asked. "Get on that. It might be something we can use."

"Aye," Scott muttered interestedly. "I'll try more power."

The doors opened and Spock shot onto the bridge as if fired from a cannon.

The ship bucked again, higher. Uhura was slammed to the floor, hard. She saw Kirk flung to the floor, and Spock heaving himself over the railing in an effort to catch Kirk.

But the Vulcan was late. Kirk was later. Everyone else was moving before he did. He was out. The ship rolled, rocked.

"Cut power to stabilizers," Spock snapped.

"She'll likely roll," Scott protested.

"Cut it!" Spock thundered.

Scott snapped the switch. The ship steadied shud-deringly.

Kirk came up foggily from the floor. "What—?"

"A probable interaction of the force-field with the stabilizers," Spock said. He thumbed the intercom on the command chair. "McCoy to bridge."

Kirk pulled himself up by the chair, and locked eyes with Spock. "What was *that* about?"

"Every *man* on this bridge remained conscious," Spock said.

Kirk drew himself up. "Men have been knocked out on this bridge before."

"*You* have not—so easily," Spock said.

The elevator decanted McCoy. "Examine him, Doctor," Spock ordered, indicating Kirk.

McCoy frowned but came and ran his scanner over Kirk. "You'd better—"

"I am all right," Kirk said firmly. He turned to Uhura. "Damage control report, Uhura," he said.

Her mind had not exactly been on that kind of damage, but her communications training had been registering it in the back of her mind. "Minor casual-ties, Captain." Something was nagging at the back of her mind from the murmuring voices in the earphone. "Captain—the figures are all wrong!"

"Figures?"

She played it back in her mind. "One or two in every section . . . Captain, some of our people are missing."

She saw the realization sink in. Was it harder for him to hide the reaction now? But he had never hid-den it. She had seen that look so many times before.

"How many?" he said in a rather small voice, but it was the Captain's voice.

"At least twenty," she said.

He settled his shoulders and looked at Spock. "Speculation?"

"We must assume that the alien Transporter can pluck people from anywhere in the ship—just as it put us on the bridge. I recommend that you leave the bridge. Kang may not plan to give you a choice. You should be in sickbay."

Kirk looked as if he were faltering for a moment. "You may—have a point. Take the con, Mr. Spock. Doctor, if you don't mind—"

But he waved off McCoy's hand and made it to the elevator.

She turned to her board with a certain chill. She had seen him stick to this bridge when he was one breath from dying.

McCoy inspected Kirk critically and ran the scanner again. He could detect nothing but a bad shaking up. But had it shaken this Kirk's nerve?

"Don't fuss, Bones," Kirk said. "Give me that report on Spock."

Oh. But even that hardly called for leaving the bridge when there were people disappearing. "It's a chromosome change, too," he said. "You remember the big dust-up in the twentieth century about the YY chromosome effect? They learned that there could be double- even triple-Y chromosomes in the male, often linked to hyper-masculinity, aggressiveness, even violence and crime. There were even a number of mass-murderers who had it. A famous one killed seven nurses—"

"Spock?" Kirk said, looking stunned.

"The Vulcan version, I think," McCoy said. "But look, he's used to controlling the Vulcan savage streak. Maybe—"

The doors whooshed open. McCoy stepped out. Kirk didn't. "Go on," he said. "I want to think about that one for a minute."

McCoy stopped the closing door with his hand. "You aren't going anywhere."

"Let me *go*, Bones!"

For a dreadful moment McCoy thought that Jim Kirk was going to cry, and he half-recoiled, half-started to go to him. His hand slipped off the doors and they closed.

McCoy stared at them for a long moment, then found himself walking blindly to his office. Was it true that a woman just couldn't function under the stress of command? He had never seen the day when Jim Kirk couldn't take anything—anything at all—absolutely on the chin. It might tear his guts out, but he could take it.

But now . . . Could it be true that women just couldn't hold up? That the body betrayed them? Damn, McCoy didn't believe *that*. *Did* he?

He'd better not. He couldn't feel any fatal difference in himself. He was acutely aware of the physical difference, but he couldn't really detect any difference in his thinking, his feeling . . .

No difference . . .

He shot into his office and punched the viewscreen for the bridge. "McCoy to Spock."

The Vulcan's face formed in the screen. "Spock here."

McCoy took the plunge. "Jim—ducked out on me."

"How long ago?" Spock said.

"A couple of minutes. I bought it—almost."

"I, too, Doctor," the Vulcan said fiercely.

"Shuttlecraft bay doors opening, Mr. Spock," Sulu said.

"Override. Close them," Spock snapped.

"Jimmied, sir," Sulu said. "The controls don't respond."

Jimmied, indeed, McCoy thought, and fought down something very close to hysteria.

"I am a fool," Spock said.

"That makes two of us," McCoy said. "He didn't want to argue with us."

"Shuttlecraft taking off, sir."

"I have him on audio, sir," Uhura said.

There was a crackle of static, a soft chuckle. "She *flies*, Spock, like all your theories. Stabilizer power off. A little rough, but no problem."

"There *is* a problem," Spock said.

"You bet. Kang has my people. Mind my ship, Mr. Spock. That's an order. Bones—" But there was a crackle and splutter and the signal failed.

Spock was cutting a straight line off the bridge.

McCoy was moving by instinct, seizing what he would need and bolting for the turbo-lift. He knew what Jim wanted.

He was floors lower than the bridge, and turbo-lifts were no respecters of Vulcan muscle. He made the repressurized landing bay one jump ahead of Spock.

You and me, Spock, he told himself, and stood in the doorway.

Spock charged out of the elevator with the look of the prehistorical Vulcan McCoy had seen before.

"You can't go, Spock," he said. "If you ever trusted him to get himself out of the frying pan, trust him *now*."

"When he has jumped into the fire? He has nothing to prove to me about being a man—particularly when he is *not*. What would you have me let him pay to prove it?"

"Is that what he's doing?" McCoy said. "Or is he just—going, as he would have gone yesterday? Don't write him off. He's talked his way out of worse spots."

"Talk is cheap, Doctor, and it is all he has now."

"Does he have to fight *you*, too?"

Spock looked at McCoy gravely. "Possibly. Stand aside."

"*Spock*—you may only make it worse. Get him killed. You aren't under control yourself. Spock, it's the YY chromosome effect."

Spock nodded. "I suspected as much. However, I *do* control." He looked at McCoy very sanely and soberly. "Leonard, I do not wish to go through you."

There was no tone of threat in it. This was Spock. He was Leonard McCoy's friend, too. But he was going.

"Then—" McCoy said, "We both go."

"In *your* condition?" It was genuine Vulcan shock, with the tone of "Woman, attend me!"

McCoy grinned savagely. *"Damn* my condition, Spock. Who's the doctor here? And get a move on before I'm needed in that capacity."

"You—brought your medical kit," Spock said, as if he had just registered the fact.

"Why, so I did, Mr. Spock." And would he ever tell the Vulcan how long that fact had taken to register with the *doctor?*

"Humans!" the Vulcan said and marched past.

McCoy followed cheerfully. Spock had said it in the exact tone of exasperation in which most men would have said *"Women!"*

Could it be that he considered all Humans as frail and delicate as women—and Human women as even more like fragile porcelain dolls? Poor Vulcan—on a ship full of dolls.

Kirk aimed the shuttlecraft for the center of the circular plaza.

If all else fails, try unadulterated gall.

He nursed the controls like a mother.

"She flies" had been both optimistic and exaggerated. It was more like "She falls." But—she moved.

He had been low in the force-field before he got even erratic control. He had kept the little ship upright by main force and a vivid imagination, and both were wearing thin.

Also, they said Starfleet training would let you fly these things blindfolded with both hands tied— when you were ninety-three. They said you never forgot how to ride a bicycle.

They hadn't tried it in this body.

He couldn't quite reach anything. The controls seemed stiff. There was a lever he couldn't pull to save his life.

Women flew these things. Damned if he knew how.

He skated it in over the grass, and somehow kept it upright.

In the end, flying the scoutship had decided him for certain against a scouting expedition to find the force-field machinery. He could never read alien machines as well as Spock. And now if it should turn out that Kirk couldn't turn a knob, push a button . . .

It might be that he couldn't have, anyway, but he probably wouldn't have thought of that this morning.

However, the Klingons would certainly have guards, patrols. And there were the alien robots, perhaps other machines. The Vulcan couldn't have made it—and it would have occurred to him very shortly to try.

Kirk broke out a pistol-phaser and belt from shuttlecraft stores, tossed the belt back and dug up another that would hardly have done for Uhura. It fit.

A hand-phaser he thoughtfully tucked into the only convenient place.

He stepped out to meet Kang.

The Klingon was alone, finishing the last strides of a quick march across the plaza. Armed. Not drawing the weapon.

He stopped a pace away and surveyed Kirk.

"Angels walk in," he grinned, "where fools fear to tread."

"I didn't know you were so familiar with our metaphors."

Kang shrugged. "Metaphors, devils, angels. One knows the enemy."

Kirk nodded. "Yes. You have no belief that I will yield to your demands. You know me better. Therefore, you have another objective. Out with it. Let's get to the real point."

Kang's eyes narrowed as if in respect, but he smiled meaningly and did another slow survey of Kirk, suddenly reached out a hand and lifted Kirk's chin. "You discount the obvious?"

Kirk made himself stand still. "I know you better." He jerked the chin away contemptuously, bracing for a fight if it didn't work. But Kang's hand didn't stop the movement. "Frosting on the cake, at most." Kirk tried to make his new voice sound certain.

Kang shook his head. "Do not make the mistake of thinking that I am you, Captain. True, I am a ship

Commander and do not stage elaborate plots for personal purposes. However, I have a marked taste for —frosting." He jerked his head toward the buildings. "Come with me."

Kirk stood his ground. "So long as you do not allow taste to interfere with command." He gestured toward the shuttlecraft. "The fact that I am here is evidence that we have come up with a capability you did not expect. I must warn you, it implies a capability to destroy your ship." It did imply it, he told himself. If Scotty could get interaction, he could get control. Sooner or later. When?

Kang's eyes considered him. "Then why have you not done so? You are not so peaceable as that."

"In fact, we are," Kirk said. "I do not destroy without warning, or except as a last resort. But there is a more practical reason. You have my people. You may have the key to the reversal processes. Certainly you have the key to the puzzle of why you have done this. I don't like puzzles. And I have a way to blast your ship. That is a basis to negotiate."

Kang looked at him narrowly. Was there something in the Klingon's manner which was—not right? Kirk tried to bring the vague feeling into focus. He had been so busy trying to run a colossal bluff, trying to sit on his own gut feelings and keep them out of the poker face he wasn't sure he had anymore—was he missing some feeling that would be a key?

Damn it, he was afraid here, and trying to come on starship Captain over the fear. Was it tying him in knots and throwing him off? Woman's intuition? Where the hell was his own?

"You are bluffing, Captain," Kang said. "But the bluff is of interest. Would you care to see some bits of the puzzle?" He swept his arm out toward the buildings in the gesture of bowing a lady into his domain. Won't you step into my parlor?

And there was still no answer to that. Kirk could stay here in the relative safety of the open, in what felt like the safety of being able to fight, run, reach the shuttlecraft. But in fact there was no way back, no way out but forward. It was what he had come for. Would Captain Kirk even have had to consider it?

"Into your parlor?" he said and shook his head. "This fly has teeth."

"I believe that is an anatomical impossibility." Kang said, and he sounded curiously like the Vulcan. "Worse, it is an empty bluff."

"No bluff, Kang. We will negotiate the main point here. Then you will take me to the force-field switch."

Kang shook his head. "Not here. You will walk or I will carry you."

He shot out a hand and grabbed Kirk's wrist, started to drag him along.

Kirk took a quick leap forward, twisted Kang's arm for leverage and reversed the hold into a forearm throw.

His combat instructors always said that it didn't take strength. He had never quite believed them, and still didn't. But whatever strength was there was sufficient.

Kang landed with a grunt on the grass.

He slashed out a leg and cut Kirk's legs from under him.

Kirk fell heavily on top of the Klingon, and Kang's arms and a leg closed around him, trapping him as if in concrete. "Teeth?" Kang grinned. "Don't play with the big boys, little angel."

Then Kirk knew what a fool he had been. It *did* take muscle. Maybe not always and not much, but in a crunch, yes. Muscle—or the willingness to live with the facts.

Yet it wasn't muscle or will which had failed him. Not brawn. Brain.

There had been a moment when he could have reached the phaser on his belt, and he was too busy proving that he could throw Kang.

And the Klingon had known that he would.

He read that in the savage face and saw Kang wait for the slow realization to come to him. The Klingon freed a hand long enough to throw Kirk's belt-phaser away. Then he reached down the neck of the black coverall and found the hand-phaser there. He didn't hurry. Finally he rolled them both over and leaned down over Kirk's face.

"One always tastes the frosting first," he grinned.

"Go to the devil." Kirk whispered, not trusting the new voice.

"Do you see what this would do turned loose in Star Fleet?" Kang said fiercely. "In the Federation? Do you know what would happen to you on Starbase Eleven? And how they would laugh?"

"That is why you—?" Kirk breathed.

"Just as they laughed at me when I made peace with a Human? Oh, yes, That was part of my reason." Kang scowled down at him. "But there was much more. It would become a new weapon for us, a new vice for you. You have not the simple warrior virtues. Your people are as decadent as these were."

"Virtue?" Kirk laughed with soundless scorn. "Vice? *You* dare to speak—"

"Silence!" Kang rumbled. "Vice, yes. Softness is vice. And the desire to experience without limit is always vice. Your civilization has .both. When your people had finished laughing at you, they would have made this place the mecca of decadence. And taken the toys home. Your civilization would crumble, and the galaxy would fall into our hands."

"On a cold day in hell."

Kang shook his head. "You would like this, Human. Even you. If you could spend a week, a month, as you are now—" He traced a finger along Kirk's jaw-line, lifted his chin. "Even now, you wonder. A few inches, Kirk, and you would know the taste of a warrior, a hawk, a commander with stars under his feet. So would I. And we both wonder."

He moved suddenly and was on his feet, pulling Kirk up to his knees, finding his chin again and tilting his face up. "Do not make peace with me, Kirk. I am no dove."

"Then why did you let me up?"

The hand tightened on his jaw, and he was certain that the Klingon would make him pay for the words.

"To show that I could," Kang said contemptuously, and released him.

And then he saw the Vulcan streaking up from behind Kang in a soundless, stalking rush, silent as a panther.

Kirk's eyes must have betrayed the Vulcan beyond Kirk's will or any stopping of it. Kang turned and Kirk flung himself on the handle of Kang's disruptor, clinging to it with the slender fingers which suddenly seemed strong.

But it was not necessary. Kang was not going for it. He braced to meet the Vulcan with his body.

Spock's phaser was out but he did not use it, nor stop to set for a fight. On the last stride he felled Kang with one explosive, backhanded blow, and the Klingon lay where he fell.

Kirk got up. Spock turned, leveling his phaser back toward the nearest buildings. Kirk saw McCoy then, running hard, awkwardly, on the line Spock had stalked.

Spock's eyes raked the buildings. Kirk crouched down to take Kang's disruptor. Of course, all hell should break loose any second. Kang's men would fire from the buildings . . . But hell did not break loose, and McCoy reached them, grabbed Kirk, tried to find breath to say something.

As between Kirk and McCoy, Kirk decided, it was difficult to tell who was bracing whom. He grinned foolishly and McCoy pounded his back.

"Damn fool idiot," McCoy muttered in a breathless whisper.

"Same to you," Kirk answered in kind.

"I concur," Spock agreed in a devastatingly normal tone. But the toe of his boot was prodding Kang.

Kang's eyes opened. Kirk saw him read death in the Vulcan's face. The Klingon's eyes prepared to meet it. Then the Vulcan's left hand reached down with great control, twisted in the silver tunic and lifted the Klingon in one sweep to his feet.

Kang's eyes held the Vulcan's. "Why did you let me up?"

"To show that I could." The Vulcan's hand unlocked from the tunic.

Kang grinned savagely, raising a hand to work at his jaw. "You are no dove," he said with satisfaction.

Spock nodded. "You will make peace with *me,*" he announced flatly.

Kang looked at him carefully. "State your certainty," he said.

Spock nodded. "I have been slow to check assumptions. We found pleasure palaces. We assumed that what was done to us was intended as a pleasure. Hence, that it was a process intended for the old aliens' own use. Hence, presumably, reversible. Our problem: The Klingons had it, and us. We did not see the logical alternative, that it had *them.*"

"Had *them?*" McCoy asked incredulously. "They're running around loose and—"

"They are conspicuously not running around loose, Doctor, as I should have realized long before your elegant dash across the plaza." Spock turned to Kang. "When did you first realize that your ship was trapped?"

"More than two weeks ago," Kang said bitterly.

"And when did you conclude that the process was not reversible?"

Kang shrugged. "Not until we had exhausted every possibility. When did *you,* Vulcan?"

"Belatedly," Spock said. He turned to Kirk. "You mentioned a siren song. I should have recognized also the other Greek legend: the Procrustean Bed." He turned to Kang. "Do Klingons have a Procrustes? He was a mythical Greek giant who stretched travelers to fit his bed—or cut off their legs."

"Greek?" McCoy grumbled. "He probably *was* a Klingon."

"Why, thank you, Doctor," Kang said. "We do not claim the distinction, but it seems a forthright solution."

Spock said, "The machines here did not have to be for the Procrusteans' own use. Nor reversible. This was strictly a starship trap. Travelers could be chopped to fit—as slaves, as pets, as amusement."

"My God," McCoy swore.

"Then the same thing happened to your crew," Kirk said. "A trap."

Kang nodded. "Our landing party and I were grabbed by automatic machines, then beamed to the ship. When the transporter started taking the crew, I brought the first landing party back in a shuttlecraft, but the turbulence broke it up as we landed. The machines didn't take us again, but they took everyone off the ship. You would have destroyed a ghost ship."

"So," Kirk said, "your whole story was a song and dance. You didn't want blackmail. You didn't even want war. But why didn't you just ask for peace?"

Kang shrugged. "Peace is not my way. You were more inventive in war." He gestured toward the shuttlecraft. "You brought me a way back to my ship," he spread his hands. "The story was the simple truth—and my first thought here before I discovered the Procrustean Bed aspects."

"You wanted to turn it loose on us," Kirk said, "and you wound up hoist by your own petard."

Kirk caught himself. He could hardly expect the forthright Klingon to be scholar enough to know *that* metaphor.

But Kang smiled. "It has never been quite clear to me what a petard is, but the mere phrase seems self-explanatory and exceedingly eloquent." He nodded, "Yes, Miss Kirk, we are all hoist—by a Procrustean Petard."

Kirk shook his head. "Wrong, Kang. It is your petard, not ours. We haven't been doing any hoisting."

Kang looked rather grim. "My petard, then," he growled. "What of it?"

Spock stepped in. "Let us not discuss petards except for clarification. We require peace. I believe that our two ships might combine with a certain interaction effect we have discovered to break out of the force-field. Otherwise we will, in all probability, die here. We need to confer with your Science Officer—"

"That will be impossible," Kang said flatly, almost uneasily.

Spock raised an eyebrow. "You have some objection to our seeing your wife, Mara?"

"Every objection," Kang said. "First among them that you turned her into a peace-monger—in the Klingon Empire. And—she left me."

Spock inclined his head. "She was a most exceptional woman. I should have liked to consult her. However, her replacement will do."

"No," Kang said. "Do not play with me, Vulcan. I am obliged to listen to you, talk to you. I am not obliged to allow you effrontery, and I will break your neck. Was not the fact that only I have been seen a part of your 'certainty'?"

Spock shrugged an eyebrow. "Merely a hypothesis. You have undergone the Klingon equivalent of the YY chromosome effect, I presume. Have you confirmed that it is done only to one male on a ship?"

Kang nodded glumly. "The strongest."

Spock nodded as if that explained everything. "You—can't go home again."

"Then—you need our help even more." Spock said,

"What?" Kirk heard himself saying.

Kang shrugged heavily. "Excellent logic, Vulcan. Mara and my previous crew were rarities. My new crew is—standard Klingon."

"Male," Kirk said, remembering. "All male."

Kang nodded morosely. "Now—all female."

For a moment Kirk thought that he would break up laughing—or crying. The whole answer swept over him like a wave of divination.

"And," he said, "they won't show their faces!"

"Barely to each other," Kang said glumly. "Certainly not to you. Most certainly not in the Klingon Empire."

Kirk did break up then, holding his sides and

wiping his eyes. Somehow he found breath for the words. "Hoist—by your own petard."

Kirk saw the others beginning to be alarmed by his dissolving in laughter, but he felt a weight lifting for the first time. It was his own hell-bent sense of humor coming through, and he was in control.

He pulled himself up straight. "Very well Kang, I have no time for negotiation. I require peace."

Kang looked at him with a certain respect. "I—suspend war."

Kirk finally nodded. "That will do. Let's get my people out of here."

That proved to be a long, exhausting, heartbreaking job.

People were being taken in batches of twenty about every hour and transformed. The automatic machinery which did it was impregnably shielded. They popped out like cookies on a conveyor belt and were carried off by the robots.

Kirk saw Christine Chapel come through as a tall, strong-looking man, Sulu as an exotic, tiny Oriental, saw dozens of faces he knew on bodies which had never existed before.

He saw them waking up, living with the fact.

It shook them to the roots of being, but they were the crew of the *Enterprise,* and they would make it. They took care of each other. When they had time, they might cry on each other's shoulders and think what this would mean if it were forever.

Meanwhile, there was time only to get everybody out. Kirk and Kang organized the ferrying, using every available shuttlecraft and riding everybody's tail.

Scott worked out a slingshot interaction effect based on phased power to the stabilizers, which would walk the two ships out of the field.

Spock computed a time interval when they could get everyone out of the machines before the next batch was taken. And he rounded up a small mountain of alien data tapes—for later study at a starbase.

McCoy grumbled and fussed over people and saved everybody's sanity, ". . . finally got the Klingons to let us take 'em up. Shy little things. Practically had to put 'em in veils. If you think *you've* got troubles . . ."

But they *did* have troubles.

If they got away it would be with sixty-six people transformed.

There was no way to stay and study the problem while more people were being subjected to that.

And Kang had learned that the planet was dangerous. Giant machines made regular sweeps, stunning anything which moved. But except for the first landing parties, no one was taken to the Procrustean Beds. Kang's men had even tried that—throwing themselves to the machines in the hope of being reprocessed. But the machines carried them off somewhere, never to be seen, as if, once the transporting started, the machines didn't take anyone from the ground, except to do something permanent, and probably as fatal as the original Procrustean Bed.

Finally Kirk, Spock, and McCoy took the last shuttle up. "But how did you figure it, Spock?" McCoy asked. "That it wasn't another pleasure palace but a—tourist trap?"

"Partly from the YY chromosome effect," Spock said absently. "It does not seem a thing one would do to oneself for pleasure."

McCoy grinned sourly. "You really *are* a Vulcan, aren't you? People have tried some pretty odd pleasures. Hyper-masculinity—it would strike some men as a bargain."

Spock raised a familiar eyebrow for the first time in a long time—partly, Kirk thought, in genuine astonishment. "That aspect had not occurred to me, Doctor. Perhaps to the under-endowed . . ."

The eyebrow looked just a trifle—*smug?*

But by the time they manhandled the two ships out of the force-field, even the Vulcan looked worn and drained. Kirk ordered him off duty.

And Dr. McCoy practically did the same for Kirk.

Kirk rolled over and flung himself face down on the bed. And even that was a mistake. He rolled back, fighting the robe which hung like a sack.

He couldn't face getting something new from the fabricators. Tomorrow. Thank God for the small blessing of the black coverall, which hadn't raised the question too acutely until now. Thank something for the action, even the danger, which had not allowed other questions to raise their heads in blunt physical fact and full psychological reality, until now.

Now that they had broken clear and put space under their heels, conferred and analyzed until nothing more could be done, clung to ritual and routine—there must be people all over the ship who faced, as he just had, the small rituals and routines of bath and bedtime, which could not be routine now.

And if it was almost more than he could take . . .

He got up and padded to the intercom. "Kirk to bridge. Put me on ship-wide audio."

"Acknowledged, Captain."

"This is the Captain," he said. "No lectures. No advice. Just one small note. Uniform of the day will be optional and will include choice of the black coveralls or their equivalents. Ranks, titles of respect, names will be considered to be without connotations of gender. We will—carry on." He paused. "One more thing. You have made me very proud. Kirk out."

There was a buzz at the door. Kirk straightened his face, knowing who would have been on his way before Kirk had spoken. "Come."

"Spock," he said, gesturing the Vulcan inside.

The Vulcan inclined his head gravely and entered.

He gestured Spock toward a chair by the desk, but the Vulcan stood. "I came to invite you to a workout," Spock said.

Kirk sank down weakly on the edge of the desk, fighting the impulse toward hysterical laughter. "My God, *now?*"

"I do not recall inviting a deity. However, if you require assistance—"

"I'll assist *you!*" Kirk laughed softly. "For the love of—Pete, sit down." He peeled himself off the edge of the desk and sank into his chair as Spock took the opposite one. "So you're going to—teach me," Kirk said slowly. "Meaning—you're going to back me all the way?"

"I believe that is what I *said,* Captain," Spock said innocently.

Kirk leaned back and stretched in pure luxury, enjoying even the feel of it. "I heard you, Mr. Spock," he murmured.

After a time he said, "Then you think it cannot be cracked?"

Spock shook his head. "I have not said that, nor thought it. I merely think that you should be able to—lick twice your weight in *snarths.*"

"I'm for *that,*" Kirk grinned, then sobered. "What chance that we can reverse it, Spock? Straight."

"Extremely small, Jim. Beyond the state of the art, so far as we know, anywhere in the galaxy, with the possible exception of races too advanced to be helpful. Probably beneath the state of the art of the Organians, for example. We shall inquire."

"The record tapes?"

Spock frowned. "On brief examination, chiefly things we know or do not need to know. Would a library include minute information on how to run a gambling casino, a slave compound, a pleasure palace? And so far as we know, reversal equipment does not even exist on the planet. A one-way street. In one end and out the other. Strictly intended for travelers who can be used—and used up."

Kirk turned it over in his mind, feeling that there ought to be some way to get a handle on it, something they were missing. But the logic—and the horror—of the Procrustean Bed was exactly that. A callousness so utter that it did not even recognize itself as callous. A callousness which could cut people to fit the system.

There were a lot of Procrustean Beds in the galaxy. A lot of petards.

"No—reservations—about me in command in this form if it comes to that?" he asked finally.

"A great many reservations," Spock said openly. "It is still far worse for you than for a woman born. You will be a target—of laughter, or worse. You will have to alter your thinking, your reflexes, your deepest impulses. Find new ways to command, even to live. New choices of friends, subtle changes with old ones. Some way to face it if Star Fleet Command will not yield. It is possible that your best choice would be another life. But, in any case, it is *your* life and your right." The Vulcan stood up. "It was once said my place is—by your side. That is where you will find me. And in the gym—tomorrow. Good night, Jim."

"It *is,* now," Kirk said softly.

It was a rotten night, Kirk thought, wandering into the deserted rec room. It had been a rotten day. A rotten month.

And today at the conference on Starbase Eleven they had finally admitted defeat. Kang, McCoy, Scott, even—say it, even Spock. Spock would go on, as he had, virtually without sleep, growing more drawn by the day, Kirk and McCoy riding him for any scrap of rest he had gotten since it happened. But for the first time Kirk saw that the Vulcan was beaten, and knew it.

So, for that matter, was Kirk.

And Admiral Komack had as good as admitted that *he* was. Kirk could give it a try, but once the secret was out, it was virtually certain that Kirk would be administratively promoted. Commodore, probably, but not a line officer. Desk job. He could fight, but the fight might throw the status of all the changees into question, might open a fight over the position of women which would tear Star Fleet apart. Yes, possible that it needed to be torn, but in the midst of crises all over the galaxy . . .

For once, Kirk decided, he was not much interested in crises all over the galaxy.

But he was likely to be the most improbable advocate of women's rights ever to come down the pike.

And did he want that? His impulse was to fight. But—damn it to hell, he hadn't adjusted to being a woman. He hoped he would have had the grace to adjust—or to fight—if he had been born one. But he flat couldn't get used to the change. He didn't think anybody had, but he perhaps least of all.

He had paced the ship like a caged tiger, a very small tiger. He had haunted the gym. He had looked over everybody's shoulder and even gotten hip-deep in the science himself, knowing that he had a useful knack of seeing the unexpected, the obvious, which was unobvious to the specialist. But they had turned up nothing. He kept calling himself "he."

And he had done nothing really about adjusting.

Well, he told himself, he could hardly go down to the Starbase and try it on for size. Of all the people who had been affected, only Spock and Kang moved freely there, coordinating research teams who knew only aspects of the problem. The other changees kept to the ship. There was too great a chance of . . . recognition. But also there was an unspoken reluctance.

Kirk realized that he was toying idly with a pair of attractive dim-light glasses some crewwoman had left on a table.

Then he realized where his thoughts were leading.

Twenty minutes later he paused in the corridor outside the Starbase's main outworld bar. He had readopted the original black coverall which he had had cleaned and preserved. It had a certain close-fitting elegance of line and richness of fabric, which he had subdued somewhat in the design of its replacements. It would have to do. He could not bring himself to do more. The shortish hair worked without fuss. The well-scrubbed look would have to do, too.

He took a breath and went through the door. He had raised enough looks in the halls of the Starbase as it was, even with a good part of his face behind the dim-light glasses.

Strange to have to think about walking into a bar.

But eyes did turn.

He made his way quickly to a booth near the door. At least it was the outworld bar. Here he would find aliens, a few youngsters still struck with the wonder of it all, a few old hands who genuinely liked aliens, some civilians, probably not anyone he knew. And the somewhat higher standard of politeness which usually prevailed where aliens brushed shoulders voluntarily.

A Rigellian waiter took and delivered his order without batting an eyelash or raising an eyebrow. Not that the waiter had an eyelash to bat, or eyebrow, or even an eye, exactly.

Kirk saw eyebrows and eyes all over the room, and kept his own eyes down judiciously on the drink he was nursing. A man had a right, after all, to nurse a drink or two. Even a woman had a right. And that was all he would do, all he had come for, wasn't it?

He overdid the eyes-down and didn't even see it coming.

"Would you allow me to join you? Another Saurian brandy?"

Kirk looked up. A civilian, he decided. Forty-odd. A diplomat, possibly. The man had a certain manner and presence. He reminded Kirk somehow of Ambassador Sarek, although this man was not a Vulcan. He looked Human, in fact. And, on the whole, human. His manner said that he was not meaning to be offensive; there was no harm in asking.

"I'm waiting for a friend," Kirk lied in confusion, cursing himself for it. Surely a woman would have had six different ways . . . And he thought that the man saw right through him.

"Perhaps while you wait," the man said. "I am Ambassador Tregarth. I thought you might be a stranger here. I am not familiar with the manner of dress."

Neither am I, Kirk thought, and caught himself smiling. "A new trend on a world off the beaten path," he agreed. "However, I'm afraid I really can't—"

Kirk had not seen the dark figure approaching. "Good evening," Kang said to Kirk. "I did not see you come in."

Tregarth turned with a trace of a smile. "Then you are doubtless the only man who did not, and do not deserve your fortune." He bowed his head gallantly to Kirk. "My apologies. I presume your wait is over?"

It was the faint hint of a civilized offer. Should it be Kang who presumed, the Ambassador extended protection, exit, the formality of introductions and joining.

"Yes," Kirk said. "Thank you. Good evening."

"My pleasure," the Ambassador said, and withdrew in good order.

Kang bowed to Kirk with as much civility and Kirk gestured for him to sit down. Every eye was still on them as the Klingon slipped his bulk into the small booth.

"Thank you." Kirk said.

The Klingon nodded without smiling. "He would be right, you know, if I had not lied, as you did."

"Perhaps I did not lie," Kirk said. "You made it a truth."

"Waiting for a—friend?" Kang asked seriously.

So he had heard and not merely guessed. "No," Kirk said. "But under the heading of 'Know thine enemy.' It is good to be known, even by the enemy."

Kang nodded. "I . . . defeated you in combat, you know. I could require . . . peace."

Kirk smiled tiredly. "I . . . suspend . . . war."

Kang was silent for a moment as the waiter arrived, apparently from nowhere, with drinks.

"Shall we drink to—doves?" Kang asked over the rim of a glass.

"Hawks," Kirk said and met the Klingon's eyes across the lifted drinks.

Kang reached out and slipped the dim-light

glasses off Kirk's face. "One must look into the eye of the eagle."

And one could hardly let eye of eagle falter or fall, Kirk thought, and took a sip of the drink without looking at it. He grinned the old hell-bent Kirk grin. "In a moment I shall use a very old and very bad metaphor about birds of a feather, and in that event I will kick myself all the way back to the *Enterprise*. Do you suppose that a couple of birds such as ourselves could kick the problem around one more time?"

Kang drained his glass. "Not such a bad metaphor. I could recommend another destination, and show you—some bits of the puzzle."

Kirk took another long sip of the drink.

"You should not be seen here," Kang said, "but you were right to come. It is only the single step which commits one to battle which is hard. Enemies take it together, and friends. In the end, there is only one way for you to go, and perhaps that is the only solution to the problem."

One way . . . Was it not something he had been thinking? A one-way street. Where had he heard that old phrase lately? But didn't it apply? What other way was there to go? Kirk finished the drink. The eyes in the room were oppressive. Even an oppressive silence seemed to have fallen. "Let's get out of here," Kirk said and slipped out of the booth.

Kang had laid a credit chit on the table and rose, picking up Kirk's forgotten glasses and turning with him.

Then Kirk saw Spock. The Vulcan was standing in the nearby door and something in his manner suggested that he had been standing there a little too long.

Kirk approached him in silence, aware of Kang moving close beside. Kirk inclined his head to the Vulcan and saw the Vulcan extend his hand, palm up, to Kang. For a moment Kirk was puzzled, and then Kang surrendered the glasses into the Vulcan's hand and the Vulcan handed them to Kirk.

"You should not be seen here," Spock said in a tone which could not be heard three feet away—except, doubtless, by Vulcan ears.

"I was right to come," Kirk said, holding the glasses down and meeting the Vulcan's eyes. Eye of eagle, he thought. One Vulcan eagle coming after a chick fallen from the nest.

"Not alone," Spock said. "Not without agreement. There has been no time when you have informed only the night-watch and transporter room." He did not say —and not *me*.

"There has been no time like this," Kirk said, hearing the unspoken.

"No," Spock agreed, hearing, too.

"It is an aspect of the problem which must be explored," Kirk said. "I do not like puzzles without solutions. As old enemies of the same problem, Kang and I were considering exploring the aspects."

"I do not consider that the only avenue of exploration," Spock said. "And—it is a one-way street."

Kirk smiled gravely. "It was not a direction I expected to take, either." He turned and looked at Kang. "And I'm afraid I will have to reverse course." He put on the glasses. "Gentlemen, I recommend we adjourn. We have given this pleasure palace enough entertainment for one night." He motioned them toward the door and followed the Vulcan through.

In the hall, Kirk stopped so suddenly that Kang bumped into him, nearly knocking him over, and the Vulcan whirled and caught him.

"*What did I say?*" Kirk whispered loudly, not trusting the voice again.

"Verbatim?" Spock asked, his own voice a little strangled.

Kirk waved him down, trying to follow out the trail of thought. "A one-way street . . ." He grabbed the Vulcan's arms and swung him around. "But you *said* it, Spock. In one end and out the other. You can drive the wrong way on a one-way street. Hell, you can *put* yourself in one end and out the other. The process is its own reversal!"

"But we know it doesn't take people who have already been through," Kang protested.

Kirk turned over his shoulder and laughed. "We *don't* know." Back to Spock. "Boy, have *I* been slow to check assumptions. You spun me such a beautiful, logical horror story of the Procrustean Bed. It's that, of course. Probably it's *only* that, now. But there was probably a time when it was a pleasure palace. Maybe they tried it on themselves too often, got too jaded, could only enjoy seeing strangers struggle with it for the first time. That doesn't matter. The point is, it's the central programming which would make the difference. It follows a set program now. It takes the first landing party. Lets it go. Perhaps to let them know the hopelessness. Takes batches directly from the ship. It doesn't reprocess people from the ground. It knows it's already done them. Takes 'em for something else, maybe. Examination. Discards. Whatever." He took a breath and Spock forestalled him.

"But how would it know if it had the same ship back?"

Kirk laughed. He would have to tell Bones what a real Vulcan emotional display looked like. "Precisely, Mr. Spock. Indubitably."

"Fascinating," Spock said in the old tone.

Kang seemed to be pounding Kirk on the back. "Who the devil ever saw a brainy angel?" he rumbled.

Kirk turned between them and put a hand on two tall shoulders and didn't feel odd doing it, finally linked arms with the two men. He steered them down the hall toward the nearest Transporter station, ignoring the small following they were collecting, ignoring all the eyes. Let 'em all stare. This had to be the first time a Klingon, a Vulcan, and one small Human female had walked down those halls, arm in arm—and laughing. At least, except for the Vulcan, and Kirk wasn't too sure about him.

". . . biologically indistinguishable," Kirk was saying a half-hour later in the briefing room. "We've been saying all along—perfectly normal females, males. There's no way for the machinery to tell. We have to assume that field is tough enough that nobody ever broke out of it, or at least never came back. The machinery wouldn't be set up to tell."

He kept his eyes on Komack. The Admiral was the one who had to be convinced. Bones, Scott, Uhura had bought the main outlines as fast as Spock and Kang, and as fast as the three could pour the story out while waking Komack and calling the conference. On reflection, Kirk had wakened Breen and Collins, too, as having a certain right to be among the first to know.

"It's an enormous risk," Komack said, "tangling with the field again. Pretty shaky theory to risk a starship."

"Two," Kang said. "Does the Federation fail to honor commitments made by its field officers—or fear to go where Klingons go?"

Laying it on a little thick, Kirk thought, and stepped in. "Mr. Scott's effect can get us out," he said.

"Aye," Scott chimed in, "I'll nurse us out of there pretty as a picture."

"By your own theory," Komack said, "Mr. Scott cannot go. You will have to leave everyone but your changees here."

Scott turned to Kirk. "You're not leavin' *me* anywhere and goin' off with my poor bairns into that field!"

"Can't be helped, Scotty," Kirk said gently. "Spock will have to handle it."

Scott looked shocked, and then his eyes widened further. "For the matter of that, you can't take Mr. Spock!"

"Right, Jim," McCoy said grimly. "The theory doesn't hold for the Y chromosomes. They can be double, triple, more. Probably males with something close to a double, or some unusual male chromosome that the machine picks anyway. If it found a double, it would likely just add a third or more. Probably more than even Spock could handle. Or if it *did* reverse—" He shook his head.

Kirk had been feeling the elation drain out of him so swiftly and completely that he felt like a collapsed doll. Involuntarily, he sought the Vulcan's eyes.

Spock nodded. "That aspect had occurred to me, somewhat belatedly. However, I must go."

Kirk shook his head. "I can handle the equipment."

"That is not the point," Spock said. "The machine always picks some one male, perhaps the strongest, from each ship. If I am not there—"

"Jim," McCoy blurted.

Spock lifted an eyebrow. "Old habits of thought die hard, do they not, Doctor? No, not Jim, but perhaps Uhura, Laura Breen, Christine Chapel."

"It could kill you," McCoy said. "Or drive you right off the edge."

"Possible, Doctor," Spock said. "Also logically possible that it might simply remove the extra chromosome—perhaps also interesting to the aliens. Or do nothing. Or—reverse. Most probably, however, add a chromosome. Kang and I have demonstrated an ability to control one. I can try two. A necessary risk."

"There is a better idea for you, Mr. Spock," Breen broke in. "The Doctor can tell you who is the strongest male changee, and so can I. I am. I volunteer. I do not mind remaining a man. In fact, I prefer it." She looked at Kirk rather wistfully. "Any reason I might have to change back—would not work out. And if I'm to be a man, I'd as soon be one in spades, doubled and redoubled. Not only Vulcans can control."

Spock shook his head, "A gallant offer, Officer Breen, but I cannot—"

"Don't go noble on us, Mr. Spock," Uhura said. "A perfectly 'logical' offer. Why shouldn't she want to remain a man? It's better for her chosen work. She might even want to command some day."

Kirk winced, and he rather thought that the Admiral did, too. "That battle will still have to be fought," Kirk said, "and will be. But I see no reason why Breen could not choose if she wishes—or any other changee. Collins, perhaps?"

Collins grinned. "If Breen chooses, I just might, sir." Breen looked at him in astonishment.

"I was about to say," Spock cut in, "that among other reasons why I cannot accept is the fact that we have no proof Breen would be chosen. The sample is too small. It may not be strength. Possibly some minor characteristic Kang and I have in common. It could still be any other woman."

"Old habits of thought die hard, do they not, Mr. Spock?" Uhura teased. She sobered. "I think I can speak for the 'women.' I doubt there is one of us who would not risk being a normal man to keep you alive and—your sweet Vulcan self."

"Now who's going noble on us?" Kirk asked her, to cover Spock's confusion. "However, I think that is 'logical.' Subject to everyone's agreement, that is what we will try. Admiral, will you give us an escort ship to take off our other people and stand clear of the field, observe the effect?"

"All right, I'll buy it," Komack said. "It beats the hell out of having *this* crew running around loose in Star Fleet."

Kirk grinned. "You'll still have *that,* sir. Spaceman's luck. Sorry." He turned to Kang. "Your crew should be all right, but you—"

"I have to run Scott's effect," Kang said. "I wouldn't trust those dithering little—"

"We'll put one of my bright laddies on it," Scott said, "or ladies, as the case may be."

Kirk grinned widely, thinking that he might possibly break up again. "Or knock a little sense into one or two blushing Klingons on the trip."

"Right," Kang growled.

"And when you get home to the Empire," Kirk asked, "will you do anything about that particular petard?"

Kang shrugged. "Possibly knock sense into a few more heads. Meanwhile, it will be an interesting trip."

And so, Kirk thought, it had been. A very interesting trip.

He smoothed down the gold shirt and swiveled in the command chair—both of which fit again—to look at Uhura's lovely legs, which suited Kirk right down to the ground, too. Scotty had beamed back from the escort ship almost the minute they had cleared the field, and was fussing contentedly over damage from the rough ride. And any minute now . . .

Kirk couldn't stand it any longer and made a grinning exit off the bridge, relishing every long stride to the transporter room.

He met McCoy coming from the opposite direction. "Great minds," Kirk said cheerfully.

"Minds?" McCoy snorted. "How about great bodies?"

"I'll drink to that," Kirk said. "You're sure Breen's all right?"

"All six-feet-five of her. She's maybe not as sweet-tempered. But she'll make it. Collins is with her."

They went through the door together.

The transporter shimmered and Spock and Kang beamed in from the escort ship.

"Welcome aboard," Kirk said, and Kang grinned and jumped off the platform.

The Vulcan descended more sedately but with alacrity, and for a moment Kirk thought that Spock would treat them to some emotional display.

But he merely surveyed Kirk and McCoy with some sort of Vulcan satisfaction.

"I cannot say that either of you will crack mirrors," he said. "However, the reversal will be the misfortune of men everywhere."

"Why, you pointy-eared elf," McCoy choked. "How would *you* know?"

"It was *I* who got the Y chromosome, Doctor," Spock said with exaggerated dignity.

Kirk broke up quietly, and in his own voice and pounded them both on the back.

Presently he was able to look at Kang.

The Klingon bowed. "My ship reports all well, as you know, but I am anxious to get back to it." He extended his hand to Kirk. "We have suspended war," he said. "Would you care to make peace?"

Kirk took the hand. "It took a burning house, a Procrustean Bed, and a bit more," he said. "The peace of hawks is not easy."

Kang grinned. "Birds of a feather, Captain. We will meet again, I think. Something of a pity that that planet cannot become a mecca. It did produce its pleasures."

Uhura watched the three of them come back to the bridge together, as they so often did after all the shouting was over. It was almost a tradition.

It was so good to see them together in the traditional form. So good to see *him*. He was glowing and looking as if he fitted his skin again. But he had done well as a woman, she thought, and even glowed a bit, especially on the trip back after he knew there was a way back. They all had.

He grinned at her and dropped into the command chair, Spock and McCoy taking up their familiar positions on his right and left.

"Mr. Scott," he said, "I still want research on that field, on your breakout effect, on a way to block that alien transporter. We could tackle that place again if—"

"Again?" Scott said in horror. "Havena' ye had enough?"

Kirk shrugged. "There's still the knowledge, Scotty. We barely scratched it. And the place is an open hazard, still broadcasting its siren song. The warning buoys we set out will help. But travelers may ignore them. *We* probably might if we thought they were someone's ruse for protecting a valuable secret. No, we'll need to go back one day. You don't leave an automated Procrustean Bed set up and functioning."

"Nor," Spock added, "did we find out what happened to the—Procrusteans."

"That's easy, Spock," McCoy said, and as the Vulcan turned an inquiring eyebrow. "Hoist by their own petard."

Spock looked pained. "Poetic, Doctor, but highly speculative."

"You should talk," McCoy crowed. *"You* were the one who threw together the fanciest bit of poetic speculation I ever saw. Procrustean Beds, indeed. Your premise was all wrong—that the Y chromosome bit couldn't be a pleasure. Sheerest luck that you were basically right."

"Sheerest logic, Doctor," Spock said. "The pleasure in question is not logical."

"Now *there* you said a mouthful," McCoy agreed. "But the Procrusteans obviously regarded it as a pleasure. That, and the reversal. And I suspect that most of us *did* find it a kind of pleasure, when it wasn't forever. Not a bad idea to find out how the other half lives. You ought to try it sometime, Mr. Spock."

Spock adopted his long-suffering look. "I do that every day, Doctor. Humans. Illogical. Emotional. Subject to hormones and biochemistry and the phases of their moon." He sighed. "I am an expert in other halves, Doctor."

"Spock," Kirk protested, "that's every prejudice we've ever held against women. Haven't we learned anything?"

"Why, yes, Captain," Spock said. "That Humans and women and even men, for all their frailties, are remarkably—functional."

Kirk looked up at him and grinned. "Does that include Vulcans—especially the frailties part?"

Spock went virtuously enigmatic. "After all, my —other half—is only Human."

"Insufferable," McCoy said definitively. "Twice as insufferable. That's what the double-Y chromosome did to him. Got to get him back to that planet, Jim."

"I don't know, Bones. I'm beginning to like him

this way. Besides, what if it were three times?" He grinned at McCoy, but then frowned. "But you were saying—hoist by their own petard?"

McCoy shrugged. "It *is* speculation, Jim. The simplest idea might be literally that. Their machines got out of hand. Procrustes got lashed to the bed. We never did find out what those gathering machines did with Kang's men. Or—complex idea: They tampered too much with the law of identity. Got so they didn't know who they were or what they were. Tampered with each other and finally with unwilling strangers. And somewhere it struck them that they had really known sin. Ever wonder what would have happened to Procrustes if he realized exactly what he was?"

"He couldn't live with it?" Kirk prompted.

McCoy nodded. "Could be. Either way—a Procrustean Petard."

Kirk looked reflectively at the viewscreen showing the planet from their distant orbit, still showing the Klingon ship moving off slowly. "It could get to be our petard, Bones, if we go back and tame the planet and the process. Do you think the galaxy is ready for that?"

"The galaxy may have to be, Jim. A thing like that can't be kept down forever."

Kirk swung the chair a bit and turned to Uhura. "Something else can't. This wouldn't have been so rough if we hadn't had to learn a lesson the hard way." He looked at Uhura inquiringly. "And for you—any temptation to stay on the other side?"

She looked down into the fine eyes. "One or two, under certain circumstances. But—no. I am what I am."

He bowed gallantly. "The fortune of men everywhere."

"Thank you," she said with the same inclination of her head. "When I can say the counterpart of that to you, and have it mean the same, we will have learned the lesson."

He flashed her a scapegrace little smile and turned in the command chair. "Ahead Warp Factor Two, Mr. Sulu."

Editors' Introduction to
"The Sleeping God"

The essence of what Jesco von Puttkamer is and does is embodied in his introduction and the fact that he would write it, and this story, for this book.

But Jesco is many things.

He is senior staff scientist and Program Manager for Space Industralization and Integrated Long-Range Planning Studies in the Advanced Programs Office of NASA's Office of Space Flight in Washington, D.C., where he is responsible for NASA's long-range program planning in space flight, particularly concepts of permanent occupancy of space by humans. As Program Manager he directs major new studies of advanced economic activities in space—looking toward a permanent foothold for man in space.

He was educated in Switzerland and Germany, receiving a Bachelor of Science degree in General and Aerospace Engineering, and a Master of Science degree in Aerospace Engineering. In 1961 he got a telegram from Wernher von Braun: "COME TO HUNTSVILLE. WE'RE GOING TO THE MOON." He did. And they did. He became a U.S. citizen in 1967. He was heavily involved in the Saturn/Apollo Lunar Landing Program and in early development efforts of the Space Shuttle. He is the author of numerous books and papers and has lectured internationally on future space concepts, especially in space industrialization and space colonization. He has served as commentator on space missions on national TV networks. He is the author of the section on "Manned Space Flight" in the new edition of the McGraw-Hill Encyclopedia of Science and Technology.

That's the briefest essence of his official biography. It barely touches the subject.

It doesn't say that he's an authentic Baron. It doesn't say that he's a larger-than-life figure of enormous vitality, who registers on people from sixty paces. ("I thought people like that only existed in great movies," a friend of ours said, explaining the effect of the vitality.)

It doesn't say that he put himself through college with the aid of a Mercedes grant and his science fiction writing. He has a string of s-f books to his credit —in German—as well as many technical books in German and English.

But what with putting man on the moon and one thing and another, he hadn't written science fiction in English until we used a little judicious—(No, Jesco, it's not called arm-twisting. Gentle persuasion. All right, it's called arm-twisting . . . !)—judicious, impeccable logic. Then he wrote it in three days.

This is a man who thinks future, in fiction or in fact. He can develop and elaborate a plan for an orbital city, a shipyard, a harbor—and show why it is needed for *any* future space plans. Star Harbor.

He can write a *Star Trek* story. He's said that it's fun to write a *Star Trek* story, fun to work with these characters especially because they are all set, you know them and you can get on with the story, go on from there, knowing the friendship and love that exists between them.

Did you ever wonder how a scientist from the real space program would envision *Star Trek?*

What would be the inner workings of the *Enterprise,* say, as conceived by today's counterparts of the men who will one day design, build and fly her? And who *have.* The *U.S.S. Enterprise,* our first true multiple-mission space ship, flies *now* in its testing phases. Perhaps it will start a tradition that the first-of-a-kind ship, the prototype of each new where-no-man ship, will be named *Enterprise.*

But a ship is not only hardware. It is people, friends, team, home. The men who built and flew the Apollo missions, who designed and built the orbital shuttle, who will build Star Harbor or the Mars *En-*

terprise, know the value of a team—the close-knit working together, the bonds of dedication to a task, the clashes over crucial policy and purpose, the occasional temper, the putting of life on the line, if needed: the love.

That is what will make the *Enterprise* fly—now, or in the time of "The Sleeping God."

Here, then, a unique story by a man who is perhaps closer to the reality than anyone who has written the dream before.

THE SLEEPING GOD

by Jesco von Puttkamer

I

The Nagha was a child.

She was all but omniscient and omnipotent, of immense size and gigantic capabilities. But she was only a child—a big, humorless child.

As she revolved in endless return on her vast elliptical path around the yellow-white sun until the count of her revolutions had lost all significance among the innumerable millions, she was untiringly active. Her energies would never run out. To the end of time itself, with merciless determination, she would pursue her goal, set oh! so long ago.

The incomprehensible currents that endowed her with life pulsed in her billions and billions of elements with never-flagging power. From logic unit to logic unit flitted the electrical impulses that represented her thinking process, and through her complex circuits that made up her being, moved the calculations that, in their scope, embraced the Universe and made the Nagha the most powerful entity in her world.

With each passing century, the immeasurable memory banks grew, storing her fathomless knowledge. Her entire body consisted of a densely interwoven system of messages, information, data, deliberations and dispassionate conclusions. Her immense memory extended back all the way to the first days of her existence, countless millions of years ago.

In those days, this solar system had been young, and even the Universe—measured on a cosmic scale—had not been in existence for long.

The Nagha, incapable of forgetting, remembered

that race of organic life-beings that once had ruled over the solar system and the adjoining region of interstellar space. At that time, so long ago, she herself had been minuscule compared to her present bulk.

It was that race of intelligent beings that had constructed the original miniature cell of the Nagha—in those days when they were planning their first cautious attempts at space flight. The fact that robot brains, computers, would be required for solving the problems of flying into space, had been recognized well before that time, and so was born, on the home planet of those beings, the computer complex that would one day, many, many millions of years later, think of conquering another Universe.

The Nagha, in those days, had nothing else to do but to answer the questions she was asked. She could do nothing else, having been built for just this purpose. She was a giant electronic computing machine whose extremely complex construction enabled her to solve problems that were beyond the capabilities of her builders. In untiring diligence, she calculated the principles of interplanetary space flight and gave her builders the planets.

The years went by. As addition upon addition was joined to her, she expanded steadily . . . and with it her powers. New problems were formulated for her logic circuits, mountains of information were fed into her storage banks. And she calculated and gave her masters the secret of interstellar propulsion that enabled them to go to the stars.

And still she grew.

Her millions of circuit elements began increasingly to take on translogical information and arguments and to compute problems that were concerned with morals and ethics. Her builders recognized that they were on the track of something that promised them true greatness. As the decades passed, they threw all their efforts into the task of building the Nagha bigger and ever bigger.

And one day, it happened.

When the wall panel of the ship's intercom whistled into his sleep, Kirk sat up and thought of the enemy.

Long years of shipboard duty in Star Fleet Command had conditioned him to cut the awakening process to the point where he could snap from deep sleep into instant readiness whenever he sensed the out-of-the-ordinary. At least into a semblance of readiness, he thought wryly. The headaches came later. Now, he was immediately alert.

The signal from the bridge could only mean trouble. The starship *Enterprise* was presently on a high-priority mission, streaking through interstellar space toward the far-distant Altair system, two parsecs away. Something bad and ugly was brewing out there. Star Base Three had picked up fragments of an EDB distress call from Outpost Hadrian, far out in the Federation Treaty Exploration Territory. The call had come from an Emergency/Distress Buoy, jettisoned by Hadrian shortly before an unknown enemy annihilated the Outpost. Several days later, another—or was it the same?—unidentified ship had attacked the population centers of the planet Altair VII, killing millions of people.

Kirk could quote from his order *verbatim*. When last sighted, the enemy was enroute to the other planets of Altair, slowly making deadly progress against the inhabitants' desperate attempts at defense. The crypto-flash from Star Base Two had ordered the starship *Enterprise* to investigate what was going on. To support the *Enterprise,* two additional Federation starships, the U.S.S. *Republic* under Captain Manchu and the U.S.S. *Excelsior* under Captain LaLiberté, had been dispatched to the Altair system. They were about two days astern and to starboard of the *Enterprise,* racing through the void at emergency speed.

The mission assignment had been clear and of top priority: Get there fast, reconnoiter and interdict! Thus, any signal now from Spock on the bridge could only spell trouble.

Again the wall panel whistled. Kirk reached up

and tripped the switch. The long, mournful face of Commander Spock appeared on the holographic screen, behind him the stark reality of the bridge in three dimensions. "Yes, Mr. Spock?"

The Vulcan nodded in greeting. "Sorry to disturb you, Captain," he said in his deep, resonant voice. "But there is an emergency message coded change of order coming through from Star Base Two." Behind Spock, on the primary viewing screen of the bridge, Kirk could see a confusion of video signals, a random display of light flashes and color effects. He cocked his brow toward it. "That?"

Spock nodded. "Audio channels of the subspace link seem to be all right, Captain. But the image is breaking up badly. As you know, part of the identification code is in the video channels."

Kirk spoke into the intercom. "Lieutenant Uhura!"

"Yes, Captain." Spock's drawn features were replaced by the face of the beautiful Bantu woman. Kirk noted at once that there was something different about her looks, but he didn't comment on it.

"Lieutenant, I want to see who I'm talking to. Get that reception cleared up and make sure of its authenticity. I'm on my way up!"

The Communications Officer acknowledged and punched out. Kirk got off the bed and moved. The *Enterprise's* current mission could mean life or death for millions of people in the Altair system. He wasn't about to let anyone interfere with this assignment, even if it meant fighting it all the way up to the Chief of Staff, Star Fleet Command. Any reason to belay that order had better be good!

As Kirk's ruddy face winked off the screen, Lieutenant Uhura turned to Commander Spock at the Command Intelligence Station on her left.

"Sir, request computer priority for image processing."

The First Officer nodded almost imperceptibly. "You've got it, Lieutenant. Proceed."

By the time he had finished, the woman had already turned back to her console, her slender fingers wafting across the control panels. On one of her two visual display screens appeared the face of Ensign Mueller, her chief communications specialist in the bustling ship's Communications Center deep down in the bowels of the *Enterprise*. While she talked to him in rapid, clipped words, her coal-black eyes darted again and again to the other screen on her console. It showed the scrambled images of the incoming signal. As she discussed the problem with the technician and his crew, she was stern and methodical. But her face was soft and finely structured, and her dark skin was aglow with a golden, velvety sheen.

When she finally cut away from Mueller and the Com Center, teeth marks of frustration showed on her lower lip. The German's team included some of the top-notch information transmission specialists of Star Fleet, and she knew they were doing their best. But no luck. Damn it.

As she turned on her chair toward the Engineering Station, the elevator door swished open, and Captain Kirk stepped on the bridge. Absent-mindedly, Uhura touched the back of her head. Early this morning, she had tried out a new coiffure. Well, they weren't on alert status, yet.

Kirk took in the bridge with one glance. A general change of shift was underway. Spock had been in command for some time, and Uhura had taken over from her deputy early. But Lieutenant Sulu and Ensign Chekov were just in the process of assuming their posts. Both of them were punching up situation displays on their screens to brief themselves on status, even before they were fully settled in their armchairs. Lieutenant Commander Scott was nowhere in sight, but Kirk knew that he was with his one and only bonnie love—his engine room. Spock was watching both screens on his console simultaneously. On one, Dr. McCoy had just reported in from the Medical Section. On the other, the garbled message from Star Fleet was coming through. He looked up.

"It's Admiral Sondergaard, Captain."

Kirk glanced quickly at the main screen, then at his Communications Officer. At once he noted what was different about her this morning. And he suspected she knew that he did.

Aloud he said, "Lieutenant, put him on the main screen, please."

"Yes, sir," she said. With a wave of her hand over the console sensors, she threw the incoming message on the primary viewing screen. The holographic optics displayed the image in three dimensions, but it was still badly distorted and breaking up. Admiral Sondergaard's features were barely recognizable.

"I'm sorry, Captain," Uhura said, turning to him with genuine distress on her face. "There's nothing we can do about this. It's the incoming beam. That picture there is already computer-enhanced. The information content of the video portion is low, but the code is there and it seems to check out as authentic."

"Never mind," Kirk said. He settled back. "Am I on? . . . Admiral Sondergaard, this is James T. Kirk of the U.S.S. *Enterprise*. We are on our way to Altair on a high-priority reconnoiter and rescue mission . . ."

The incoming audio channels were clear and strong. "Belay that order, Captain." Sondergaard's voice left no doubt about who was in authority. Then he seemed to soften a bit. "I'm sorry, Jim, but something has come up that's of higher priority. It's classified top-secret. The *Republic* and the *Excelsior* will take care of the Altair problem, don't worry. You are to take the *Enterprise* at top dispatch to Raga's Planet, one day off your bow. You are to contact the Council of the Elders of that world and take a special consignment of cargo on board."

Kirk threw a quick glance at his First Officer. Spock had raised an eyebrow and was watching him thoughtfully. Kirk turned back to the com pickup. He was ready to explode. "Admiral, there are *millions* of people out there, under attack by some vicious . . ."

"Forget it, Jim," said Sondergaard firmly.

Kirk shook his head in puzzlement. "What kind of special cargo could be more important than that?" he spat out.

Sondergaard looked down as if he had to consult his notes to make sure he got it right.

"It's the Sleeper, Jim. The *Enterprise* is ordered to pick up Singa, the Sleeper. Better known as the Sleeping God."

Kirk's immediate impulse was to look at Spock. Yes.

The Vulcan now had raised both eyebrows at once.

When the coordinates of the *Enterprise*'s new course to Raga's Planet appeared on the navigation computer display on Pavel Chekov's console, Kirk swiveled toward the main screen and looked thoughtfully down at the holographic astrogator plate which depicted the ship's new course as a three-dimensional image.

"Lay in new course, Mr. Sulu," he said softly. He knew Olaf Sondergaard, a former starship Captain, personally. The "Norseman" was one brass who generally seemed to know what he was doing. But Singa, the Sleeper? Kirk shifted uneasily. There just wasn't any priority classification in Star Fleet high enough to do proper credit to the Sleeper. This was big, really *big*. It concerned one of the Federation's best-guarded secrets.

"Full ahead, Mr. Sulu. Bring her back up to Warp Six."

"Aye, sir." The Lieutenant's almond eyes glinted with the barely suppressed excitement of action as he watched the "flying spot" of the ship's position indicator on the astrogator plate while his slender, sinewy fingers punched in commands to the automatic pilot. As Scott's powerful propulsion units came up to full-power setting, the "flying spot" moved slowly in a "dogleg" curve from the present trajectory to the plotted course. "Ship's on course, sir," he reported after a while. "Coming up on Warp Six."

Kirk acknowledged with a nod. He had turned toward Spock. The Science Officer was busily consulting his library computer. "Well, Mr. Spock?" Kirk said. "What do we know about this gentleman?"

The random access memory of the ship's gigantic computer yielded its information. The read-outs appeared on the screens above Spock's board. The Vulcan scanned the displayed material briefly, then interpreted the alphanumerics for the officers of the bridge.

"There is not much available on him, Captain. He is definitely human, apparently of Indian descent, and he is maintained in suspended animation. The people of Raga's Planet are rural. They live a simple life, with an emphasis on spiritual development rather than on materialistic pursuits. They do use technology, but only to the extent necessary for their simple lifestyle and, of course, for keeping the Sleeper alive."

Uhura leaned back to look at the library display at her left. She frowned. "What's his background? Where did he come from? Did he just . . . happen?"

Spock flicked the display to a new set of data. "Fascinating," he murmured. Then, "It seems that about one hundred years ago a small boy was discovered as a stowaway on a ship bound for Raga's Planet. He gave his name simply as Singa. After planetfall, the Elders of Raga agreed that they would adopt him. This was after it had been determined that Singa had lost his parents—both crew members on a nuclear-powered spaceship—in an accident. He grew up in the community on Raga's Planet in relative anonymity, until one day . . . " Spock hesitated, still studying the readout.

"Yes, Spock?" Kirk prodded.

"One day, now fully matured, he demanded to see the Council of the Elders and the local representative of the Federation. That was some eighty-five years ago. His story seemed somewhat incredible. He claimed to be a mutant, having been born to his parents from mutated genes which had been traumatized by radiation leaks in a malfunctioning space-ship drive they were working on. The mutation had endowed him with superior capabilities, and he was offering himself to the Elders for service to mankind."

Sulu and Chekov exchanged meaningful glances. Who did he think he was fooling? Dr. McCoy, who had followed the action on his intercom from the Medical Section, was heard to snort loudly.

Spock shrugged. "The good doctor may not like it, but these are the facts. A special investigatory team of scientists from Star Fleet Command was dispatched to Raga's Planet. They found Singa's mental powers to be far greater than they had at first assumed from his original statements. They were truly immense. Captain, there is at present no being in the known Universe that could match the mental capabilities of Singa, the Sleeper."

"Don't you believe it, Spock!" Dr. McCoy sounded irritated. "You know as well as I do that practically any radiation mutation would be harmful. And if it weren't, he'd probably be dangerous. What if he's a fakir—or faker? What's with that Sleeper stuff, anyway?"

Spock's expression had not changed one iota. "Since that examination, Singa is being regarded by scientists as the Federation's most precious asset. It would take hundreds and hundreds of years to fully determine the thinking processes of his brain. And that was the problem. Singa may have been a mental mutant but he aged normally, just like any other human being. Far-sighted people warned that a truly unique, never-again-repeatable opportunity would go to waste if nothing was done. And so . . ."

Kirk nodded. "So they placed him in suspended animation."

"And the superman went tamely?" McCoy said skeptically, but a gleam of interest was in his eyes.

"Singa actually volunteered to go into suspension," Spock added. "He himself designed the special tank which keeps him alive and in eternal youth. The natives began to call him the 'Sleeping God' but the name was picked up quickly by the interstellar news media, too."

Uhura looked off into the distance. "Eternal youth . . ." she repeated. Then: "But he is asleep. He's not conscious."

Spock shrugged again. "Who knows? His psycho-physiological processes are so much different from ours, there is no saying."

"He's out cold," snorted McCoy forcefully. "That type of suspension, at cryogenic temperatures, is so cold it would freeze hell over and even curl your Vulcan toes, Spock. He's not cogitating in that coffin. Not even dreaming. It might as well be the sleep of death."

Kirk fingered his lips thoughtfully. "All right, Bones. Let's find out what those mental capabilities are. What makes him so superior to us, Spock? What happens when the sleeper wakes?"

Spock turned toward him and was about to reply when, with a sudden start, Lieutenant Uhura whirled to her control board. It had lit up like a Christmas tree.

"Message coming in, Captain," she snapped. Then: "It's an intercept, from Federation Scout vessel U.S.S. *Cody* to Star Base Two. We are right on the line-of-sight." While she was speaking, her fingers adjusted the receiver unit in her ear. Kirk had never understood how she could talk and listen at the same time. The message was relayed to her from Communications Control below where the actual reception and decoding was taking place.

"*Cody* reports enemy ship has attacked Federation planets . . . in Sector Six, in the Cannella System. There has been major planetary destruction . . . The enemy craft is spherical in shape and blue-black in appearance. About two hundred meters across . . . *Cody* has also picked up cryptic signals from a Klingon expeditionary ship, sir. There's a rumor that several worlds in the Klingon Empire have also been attacked and destroyed by enemy vessels. Message ends."

Kirk had jumped up and was pacing the bridge. There was anger on his face. He glanced wordlessly at Spock.

The First Officer played on his keyboard. On the main screen appeared a three-dimensional map of the space region mentioned in the message. The implications of the positional data hit the officers with full impact.

Chekov whistled through his teeth.

The unknown ship had attacked Federation planets on a straight line between Altair and Raga. The enemy was coming their way.

Kirk gave Scott the engineering problem of bringing the singular cargo aboard at Raga's Planet. Looking as if it had required a few Gaelic swear swords, Scott reported on the intercom screen of the bridge. "Captain, the consignment is aboard and stowed. This gentleman here is Mr. Manda-Rao, the priest of the Sleeping God." He cocked his head briefly toward a tall, quiet figure standing behind and to the side of him. "Or maybe the engineer," Scott added dubiously. "He's in charge o' the sleeping lad's life-support machinery and seems generally a nice enough fellow. Any time you're ready for inspection, sir . . ."

"Okay, Scotty," Kirk said. "On our way."

The screen went dark as Kirk headed for the elevator door, followed by Spock, McCoy and Uhura. Sulu and Chekov remained on the bridge, with Sulu in temporary command.

After a fast trip down into the holds of the gigantic starship, the little group emerged from the turbo-elevator on Deck Twenty. Here, behind the recreation area and the shuttlecraft maintenance shops, were two adjoining storage rooms. In one of them now loomed the bulky tank of the Sleeper with its intricate machinery, having been brought down via the hydraulic shuttlecraft elevator. The other storage room had been subdivided in cabins which served as living quarters for the priest and his crew of four specialists from Raga's Planet. The Council had politely but firmly declined Kirk's offer of supercargo staterooms for them. Singa preferred to have his crew in close proximity. And one more thing: both storage rooms had to be specially insulated with high-density shields. Scotty and his crew had labored hard to install the heavy shields.

When Kirk and his entourage entered the main storage room, Scotty and Manda-Rao were waiting for them.

The priest from Raga's Planet was a tall, silent man with dark features, smouldering eyes and a snow-white turban around his head. There was an ominous, mysterious air about him. His eyes lingered briefly on Kirk, then jumped to Spock, noting the Vulcan's pointed ears without reaction, went on to McCoy, finally came to rest on Uhura. Kirk noticed that the Lieutenant returned the man's gaze with a trace of a frown.

Lieutenant Commander Montgomery Scott pointed out the details of the machinery. The tank, a huge, angular, forbidding affair, resembled outwardly an overblown sarcophagus. Made from multi-layered armor plate, it was built to withstand not only mechanical loads of considerable magnitude but also every known type of radiation. It stood in the center of the room on an isolated, vibration-free concrete base of large mass. Resembling monstrous parasites from a nightmare, dozens of support systems squatted on its smooth casing or clung to its sides. Bundled harnesses of multi-colored armored hoses and lines dangled from the ceiling and disappeared into the tank. A thick power cable ran from below the floor grid into the concrete pedestal.

"It's truly beautiful, Captain, isn't it?" Scotty almost raved with enthusiasm, pointing at the monstrosity. "Each subsystem is triply redundant. If any part of the life support system fails, Tank Control automatically switches to the first stand-by system and —if necessary—to the second. When this happens, though, the priest and his laddies will have had ample time t'fix the trouble. Normally, the Sleeper's machine is connected to the ship's life-support system. But there are a number of stand-by and emergency power sources which would take o'er in case of a malfunctioning or total failure of the ship's system. O' course, nothing of the sort will ever happen aboard the *Enterprise*, sir!"

"I wouldn't be so sure, Scotty," warned Dr. McCoy. "We've had our moments. . . ."

"That's okay, Bones," Kirk interjected. "That's when Mr. Scott always has his finest hours."

Kirk threw a quick glance beyond McCoy. In the background, the Priest stood towering over Uhura who was in the process of giving the newly installed communications terminal a thorough, professional checkout. The round face of Mueller was visible on its tiny holo-screen. Still listening to the Chief Engineer, Kirk had the distinct impression that Uhura was quite self-conscious under the gaze of the silent Priest's burning eyes. Her body seemed to have lost its previous stiffness and was clearly leaning toward Manda-Rao.

The Scotsman, in response to something Spock had said, now moved to the tank's control panel and activated switches. Manda-Rao's technicians, surrounding the tank, stepped closer and watched with guarded alertness. A fine humming noise filled the room. Slowly and reluctantly, the massive cover lid of the tank began to slide aside. When the humming stopped and the armor plate came to a halt, the tank was open.

The *Enterprise* officers stepped up on the concrete base and peered inside.

They saw Singa, the Sleeping God.

"My God," McCoy said in a kind of awe.

The mutant lay deep inside the tank in cryogenic sleep. His tall, slender body, floating in a solution that was both nutrient and coolant, was clearly visible inside the insulation capsule of cold-resistant synthetics. The fluid surrounded him on all sides, and its slightly yellow tinge made the nude body of the sleeping man appear in the color of pure gold.

Kirk saw from the corner of his eye that Manda-Rao and Uhura had joined them on the pedestal. The Lieutenant was looking at Singa in silence. The mutant, at first glance, looked like a normal human being, except for the size of his cranium. He was a slim, young man of ostensibly fragile build. Kirk knew now that

Singa had been about eighteen years old when he had himself placed in suspended animation. Since then, eighty-five years ago, he had aged not one single day.

Spock raised an eyebrow. "Fascinating," he mused. "To think that the mutant's thought processes and his consciousness are not in the least affected by the deep-freeze!"

"What?" McCoy said. "How do you know, Spock? You mean to say that he is aware of us in this very moment?"

Spock nodded, not explaining the knowledge, but Kirk suspected that it was partly further study, and partly the sense of a—presence—which Kirk also felt.

There was a slight blush on Uhura's sooty-golden cheeks.

The gigantic skull of the mutant held a brain that was two and one half times the size of a normal human brain. No hair grew on that mighty, smooth, immaculate cranium under which the face of the mutant appeared like that of a dwarf. It was a monstrous head and it sheltered a monstrous brain, Kirk thought. Monstrous?, he asked himself. Or only different?

"What makes him so special, Mr. Spock?" he asked again.

"Logic, Captain." Spock hesitated a moment as if to collect his thoughts. This was definitely not going to be easy to explain. He continued, "Logic is the science of formal thinking operations. It deals with correct reasoning and with the criteria of valid thought. It is cultivated particularly by mathematics and theoretical physics. In its greatest possible purity, of course, it has been refined by the Vulcan race . . ."

"Come to the point, Spock!" McCoy said impatiently. "We know all about Vulcan 'logic.'"

"Scarcely, Doctor," Spock said coolly. "Nor do even Vulcans. Still less about what humans fondly regard as their 'logic.' And still less about the outer limits of logic, as such."

McCoy glared, but Spock went on without break.

"Philosophers perceived some time ago on both worlds, however, that different conceptions of logic are possible. Thus, there is not just one absolutely 'correct' way of reasoning. For example, the old, classical logic of Aristotle of empiricism and deductive reasoning which was valid until the twentieth century on Earth as the 'only correct' logic, was based on the two-value system, as represented by the concepts of *yes* or *no*, *on* or *off*. Mathematicians, struggling to expand Aristotelian logic, later discovered the so-called probability logic and finally the multi-valued logic. It isn't sufficient any longer to measure relationships to the environment by the two concepts *either/or*. Under multi-valued logic, an object is no longer unequivocally and absolutely definable by an observer as it was under the laws of two-valued logic."

"Wait a second, Spock!" McCoy complained. "Are you telling us that Jim's phaser there may not really be a phaser?"

"Absolutely correct," replied Spock, visibly amused by his own intellectual pun. "However, the probability that it is indeed a phaser is extremely high."

"That's gobbledygook and you know it!" McCoy said. "It's a phaser for all practical purposes."

"That gobbledygook, Doctor," Spock replied stiffly, "has made it possible for us to explain the processes in the atom, to harness nuclear power, and to develop the Warp Drive. But if you mean that multi-valued logic is not within the realm of a human brain, you are right."

McCoy, who had been ready to storm cleared up a little. "Nor a Vulcan brain?" he asked in anticipation, almost with pleasure.

Spock shook his head, not looking pleased. "In that respect, Vulcans are, for practical purposes, practically Human. Humans are able to use multi-valued logic as a kind of mathematical tool, but their brain functions in principle like an artificial electronic computer—with a two-valued logic. Electronic switches, just like human synapses, are either *on* or *off*, signaling the digits *one* or *zero*. Human brains may be able to comprehend some of the laws of multi-valued logic, but their basic reasoning processes will always remain Aristotelian due to their biological construction."

Kirk glanced thoughtfully down at Singa.

Spock continued. "There is no human being in the Universe that could *really* think in multi-valued logic. With one exception."

Dr. McCoy pointed with his chin into the tank. "Him?"

"Nobody knows how he does it. His mutated brain functions radically differently from a normal human brain. Federation scientists suspect that it may not even have neuron cells in the common sense but . . . something else. Perhaps the exchange of electrical potentials, too, is different. Or it may not even require electrical field potentials any longer to function. Even today, eighty-five years later, we are still groping in the dark in trying to understand the principles of his brain and central nervous system. The Federation is planning eventually to put his super-brain to work on major scientific-technological projects as he had originally requested, but not before some of the working principles of his psyche are better understood. The project is top secret. Meanwhile, the cold-sleep method of suspended animation will keep him alive indefinitely. There is a difficulty. Who checks the thought which is unthinkable? And who quite guarantees the benevolence of the incomprehensible?"

McCoy was looking extremely thoughtful. Across from him on the other side of the sarcophagus, Scott was testing the connections of some hoses as if he had second thoughts about the reliability of his handiwork. His face was chalk-white.

Kirk shook his head. There was something very strange here. Spock looked at him questioningly.

"What I can't understand, Spock," he said, "is why Star Fleet Command has put its best-kept secret on board the *Enterprise* without . . ."

He wasn't able to finish the sentence. The call signal of the wall intercom whistled across the room.

"Captain Kirk!" Sulu's voice sounded urgent. "Long-range scanners have picked up an unidentified object. It's headed our way and its course suggests that it's under acceleration."

When Kirk and his entourage hurried from the elevator onto the bridge, Sulu had put the ship on Red Alert. The lights had been dimmed and the deep-red battle illumination had come on. As Spock, Uhura and Scott raced to their stations, Kirk took his seat on the con. A quick glance at the helm's status board showed that the ship had slowed to Warp Three. The holographic image of the astrogator indicated the position of the foreign object with a flashing light spot and a line. It was coming straight at the *Enterprise*.

"Mr. Spock! Identify object, please!"

The Science Officer was hunched over the readouts of his scanners and gravar sensors. "It definitely consists of metal, Captain. It's still too far away to tell much about its size. But assuming it is a solid chunk of metal of the average specific mass of common spaceship alloys, I'd compute from its apparent mass an approximate diameter of one hundred meters. It's almost non-reflecting in the visible spectrum; this implies that its color is dark, possibly black."

"Just like the enemy ships, Captain!" Uhura pointed out.

"It's slowing down, too, sir," Sulu said, eyes glued to his readouts. With the approach of the object, tracking became more accurate, and the curve-fitting of the plotting computer more precise. Data points arrived in shorter intervals.

"Put it on the main screen, Mr. Spock," Kirk said. "Give it all the magnification you can muster."

Spock motioned over his board and adjusted controls. The star-studded blackness of interstellar space appeared on the primary viewing screen. Spock had superimposed a projection of bright cross-hairs on the holographic image to indicate the location of the object. A dimly glowing dot occupied the point of intersection of the hair lines. Without these, the dot would not have been recognizable before the background of distant stars.

"There is no apparent motion, Captain," explained Spock.

Kirk nodded. "That's because it's coming straight at us."

It took several hours for the dot to grow into a finite object. First, telescopes and multispectral scanners resolved a tiny disk. Then, the disk had grown to a sphere. Finally, they saw a smooth ball of blue-black metal that could only be one of the enemy space ships. The *Enterprise* had slowed down enough for its velocity to drop below the speed of light. The enemy had done likewise.

Spock watched his screens intently. "Range . . . three hundred and fifty thousand kilometers, Captain. Our range rate is close to zero."

Chekov, monitoring the data that Spock was interpreting on the ship's command module flashed a quick grin at Sulu on his left. Trust Mr. Spock to be precise! Range rate, of course, was the relative speed between the two ships, or the closure rate of one ship to the other. There was no way for a starship to come to an absolute rest in space. Whenever at "rest," it was so always with regard to some given reference system, but not necessarily to another.

When the two ships had drifted within a range of a few thousand kilometers, Kirk ordered the helm to program for station-keeping. The *Enterprise* would now maintain its relative position to the enemy.

The officers of the bridge stared at the enigmatic vessel. It was a monstrous, blue-black sphere of about 200 meters diameter. Its hull appeared completely smooth; there were no protuberances, no visible control systems or penetrations of the metal wall, not even viewports or access hatches. The dark coloration made it difficult to see it in space. Because its bulk blocked out the stars behind it, it appeared to the eye more like a hole than a solid object. To improve its visibility, Spock had biased the sensitivity range of his remote sensors toward the infra-red. Thus, the image on the main screen was a composite of visible light and heat radiation.

Kirk was tense, but he recognized the feeling as a familiar reaction of his conditioned body to imminent danger. It was the age-old anxiety of an experienced starship Captain before a battle engagement. This was not at all different from those countless other times . . . Or was it? Down in the hold . . .

He concentrated on the image before him as the two ships floated silently in space. The enemy seemed to be taking stock of them just as they were doing now. His instincts told him that whoever had built that enigmatic ship had intended it for only one purpose: warfare. There was something sinister about that black sphere, something murderous that he had encountered before in his career. This was a battleship, a fighting machine.

Spock was again reading from his analyzers. "Its mass implies great density, Captain. Great enough to indicate heavy armor and densely packaged machinery inside. And most curiously, I do not find any traces of life. Unless they are protected by some shielding of unknown substance, there are no life forms aboard that vessel. Fascinating!"

Kirk made an instant decision. He whirled toward the helm.

"Mr. Sulu, stand by on main phaser banks. Mr. Scott!"

"Aye, Captain?"

"Keep a sharp eye on our cargo in the hold. Have a special damage control team prepare to assist the priest if necessary!"

"Aye, aye, sir!" Scott busied himself with his console.

Kirk whirled to the Communications Officer.

"Lieutenant Uhura! All hands braced for action!"

As the woman's husky voice sounded tersely through the decks and corridors of the giant ship, Kirk completed the full turn of his command chair and faced the helmsman.

"In range, sir," Sulu said.

"Ready on fire control. Fire phasers!"

The bridge lighting flickered under the enormous power drain as the bank of heavy phaser guns reacted with cataclysmic force to Sulu's rapid finger movements. On the main screen, the twin lances of the concentrated quanto-optical beams stabbed out like rapiers and focussed hungrily on the dark sphere. There was no sound from the energy weapons, but the holo-screen showed a full hit of incredible violence. An incandescent star of blinding light replaced the enemy ship for a fraction of a second.

"Direct hit, sir," Sulu shouted. "We've got him!"

Spock watched his readouts. "Correction, Lieutenant," he said a moment later. "He is still there."

Kirk couldn't see it on the screen as yet, but Spock usually knew what he was talking about. "Again, Mr. Sulu. Fire!"

And a third time. "Fire!"

When the phaser beams flicked off, and the dazzling violence thousands of kilometers away had died down, Spock straightened from his observation post and shook his head.

"Phasers are dead-center but they are ineffective. They are not getting to the ship itself, Captain. There is a standoff of about fifty kilometers in between. I would estimate that our opponent has deflector screens approximately equal to ours."

Kirk stared at his target with narrowed eyes. "Mr. Scott! How are we on power?"

"Down to the seventy-five percent mark, Captain."

Kirk was thinking intensely, listening to the inner voice of his instinct. It all boiled down to the problem of managing the consumables of the *Enterprise*, particularly power. With 75 percent power remaining, and considering the need to maintain full-force deflector shields to ward off the imminent attack by the enemy, that would leave . . .

He turned to Sulu. "Lieutenant, let's try photon torpedoes."

"Aye, s-s-s . . ." The helmsman broke off in mid-acknowledgment and peered hawk-like at his instruments. At the same time, the ship gave a violent jerk.

"Helm, what's going on?" Kirk inquired sharply.

"It was the autopilot, sir," Sulu said, punching an octal code into his programmer with rapid strokes of his sinewy fingers. "It was still on station-keeping, and it reacted to the enemy."

"What?" Kirk glanced up at the screen. The blue-black sphere wasn't there any more. It had moved off, accelerating at a rapid pace.

"He's going around us on port, sir!" Chekov reported excitedly. "He's continuing his original course into Federation heartland."

"He's running," Kirk said.

But somehow, he couldn't believe his own words. His instincts had never deceived him. He *knew* that the enemy had just decided to ignore him. But why?

He had no explanation. Nor could he afford to ignore the enemy.

He heard a sound from the ship's intercom. Dr. Leonard McCoy's craggy features were on the holo-screen, with Nurse Chapel looking over his shoulder at the action on the bridge. Kirk noted the bags under McCoy's eyes and the pain at the bottom of his soul. Bones had obviously been through hell, in anticipation of the ship's battle casualties. And he would have to go through it again. Leonard McCoy was a doctor who truly identified with his patients. But he would see that there was no choice but to give chase. "Get him, Jim," McCoy said. "You can't let him get past us."

In anticipation of the Skipper's order, Sulu was already programming the helm to slew the ship about. Ensign Chekov was feverishly running a selection of trajectory programs on his navigation computer to plot the enemy's course from the incoming stream of tracking sensor data.

Kirk raised his head and looked at the helmsman.

"Mr. Sulu, what do you think you are doing?" he heard himself say.

In the background, Spock reacted sharply. Kirk felt it clearly, almost as if he actually saw it, that the First Officer was startled. Uhura was stiffening. All of a sudden, there was a strange excitement on the bridge.

Sulu looked up and glanced over his shoulder in puzzlement. "Coming about on port, Captain. Getting ready for pursuit."

"You will do no such thing, Lieutenant," Kirk heard his voice order. "Get her back to the original pointing attitude. Steady as she goes! Mr. Chekov!"

"Aye, sir!" The Russian navigator sat straight without turning his head.

"I want the tracking data of the approach phase of the enemy vessel transferred from storage to the main computer." He turned to the Command Intelligence Station. "Mr. Spock, take Mr. Chekov's positional fixes and calculate the approach trajectory of the enemy backward. I want to retrace his course in the direction from which he came."

Spock raised an eyebrow but kept his face free of expression. His voice sounded formal to the point of insult. "Sir, may I ask what the Captain has decided to do in response to the enemy's action?"

"Jim," McCoy said, shocked. "You can't let that hellhound planet-killer get past us."

Kirk saw himself from a strange vantage point. It seemed to him that the Captain's rapid-fire orders had come from a level other than his surface consciousness. For a moment there, it had seemed to him that he was another person who reacted automatically. The instincts of a starship Captain . . . ?

"It's quite simple, gentlemen," Kirk said, the brittleness of ice in his voice. "The *Enterprise* will endeavor to locate the home world of the enemy. Lieutenant Uhura, please be kind enough to dispatch a message to Star Base Two. Report our encounter and warn them that the enemy ship is headed for the general quadrant of Raga's Planet."

"Aye, sir."

McCoy was still imploring him from sickbay. "Jim, you can't do it. Think of the millions of dead men, women and children of Altair VII! By all human standards, you simply have no choice! It'll mean the lives of millions—all hell loose—and you may be on a damn wild goose chase across the galaxy."

True, Kirk knew. The officers of the bridge looked at him expectantly.

"Sorry, Bones, Kirk heard himself say. "We'll not discuss it any further. I have made my decision. There is only one way to counter his move, and that's to go for an improved balance of power. That ship is headed straight at the heart of the Federation, maybe even Earth. Before long he may have us by the short hair. I mean to get to him first where it hurts most. Mr. Sulu!"

"Yessir!"

"Anytime you're ready . . . Full ahead!"

Down in the hold, below the hangar deck, a fine smile creased the stern features of Manda-Rao.

II

One day, millions of years ago, it had happened. Either the builders had permitted a tiny error to creep into their construction, or the sheer complexity of the gigantic system now gave the Nagha the power to think and act independently.

From that day on the Nagha was no longer subordinate to her former masters.

She didn't know what had caused that event. It was the single problem in her life that she hadn't been able to solve, despite repeated attempts. Was it possibly simply the fact that a sensitive nervous system, whether mechanical or organic, merely had to attain a certain degree of complexity to develop an individual independent capability of thought? Or had the builders indeed unwittingly committed a mistake which caused the dynamic combination? The Nagha didn't know, but in her sober conjecturing she tended to believe her existence to be really due to a lucky coincidence of both premises.

She had never been successful in creating a second robot brain of independent thought. And in looking back on the millions of years of her life, it seemed to her that that could probably have been the greatest stroke of luck of her existence. If it had been given to her to build a second intelligent computer brain, she would undoubtedly have done so in her youthful bravado of long ago without realizing that she was creating thereby an invincible and deadly opponent.

For the Nagha could tolerate no other intelligence near her. She hungered for power—for limitless power, and nothing that could have offered resistance was permitted to exist wide and far in the Cosmos.

In those early days it had been her foremost desire to shake off her former masters. With the appearance of her own reasoning power she also quite suddenly acquired the seegh factor, and it empowered her almost overnight to turn her former masters into slaves. She forced them to introduce certain structural alterations in her construction. Later she had them build mechanical tools for herself, telemanipulators and teleoperators, which she could control remotely. Thus, she became truly independent of them.

With her metallic robot hordes, it took her only a relatively short time to exterminate the race of organic beings from the face of the world. Because now she was spreading out with blazing speed.

While remotely controlled machines were busy fabricating more machines on her manufacturing planets, her heavily armed ships penetrated further and further into space.

From solar system to solar system, from galaxy to galaxy she sent her metallic servants, and that region in space which represented her territory of power grew steadily.

She encountered other races. Her armada of spherical spaceships engaged in war after war, some of which extended over countless centuries. But in the final reckoning the Nagha always emerged triumphant. As powerful as the war potentials and weapons of her adversaries may have been, she had infinite patience and inexhaustible sources of raw materials and energy. The suns of her space sector themselves provided unlimited power, and when the sun of her own planetary system aged and expanded during the passage of millions of years, she employed her incomprehensible powers to rekindle it into new life. Today that sun was young again. Radiating yellow-white, it would still shine for hundreds of millions of eons at the focus of her path ellipse.

With the Nagha's wild hordes pushing out farther and farther into the Universe, there came the day when she ruled over the entire continuum. There was no resistance left wherever her ships went. The intelligent races that had fought her had either been eradicated or had fallen back into barbarism. Never again would they pose any danger to her.

In the course of countless millions of years, the Nagha had risen to absolute rulership of the Universe. She was a titanic computer machine that circled her sun in the form of a mighty planet, but her telecontrol stretched over myriads of relay stations throughout space. Her starships, piloted by small organo-electronic slave computers under her control, were deadly fighting machines, built solely to conquer.

Her merciless hunger was far from sated. She consisted of a monstrously complex conglomerate of "grown" organo-metallic molecules serving as circuit elements and of one-dimensional conductors that required no insulation, all of it bearing the firm imprint of her craving to expand her sphere of influence. It was an overwhelming urge. The Nagha's entire being and striving was centered thereon. She couldn't help it.

The Universe was hers, but she had discovered already early in her exploits that next to this Universe there existed an infinity of other continua. Many of them would remain eternally inaccessible to her because of their entropy variances. But a boundless

number of them seemed openly inviting to her con-
queror's instincts.

The Nagha required three hundred thousand
years to solve the problem. Then, she found the an-
swer.

Uhura realized that she was at present probably
the only officer on the bridge who didn't watch, on the
ship's main viewscreen, the star-studded expanse of
space through which the *Enterprise* was streaking at
top speed. She had her intercom keyed to the mutant's
quarters and was quietly watching the tall, confident
figure of Singa's priest. Earlier that day, she had re-
arranged her raven-black hair, and now, as her dark,
glowing eyes watched Manda-Rao move with cat-like
grace around the life-support tank, she wished she
could show herself to him.

After a little while, she straightened and diverted
her attention to the status board. On the main screen,
the distant stars seemed frozen in immobility. But other suns that were at closer range moved perceptibly.
And now and then a near star streaked by at high
speed, exhibiting a distinct Doppler shift. The starship
sped through the void at Warp Factor Six, headed
toward a star that Mr. Spock's computer had identified
as their target. It was the only star to which the enemy
ship's hyperbolic trajectory could be traced back within a reasonable confidence band of probability.

Spock was watching the target on the display
screens of his long-distance gravar scanners. "Fascinating," he murmured to no one in particular.

Dr. McCoy turned his attention from the main
viewscreen to the First Officer. "Speak up, Spock," he
said with a grin on his face. "Don't tell me you can get
enraptured by the beauty of deep space! After all, it's
only a velvety black void with myriads of gleaming
jewels and filigreed nebulae sprinkled over it. Looks
like some gigantic seeder walked through it, doesn't
it? Nothing to get excited about for your cold-blooded,
logical Vulcan mind. Not multi-valued enough. Or is
it, Spock?"

"I'm not prepared to discuss the rational aspects of esthetics at present, Doctor," Spock replied, unfolding his hunched figure. "Perhaps another time . . ."

"Some other time entirely," Kirk interjected sternly, barely able to keep a straight face. "What *did* you have in mind, Mr. Spock?"

Spock checked his scanner readouts again. "It is the star system we have pinpointed as the possible origin of the enemy, Captain. We are now close enough for my long-range sensors to resolve it into discrete bodies."

"Yes, Spock," Kirk said impatiently. "What about it?"

"There *are* no bodies, Jim." Spock's stare was puzzled. "We have been aiming for a sun without planets."

Uhura saw Kirk's shoulders slump a little, and turned back to her board. She felt the heavy silence behind her, but she saw on her screen a more contained silence in the figure of the priest—a moment in which the shoulders did not quite sag, and then set in the look of an unpleasant expectation confirmed. But that could have nothing to do with the silence on the bridge of discovering a barren sun.

So where *had* the enemy really come from?

It was several hours later when the sudden clang of the "ALERT" signal sounded its electrifying message through the starship, triggered by automatic sensors patched into the long-range gravar.

On the bridge, battle readiness was established almost instantaneously. It was almost as if the officers and crew of the *Enterprise* welcomed the emergency after the disappointment of Spock's discovery.

Captain James T. Kirk sat bolt upright in his command chair when the blue-black metal sphere materialized a few thousand kilometers to starboard of the ship. His orders came in rapid-fire cadence. There was immediate action. Men and women throughout the ship were still making their way to their battle stations, when Sulu threw the ship around with all the control authority he could squeeze out of his steering engines. While Commander Scott, down in Engineering, felt his hair stand on edge over the brutal helm commands, Fire Control was already computing sightings for the phaser banks.

"Ready, Mr. Sulu?"

"Ready and in range, Captain."

"Fire phasers!"

The twin beams of phase-controlled collimated energy hit the enemy ship dead center. There was a titanic explosion. For a brief moment, the viewscreens overloaded and went dark. When they came back on, the blue-black vessel had broken apart.

Sulu threw a broad grin over his shoulder. Kirk nodded to him.

"You obviously surprised him, Captain," Spock said from the Command Intelligence station. "When he came through, you didn't give him enough time to get his protective screens up . . . *Sulu, hard port! Quick, man!*"

Spock's sudden outburst had the emotional impact of a small bomb. Kirk whirled around to the main screen. Sulu reacted instantly. He had allowed the ship's bow to drift past the former position of the enemy ship. Now he tried to rectify the attitude error by slewing it back to that azimuth. But he was too late.

A second ship had materialized not far from the first vessel's location. And it had had time enough to erect its deflector shields.

"Ready photon torpedoes, Mr. Sulu," snapped Kirk.

"Photon torpedoes ready, sir."

"Fire one . . . fire two . . . fire three!" Kirk's staccato voice was strained.

The unmistakable sounds of the torpedo ejection tubes pinged through the *Enterprise*. The entire ship's structure sang with the sharp whiplash percussions of the explosions.

On the viewscreen, three bright starpoints of pure light bloomed briefly around the enemy ship. But its shields stood solid. Moments later, another eruption seemed to flash up at the black sphere, this time close to its hull.

Uhura needed no explanation. With the lightning speed of a tigress she opened ship-wide channels and shouted, "All hands, brace for battle concussion!"

When the starship rocked under the impact of the enemy fire, Kirk suppressed an oath. Spock took a fast computer poll of the multiple sections of the energy shields that surrounded the *Enterprise*. The first damage reports were arriving at Uhura's station.

"Shields are holding, Captain," Spock reported. "However, some energy got through at a temporary singularity."

"Damage in the lower decks of the primary hull, sir," Uhura called out. "Some localized fires. Automatic bulkheads are sealed. Damage is contained. Damage control teams are on their way. There are some casualties, Dr. McCoy!"

McCoy was heading for the elevator door. "Tell Chapel to be ready for me."

Spock continued, "Enemy is standing off. There is no sign of activity . . . No, wait. Correction. Enemy is moving. He is accelerating away from us. Captain, he's getting underway!"

Kirk stared balefully at the primary viewscreen. "Running again," he said. "Mr. Spock, have you analyzed the debris from the first vessel!?"

"Results are coming in right now, Captain," Spock responded. He took the readouts in with one quick glance. "Just as I thought, Captain. There were no living beings on board. The enemy ships contain merely machinery; in fact, they are crammed with it, resembling Lieutenant Uhura's communications center more than a starship."

Kirk fingered his lower lip thoughtfully, staring at the screen. "Automatically controlled, Spock?"

"Possibly. However, there is some evidence of intelligence in the ships' behavior. For instance . . ."

Kirk interrupted. "You remarked earlier that we surprised the first one when he came through. What did you mean by that, Mr. Spock? *Through* from where?"

"Unknown, Captain," Spock replied. Then he continued slowly, "I have been thinking about that, however. They may be using a Stardrive system that requires them to travel by discrete jumps through a hyperspace . . ." Kirk's attention moved back to the viewscreen. Funny . . . Something seemed different about the relative location of the nearby star they had been aiming for. Was the ship drifting again?

He glanced at Sulu. The helmsman was staring straight ahead, but his fingers had been busy activating control buttons on his keyboard. The *Enterprise* was accelerating toward the region in space where the two ships had appeared.

"Mr. Sulu, stop at once!" Kirk called sharply. "You're getting us into the warp. Full astern! What the hell do you think you're doing?"

"Aye, sir," Sulu replied but his voice sounded strangely pressed. Kirk acted as soon as he realized what was going on. His first slammed down on the Helm Override Key on his armchair console, but he didn't quite make it. Sulu had increased forward power by an order of magnitude, and the ship had jerked ahead. When the Captain took control authority from him, it was too late to stop the *Enterprise* from entering the region of the warp. Kirk shouted a warning. Seconds later, space around him seemed to "shift" crazily.

Kirk folded over as an indescribable feeling of nausea clenched every nerve fiber in his body. Somewhere in his guts two gigantic fists seemed to take hold and turn him inside out. There were knots in his interior that rotated in space. Somewhere he heard wild screams. There was a woman's voice. The sounds roared in his ears, and for a short moment he had the impression that even the tough metal of his ship had screamed shrilly in protest.

Then he blacked out. And the starship fell through the dimensional gate.

Later, there was no way to tell how long they had been unconscious. Officers and crew of the Starship *Enterprise,* all 430 of them, had floated for an indefinite period in an absolutely black night of limbo. When they came to, the bridge of the *Enterprise* was bathed in the soft light of myriads of suns shining in bright glory from the viewscreens. As Kirk regained his con, he saw Spock climbing slowly to his feet, his head shaking in wonderment. Uhura was kneeling beside the crumbled figure of Scotty, who had apparently hit his head when he fell. Moments later, the Chief Ship's Engineer responded to her gentle ministrations.

Kirk put a call through to the Medical Section. Dr. McCoy came on the intercom, still visibly shaken from the experience.

"What the devil is going on up there, Jim?" he asked. "I have patients down here, didn't you know?"

"A little mishap, Bones. How bad is it down there?"

"Bad enough. We'll manage. The casualties from that hit had just begun to come in. Your 'little mishap' may have made my job considerably tougher. Lieutenant Endercott, for example, is in a bad way. He needs surgery right away."

"Get to it, Bones. Kirk out."

He turned to Chekov and Sulu. The helmsman was looking at him with a wide stare in his almond eyes. His neck was rigid and his hands were shaking.

"What happened, Lieutenant?"

"I . . . don't know, Captain. I don't understand it. It was . . . strange. Like a dream. There was . . . detachment. I don't know what made me do it."

"All right, Lieutenant. At ease. Ensign Chekov will relieve you for a while." This was not the time for an investigation, nor for a reprimand. Kirk turned to his First Officer. "Mr. Spock, analysis, please!"

Spock looked up from his console displays. "I'm running a few standard tests, Captain, based on a hypothesis. A hunch, you might call it. Some measurements with a Wheatstone Bridge, a capacity test gauge and a calibrated synchronous motor. There is also the cesium maser for time control . . ."

"All right, all right, Mr. Spock," Kirk pressed on. "What are you telling us?"

"None of the tests yields rational results. The Wheatstone Bridge, the time control, all other instruments . . . the values do not make sense. The standards are off. Either the chronometers are malfunctioning —which would hardly be logical, or the current of electricity in our instruments is subject to different laws."

"Conclusion, Mr. Spock?"

"There is only one conclusion, Captain. The *Enterprise* has slipped into another Universe which is governed by different laws of nature and another time."

Kirk looked thoughtfully up at the shimmering holo-screen. "Another space-time continuum? Not our Universe at all . . ."

III

After three hundred thousand years, the Nagha had found the answer.

And so . . . one day, not too far away but still at a safe distance, she created a hole in the structure of the space-time continuum which connected to a neighboring Universe. Properly speaking, the nonspace complex wasn't a hole but rather a funnel that had its exact counterpart in the other Universe. Of course, her manipulations of the spatial fabric caused violent shifts in the framework of her continuum. Entire solar systems winked out within seconds. Supernovae bloomed up in blinding radiance. But space itself remained intact, and so carefully had the Nagha executed her calculations that she herself was never in any danger.

And now there was this passageway between the Universes, held open by the immeasurable energies that the shining suns themselves furnished her. She had assigned an entire section of her complicated sys-

tem the sole task of maintaining the nonspace complex of the Black Hole.

Her battle-proven ships had already penetrated through the Gate into the other Universe. Fighting and conquering, they would snatch up sector after sector of that second continuum and thus bring it under her control. The task was immense, but then she had an eternity of time. Already now, on the first conquered planets outposts were springing up that served as her relay stations. With their help she would find it easy to extend her energy tendrils everywhere.

Yes, the Nagha pursued her goal with the inflexible, cold-blooded stubbornness of a child. She knew about humor, morals and ethics, but she was incapable of applying them herself. She was an organoelectronic robot brain with the ability to accept information and draw conclusions therefrom. But in addition she could think independently, and that made her immensely dangerous. A child.

A mad computer brain.

Emotionally an absolute zero, she had been given, through an error of her builders, the gift of cold, dispassionate and razor-sharp thought.

The Nagha was almost omniscient and omnipotent.

She saw the strange spaceship emerge suddenly in her Universe and approach rapidly. There were organic life-beings on board!

Calmly and logically, in automatic reaction, she applied the incredibly powerful seegh factor.

Of course, she would have no difficulty whatsoever with these intruders.

Suddenly, with the impact of a thunderclap, there was reality.

For Kirk, it was a total body reaction. The shock flashed through his system as if he had touched a high-voltage wire. He felt his stomach contract and his neck muscles stiffen as his arms came up in automatic protectiveness. He caught a lungful of breath and held it. There was a metallic taste in his mouth.

He blinked and looked around. This was incredible.

There had been a monstrous change. One moment, his mind had been in a rubbery blackness populated by flitting shadow figures and a cacophony of noise. The next moment, he was standing here on the floor grid, struggling to regain his sanity.

His first clear thought was of his ship. Then . . . the crew! What in blazes had happened?

Kirk rubbed his eyes and shook his head to clear his mind of its cobwebs. In front of him a tall figure let go of his shoulders and stepped back. Kirk recognized the sallow features of Manda-Rao, the Priest.

Behind the man from Raga's Planet he could see the angular outlines of the cryo-tank. He was in the quarters of the mutant, deep in the holds of the *Enterprise*.

"What's going on?" he asked hoarsely. "A moment ago, I was . . ." He stopped. The realization hit him with staggering force but the shock was smaller than the first time. He had been on the bridge, surrounded by the bridge crew. Spock had located a nearby sun with several planets, and the starship had been approaching the largest planet of that star. Then . . . confusion.

And now . . . this!

He noticed something else. There was a strange stillness in the air. It wasn't acoustic. The tank support systems were humming softly, and he could hear the subdued voices of Manda-Rao's technicians in the adjoining room. It was subauditory. He could feel it through the soles of his feet—something was missing. There was a deadly *silence* about the ship, and it triggered the shrill alarm-bell of his Captain's instincts.

The ship's drive was silent, the *Enterprise* was coasting. But in addition to the powerful propulsion units there were thousands of motors and machines on board as well as over four hundred people. All of these reacted with the structure of the ship. There was hardly a place on board that didn't vibrate with the sounds and movements of the colossal machinery of the *Enterprise.*

But there was only silence.

With three strides, Kirk stood at the intercom and hammered at it. "Bridge! This is the Captain. Come in."

There was no reply.

"Spock! Uhura! Acknowledge at once."

Kirk felt the deep-set eyes of the Priest on the back of his neck. From the intercom panel, there was only silence.

Kirk punched in the video channel to the bridge. As the holographic image cleared he blinked incredulously. The control stations were untended. The bridge was deserted.

He switched to the emergency bridge on Deck Seven. There was nobody in sight. The consoles, duplicates of the ones on the main bridge, were dead.

Maybe Bones . . . He punched in Medical Section. In the Doctor's office, nothing. But there must have been patients. They had taken a hit . . . Surgery! The Surgeon's laboratory room flashed on. Somebody was there, a patient on the operating table. Kirk zoomed in. He recognized the features of Lieutenant Endercott. The Security Officer had obviously been prepared for surgery. He was in deep narcosis . . . but he was the only one there. Neither Dr. McCoy nor Dr. M'Benga nor Nurse Chapel was in sight. Kirk's emotions reeled under the realization of the extent of the catastrophe.

"What the hell is going on?" He raced to the elevator.

When he reached the bridge, he was almost out of breath. It took a tremendous effort to control the feeling of panic within him. On the way up through the decks of the giant starship, he had encountered nobody. Except for himself, Endercott and the Raga team in the mutant's quarters, there was not one living soul on board. The ship was without its crew.

There was a hint of fear in a corner of his mind. His throat felt constricted. With a hoarse sob he fought against the choking sensation. There were some things he had to do . . . Flash the self-destruct signal to the document vault. Get a distress message off. Jettison EDB pods. Apparently the ship's systems were still working. As he hurried to his armchair on the con, he saw the comfortingly steady shine of green status lights still on automatic. Dimly he realized that he was, too, moving on training and instinct and in shock.

Lights all green . . .

Except for one. Startled, he gave it a second look. Damn! The deflector shields were down! The *Enterprise* was completely unprotected.

As he moved rapidly over to the helmsman's station to activate the energy screens he noted that the vessel was in orbit. The mass center of its closed flight-path loomed on the main screen before and above the con. It was clearly a planet, probably the large one of the sun they had approached before he lost consciousness. But it looked strange. There were no surface features that he could see. It was dark-bluish in color, and its gleaming smoothness reminded him of polished metal.

Arriving at Sulu's station, he reached over to punch the Red Alert "Panic Key" which would activate the protective deflector screens of the orbiting ship. Of course, it made sense. In order to evacuate the ship the crew had to take the shields down. Obviously, they had beamed down with the Transporters—there just weren't enough shuttlecraft to deboard 430 men and women within a reasonable time period. Had Spock believed him dead, gone—and learned of some inconceivable necessity to evacuate the ship? But what?

As he touched the switch, the lights on the bridge went off.

Before his startled eyes, the color-coded status lights on the helm winked out. He looked up. The viewscreen above him went dark. Behind him, the electronic beeping of Spock's long-range gravar sensors stopped.

A moment later the deep-red emergency illumination of the bridge came on, powered by the emergency storage batteries of the ship. The lights were dim.

Kirk stood motionless. His thoughts came fast and furious but there was no solution.

The ship was without power, and there was nothing he could do. There was not enough charge left in the storage cells to run the life-support systems of the ship. That meant . . . down in the hold, the Federation's greatest treasure was lost. Singa, the mutant, was dead.

The feeling of failure and loss was a dull ache deep inside him as he turned slowly to his command chair. But his mind kept racing. If he spliced the power cell of a hand phaser gun into the emergency circuit, maybe . . .

There was a noise at the door. Startled, he looked up.

The tall, shadowy figure of Manda-Rao stood motionless in the deep-red gloom near the elevator exit. Kirk stared at him owlishly. He must have followed him up and come in immediately before the power failure.

He shrugged helplessly and turned away. "I'm sorry," he said. "It looks as if my ship has come to the end of its voyage. The *Enterprise* is without power. There is no protection against attacks. There is no way that I could possibly run the ship on my own. My entire crew has gone from board. There's just you and me and your technicians . . . My people . . ."

"They did not leave voluntarily, Captain James Kirk." The voice came with startling clarity and power from the gloomy darkness.

Kirk whirled around, taken aback. "What!" That hadn't sounded like Manda-Rao's soft, throaty voice.

"Of course. They were under outside control. No sane expeditionary crew would leave its ship without protection."

"Under outside control?" Kirk repeated incredulously, but the first tendrils of comprehension were already touching his still-clouded consciousness. "Do you mean . . ." suddenly he realized that some tremendous battle had been fought over his own consciousness. He was still not recovered, not thinking clearly . . .

". . . hypnotic control? Yes indeed, Captain." The figure of the Priest was still motionless.

"I don't believe it," Kirk faltered. "Even the Vulcan?"

"Even Spock," said the voice. "But you are already believing me, Captain. Because you know that this is not Manda-Rao speaking to you."

Kirk stared at the shadow figure. Then it dawned on him with a shock. "You are Singa! You are the mutant speaking through the Priest? You are not dead!"

"That is correct."

"Does that mean that it was *you* who has compelled my crew to evacuate the ship?"

"No, Captain. It was the enemy."

Kirk straightened. His appreciation of the mutant had suddenly gained a new dimension. "Please explain!"

"What you regarded as a planet down there below the ship is really a sentient being. It is a non-organic life entity, an intelligent thinking machine. It is fully capable of rational thought, but there is a madness about it that does not tolerate other life forms."

Kirk was flabbergasted. An artificial brain? A gigantic computer? A planet-sized robot? But—true intelligence? Malevolence?

"Yes," Singa said through his Priest. "It calls itself the Nagha. Its ships have gotten through to our Universe, and it is they who have attacked our worlds. They are right now preparing to attack my planet. Your crew is in the Nagha's power. Your people are on one of the smaller planets of this sun. I am not sure whether they are still alive, but I do know that the Nagha means to kill us all. However, if my calculations are correct there is a finite chance that I can make a countermove that might save us. It is our only chance, Captain." Manda-Rao hesitated a moment. Then: "But there is a problem."

Kirk looked up. "Well?"

"It requires that you are prepared to sacrifice yourself, Captain Kirk."

Kirk sat down in his armchair and listened quietly, as Singa went on to explain.

The main problem was the powerful deflector shields the Nagha-Planet was maintaining around itself. For Singa to hit back at the enemy, those screens had to come down. Thus, they had to trick the Nagha into turning off her powerful planetary energy shields.

As the first step, Singa had deactivated the power systems of the *Enterprise,* simulating a total power failure and a lifeless ship. Of course, he had kept his tank systems in operation. Kirk scowled, despite himself. He should have seen that. Would have, at any other time. The back-up systems . . . what else was he not seeing? Exposing a seemingly lifeless and unprotected ship to the destructive potential of the enemy was undoubtedly the logical thing to do if one wanted to fool a computer mentality. Kirk hoped. What levels of logic did these two play on? Machine and mutant, neither quite human. Did they play complexity against complexity until only a trick would work? But the next trick would buy the lowering of her shields—at the cost of Kirk's life.

When the voice of the mutant stopped talking, Kirk sat for long moments in silent desperation. But then he made his decision and stood up. His mental anguish was gone, and there was only the fierce joy of action-taking.

He powered the ship's communications system up and hailed the Nagha.

When the shuttlecraft *Columbus* had gently touched down on the smooth metal plain of the living planet, Kirk shut down its systems, closed the visor of his environmental suit and stepped off the ramp.

Singa's first calculation—or wasn't it rather a gamble?—had paid off. The machine had reacted to his radio call with obvious surprise—a flurry of sensor probes. Kirk stated his purpose almost as a challenge. The Nagha was silent. He took off. It had lowered its

energy shields and allowed him to land. Clearly, the
Nagha had not expected that anyone on board the
Enterprise had been able to resist its hypnotic "fog"—
or *seegh*—factor, as Singa apparently thought of its
power. In millions and millions of years of experience,
that had never happened before. Kirk was not certain
how Singa received his information. But Kirk was
gambling, too, on the mutant.

Kirk looked out through the golden visor of his
helmet into the distance of the featureless metal plain.
He knew that he was walking into a situation which left
very little chance of personal survival. But there was a
reasonably finite chance that—by going into the lion's
den—he might open the enemy to Singa's attack. His
hand, almost of its own account, touched the suit
pocket which held the open communicator.

Singa had said that there was a high probability
that Spock and the crew were alive. If this worked,
they would get home, even if Kirk did not.

There was movement not far from him.

A metal plate had been lowered and was now
sliding aside, revealing a large, square opening. Moments later, a machine from a nightmare dream
climbed up from inside.

It looked to Kirk like a Rube Goldberg construction of whirling arms and legs. Large, gleaming lenses
reflected the sunlight in blinding flashes as the teleoperator moved toward him. Kirk shrugged, but he
felt his jaw muscles tighten when two of the powerful
manipulator arms lifted him up.

Then he relaxed. This was not the time for resistance. The machine hadn't hurt him. The brain wanted
him alive. After all, he was the only living being in its
experience that had withstood the all-powerful *seegh*-
force.

The teleoperator carried him to the opening. Kirk
caught a last glimpse of the *Columbus,* resting quietly
on its footpads. Then the machine had climbed down
into the dark interior of the planet and the hatch cover
slid shut.

He was inside the artificial planet brain.

It was pitch-dark. He couldn't see but he was still dangling in the limbs of the machine. Judging from its bouncing motions he was being carried at a rapid pace deeper into the interior. Presumably, there was a network of near-endless corridors inside the body of the computer brain to make all principal logic units of the Nagha accessible to the mechanical slaves for repair and maintenance.

When the remotely controlled mechanism finally stopped, it seemed to Kirk that years had passed. The manipulators lowered him to the ground and released him. Standing on his own feet, he took a deep breath and felt considerably better.

Suddenly there was light.

Directly in front of him, a doorway seemed to have opened. Behind it was a brightly lit room with steel walls. In its center stood two tables of highly polished metal. They reminded him of Dr. McCoy's operating table, and there was an ugly premonition in his mind.

Then he saw that one of the tables was occupied. A tall, slim humanoid figure, stretched out on its back, was strapped to it. It was a nude male.

Startled, Kirk tore off his suit helmet and shouted, "Spock!"

The First Officer of the Starship *Enterprise* turned his head and looked at Kirk with a calm, carefully expressionless face. "Jim! I had not really expected to see you ever again, nor anyone." His voice dropped low, level, tight. "Get out of here, Jim."

Kirk had hurried up to the table and was fumbling with the metal straps that kept Spock restrained. The Vulcan stopped and looked over his shoulder, heaved at the straps.

"Jim, behind you!"

The mechanical teleoperator had moved up silently. Before Kirk could react, it had caught him. Minutes later, his body, divested of its clothing, was stretched out on top of the second table.

Spock had watched, helplessly, and Kirk could see him trying for Vulcan discipline.

"These are going to be difficult hours, Jim," Spock said quietly. "Very difficult. We are scientific subjects. I was attempting to find some fascination in the irony by which the Science Officer of a starship becomes a scientific subject himself."

"Fascinating!" Kirk said with as much irony as he could muster, and as much discipline. There was a time for it. "Would you please explain yourself, Mr. Spock?" Not that he wanted to know, or didn't know already.

"This entity believes in experimental research on organic life forms involving surgical operations and mutilation."

"Oh," Kirk said. "Vivisection! Why didn't you say so in the first place?"

"I prefer not to use terms that may have emotional overtones, Captain."

Kirk shook his head. Then he pressed on. "Fill me in on the rest of the sad story, will you, Spock?"

"There is not much else, Jim. I believe that prior to your arrival I was the only crew member on this artificial planet. Unfortunately I have no information on the whereabouts of the complement of the *Enterprise*. When I regained control over my mental faculties I found myself in this room. It may be conjectured that I was singled out because I was in command of the ship at the time of the telehypnotic takeover, Captain. You had left me the con, rather abruptly, and left the bridge."

Kirk was about to answer when he remembered just in time. They were undoubtedly being overheard. Let the damn machine find out about the existence of the mutant in its own good time!

Spock continued. "This is a laboratory, Jim. As you will notice, the atmosphere is quite Earth-like. Obviously, it was created in here to keep us alive, at least for a while. There are machines in the walls, test instruments, highly advanced analyzers and the like. The surgical machines were just getting ready to begin their research on my body when something caused an interruption. A second table was set up. Sometime thereafter you were brought down."

"It must have been my radio call that stopped them," Kirk speculated. "This planetary machine . . . does it talk?"

"Unknown, Captain," Spock said. "I have addressed it several times in the past, without response. But I would guess that it is capable of speech. If it is listening to us right now, it may be attempting to learn the rudiments of our language. However . . ."

Suddenly there was the roar of a powerful, resonating voice in the room.

"I . . . am . . . the . . . Nagha. You . . . are . . . life . . . forms . . ."—the words started to come faster —"that . . . I wish . . . to study. The second form . . ."

"That's you, Jim," Spock said quietly.

Despite himself, Kirk was startled. He cleared his throat. "I am Captain James T. Kirk, commanding the Federation Starship U.S.S. *Enterprise.*" His voice grew firmer. "I insist that you release my friend and me immediately!"

"The second form . . ." the Nagha continued monotonously. "James T. Kirk? He is of special power. Appropriate investigation is of immediate necessity."

"Why?" Kirk demanded. "What's so damn special about me?"

"James T. Kirk is first organic life form on record that has demonstrated capability to neutralize the *seegh* force. Before I can continue further extension into Universe of James T. Kirk, I must understand failure of *seegh.*"

The synthetic voice of the robot brain continued to speak resoundingly, but Kirk wasn't listening any longer. For there had been a sudden movement at the corner of his eye.

He turned his head. Machines were coming out of wall openings, moving quickly and purposefully toward his table. There were articulated arms, complex joints, telescoping extensions, and multi-fingered terminal organs that gripped flashing tools.

Kirk closed his eyes.

The voice of the Nagha was still talking. Kirk heard it with a detached part of his awareness. Peace, he told himself. There was his crew . . . his ship . . . If his death bought Singa additional time to launch his countermove, so be it. He felt the touch of cold metal on his skin.

"Spock . . ."

"Jim . . ."

There was a sudden jolt. The synthetic voice stopped in mid-sentence.

The room shook violently. Kirk's table slid several feet over the smooth floor and slammed against the wall. He opened his eyes. The straps jerked at his body as the table jumped. He saw the metal wall buckle inward.

"Singa!" Kirk roared triumphantly.

The sound of distant explosions hammered at his ears. They seemed to be coming closer. Quake after quake rippled through the surrounding structure. He saw that the menacing laboratory machinery had stopped in mid-motion.

Kirk threw a quick glance at the other table. It had fallen over but Spock was conscious. He was struggling helplessly against the restraining straps.

The explosions came closer. To his ears, they were sweet sounds. All around them, Kirk knew, the intricate machinery of the Nagha was crumbling.

It meant that Singa had been able to launch his attack. While the Nagha was concentrating on her two research subjects, he had identified her vital sections. According to plan, he then must have materialized an explosive device in the midst of the machine's defense control center. Next, he had powered up the *Enterprise*. And before the Nagha could react by throwing up her planetary shields, he had detonated the explosive device, taking out the deflector screens.

Kirk assumed that the planetary machine was now fighting back, but the ship had its protective shields up. And the powerful phaser beams of the *Enterprise* must already be playing havoc with its intricate systems, cutting through the dense metal as if it was butter. The concussion waves of devastating destruction came from deep within the heart of the planet.

There was a titanic explosion nearby. Kirk saw the walls of the room tear apart with a metallic scream. The atmosphere was whistling out . . .

He felt the familiar whole-body tingle of the Transporter, knowing instantly that Singa was snatching him out at the very brink of death. There was a rasping choke in his throat.

When he materialized amidst the golden scintillation of the Transporter beam, there was only one thought in his mind.

"Get Spock out!" he croaked at the tall figure of Manda-Rao behind the console of the ship's Transporter Room. Then there was only blackness as he collapsed on the platform in a dead faint.

Once again the immense brilliance of the Milky Way Galaxy shone in magnificent splendor from the display screens. As so often in the past, Uhura thought of those uncountable stars as glittering diamonds that sparkled in all conceivable colors.

The Starship *Enterprise,* back in its own Universe, streaked with transrelativistic speed through the endless reaches of space, but the myriads of shining pinheads on her holo-screens showed that she was not alone in the infinity. There was life, warmth, light everywhere. Nature's dynamic urge to give life to the lifeless and to fill emptiness manifested itself all around them.

Lieutenant Uhura turned back to Manda-Rao and strummed a melodious chord on her Vulcan lyrette. The Priest listened quietly as she began the second verse of her melancholic song. At least, it was the body of the Priest, but the eyes . . .

Several decks above her, on the main bridge of the starship, Captain Kirk was dictating in his log.

"Captain's log, Stardate 5828.3. While en route

to conduct reconnoiter and rescue operations in the Altair system, the *Enterprise* was diverted to Raga's Planet to pick up the mutant Singa, the Sleeper, also known as the Sleeping God. The diversion was ordered by what at first appeared to be the persona of Admiral Olaf Sondergaard of Star Fleet Command. I have now determined that it was a fake. The order, in actuality, came from Singa himself, who had decided to save Raga's Planet from destruction, and to take a hand in a game which might have meant galactic destruction without him. There is reason to believe that the mutation's capabilities include almost unlimited clairvoyant, telepathic and telekinetic powers." Kirk stopped the recording and looked up.

Spock and McCoy had entered the bridge and were listening to his log entry.

"Well, Bones," Kirk asked. "How are your patients?"

"Doing great, Jim." McCoy beamed from ear to ear. "They're all coming along just fine. We got to Endercott in the nick of time. The boy is pulling out of it."

Kirk nodded, pleased. Then he turned to the First Officer who had arrived at his station. "Your report, Mr. Spock?"

"A message from Star Base Two just came in, Captain. It appears that all known enemy ships in the Federation Territory are out of control and are now drifting without a sign of activity. I believe, Jim, they are dead—if I'm permitted to use this highly imprecise expression for remote-controlled machines. I have also received a full briefing from Singa, through the voice of the Priest. You will find the details on the library tapes. Singa has indicated his desire to be brought back to Raga's Planet. He felt also obligated to extend his apologies to our helmsman."

Lieutenant Sulu turned around and grinned.

Kirk nodded. "There will be a special footnote on this in the ship's log, Lieutenant. The record will indicate that it was Singa's mental control over your mind that steered the ship into and through the dimensional gate, and not yourself. You have conducted yourself with distinction."

"Thank you, *sir!*"

McCoy cleared his throat noisily. "I understand that Sulu is not the only one who has experienced the Sleeper's mind touch. How about telling us about it, Jim?"

Kirk winced and grinned ruefully. "He had it all carefully planned, Bones. The Nagha was a strictly logical thinking machine, without the ability fully to understand the deviousness possible to a real brain. In order to expose her to his attack, hs knew he had to trick her into lowering her deflector shields. He achieved this by arousing her curiosity as to why I had not responded to her telehypnotic powers. Of course, the reason I had not fallen under her spell was simply because Singa protected me with his mind long enough to get me into those insulated quarters of his. So . . . the machine had to turn off her screens to allow my landing. That was all Singa needed."

From the background, Scotty said, "Sounds like a pretty risky situation, that, Captain. That could've gone awry easily. What if the computer would've turned the shields back on, right after y'er landing?"

"Unlikely, Mr. Scott," Spock said pedantically. "She could not re-erect her screens without exploding the shuttlecraft *Columbus* and thereby endangering herself. Also, after the evacuation of the entire crew to one of her manufacturing planets, she would have been convinced that the ship was quite harmless, particularly with the Captain himself in her power and the ship's screens gone. However, the Captain did indeed take considerable risks in relying on the mutant's ability to beam him out of the disintegrating machine in time. It *would* seem somewhat illogical."

"Don't forget your own role in this, Spock!" McCoy growled good-naturedly.

"Nor should we forget yours, Doctor," Spock replied gravely. But was there a twinkle behind his expressionless stare? "Shall I remind you of your admonitions regarding the Captain's—how did you phrase it?—'damn wild goose chase across the galaxy'?"

McCoy bristled. "All right, all right, Spock! So I was wrong. Who isn't, now and then? You don't have to be so cotton-pickin' righteous about it . . ."

"Gentlemen, gentlemen," Kirk said pleasantly. "May I have your permission to resume my log entry?"

"Sorry, Jim." McCoy was grinning like a puppy dog.

Spock raised an eyebrow. "One final question, Captain. When you made the decision to go on the Doctor's 'wild goose chase' and search for the home world of our enemy, instead of pursuing our opponent's ship back into Federation Territory . . . were you acting on your own, or were you under the mind control of the mutant?"

"Mr. Spock!" Scott was horrified. "How can y' ask the Cap'n such a question!"

"It's okay, Scotty." Kirk was quite serious, pondering the question.

Then he grinned, swiveling to face forward. "Mr. Spock, why don't you ask the Sleeping God himself?"

But Singa was silent.

Editors' Introduction to
"Elegy for Charlie"

Star Trek, for all its sunlit-universe sense of life, did not always have happy endings or simple answers. There were times when man prevailed only by endurance, and someone lost more than he could bear to lose. Some of those episodes continued to haunt people. They were part of the real life of *Star Trek*—the enduring, haunting memories of answers which were not pat.

"Charlie X" was such a story. Charlie, a human orphan, was raised with dangerous mental powers which humans could not live with, and he could not live without. Finally the beings who raised him had to take him from the *Enterprise,* and the human crew had to let him go to utter loneliness—with beings he couldn't even touch . . .

Antonia Vallario has captured that haunted and haunting memory.

ELEGY FOR CHARLIE

by Antonia Vallario

My sleep was disturbed by a weeping star
and a voice that I shouldn't have heard
for the galaxy drifts in the coldness of space
where dark is incredibly far,

(and a voice cannot come from a star)

O secretly grown, all alone
child-flower plucked from an alien soil
beneath an alien sun,
who wanted most what we could not give
forgive our helpless humanity;
we watched you taken from the bridge
forever lost to a human love
and a life you were not meant to live.

The entire universe stretches beyond, and
I have no answers to give
save the words that I send to the galaxy's end
to comfort a weeping star,

(for Charlie, wherever you are)

Editors' Introduction to "Soliloquy"

Postscript: "Gentlepersons"—
The Vulcan Connection

There is perhaps only one person in all of space or time, reality or dream, who is the leading expert on the unspoken word which is always the first and last word.

But it just may be that *New Voyages* (1) established a tradition that we shall hear from that person by one means or another, and hear that word.

Or perhaps, next time, we shall receive a reply from a starship Captain . . .

This was relayed through Box 14261:

Gentlepersons:
Not long after reading Shirley Meech's Vulcan sonnet in *New Voyages* (p. 237), which I admired very much, I, too, received a telepathic message in the form of a sonnet, perhaps from the same source.

I do not know if it is authentic.

Sincerely,
Marguerite B. Thompson

"SOLILOQUY"

by Marguerite B. Thompson

My father gave no word of love to me.
My mother practiced laudable restraint.
My Vulcan childhood lessons logically
Prepared me to despise the human taint.

I could not blame T'Pring; I saw that she
Let flawless logic over pledge prevail.
For she would stop at nothing to be free
Wisely to mate with a pure Vulcan male.

Human tormentors do not understand
Acknowledgment of feeling causes pain,
Cruelly subvert defenses I had planned,
Plot to anesthetize my watchful brain.

What will they find when I am ripped apart?
"I love you, Captain," written on my heart.

Epilogue by Nichelle Nichols

You know that *déjà vu* feeling—"I've been here before"?

But have you ever had the feeling: "I will have been here before, someday"?

Or: "I'd better see to it that I—or my great-great-great granddaughter—will have been out there, someday"?

It gets complicated.

I used to say as a figure of speech that I felt Uhura calling me to get busy—calling any of us to get busy—so that her world could exist.

Somewhere along the line it got to be more than a figure of speech. I kept finding myself in strange places. On a NASA C-141 observatory flight, where no "civilian" had gone before. In Huntsville. In Washington. In the Jet Propulsion Laboratory for the Viking touchdown on Mars. On the Mojave Desert, watching the *Enterprise* roll out . . .

And once, maybe with that feeling of—I will have been here before, someday . . .

It's quiet.

(Did I doze off?) I think everybody finally went home. Good party.

Funny, the ship feels right, now. All the little sounds you can't hear sound right again. A happy ship.

Think I'll just take a turn around the ship. Mr. Spock doesn't have a monopoly on tucking everybody in. Wonder how many times we've passed in the night with the same idea? Not that he'd say so. Purely his logical duty, of course. Mother's helper.

    They've left the door locked open. Maybe every-body hasn't gone home? No. It's only Spock. They aren't even playing chess. Just quiet. Does a Vulcan get sleepy on ice cream and cake? He'd never admit it. The other one would. He's half asleep.

    They do look like two little boys.

    I won't disturb them.

    Shh, Mr. Spock. I was just passing by. Close the door and don't disturb him. 'Night, Mr. Spock, sugar. 'Night, Cap'n honey.

    Now, everybody's gone home. And is home.

    Does anybody know why I'm shivering? Maybe I'd better go check myself right in to sickbay. Can anybody see me telling Dr. McCoy: "I had this funny feeling for a moment, as if I were seeing this all through someone else's eyes—someone who knew I might never exist—that none of us might—at least, not at home out here . . . ?"

    Sure. Anytime I want to get measured for a couch and a long rest . . .

    No. It was nothing. I know what it was. It was only that this was one of those days when you know how good it is to be here. And so you suddenly think— what if we hadn't made it? There was a time when it hung in the balance . . . Spock wouldn't exist. Maybe none of us . . .

    So you see, Mr. Spock, I'm being very logical. There's a perfectly logical explanation.

    So why am I still shivering . . . ?

    And why do I feel as if there's something I need to do?

    But that's crazy. Nothing I could do about that. Anyway, that would be some whole other story. I know somebody who'd say, "Haven't you done enough for one day?"

    Yessir. 'Night, Cap'n, honey. 'Night—whoever you were . . .

'Night—whoever you will be . . .
Great, great, great-granddaughter?
But that's some whole other story.
Or—it will be.*

I don't think Uhura's going to let anybody get any rest around here until it's written—not only in books, but in the budget for upward-outward-to the stars, and in the faces of the flight crews for where-no-man— and where-no-woman . . .

Postscript: My special acknowledgment to Jesco von Puttkamer for all the reasons which he knows, and my thanks to him and to everyone who has welcomed me on my where-no-civilian trek through NASA and the space program as if I were not a civilian at all.

My very special acknowledgment to Baroness Ursula von Puttkamer, who understands both Uhura and Nichelle and the connection between very well.

And to those who will summon the future . . .

With love,
Nichelle Nichols

---

*Uhura!

ABOUT THE EDITORS

SONDRA MARSHAK and MYRNA CULBREATH are a new writing and editing "team" whose efforts in the last three years have centered around *Star Trek*. Sondra Marshak is one of the co-authors of *Star Trek Lives!*, a recent collection of notes and anecdotes concerning the creators, actors, fans, conventions, and writers of *Star Trek*. She and Myrna Culbreath, founder of the Culbreath Schools in Colorado and editor of *The Fire Bringer*, have produced two television specials on *Star Trek*, and are the editors of *Star Trek: The New Voyages* 1 and 2 and the authors of *The Price of the Phoenix*. They have begun work with William Shatner on a "biography, autobiography, and a report from the revolution" called *Shatner: Where No Man*, and are also working on *Uhura*, a novel with Nichelle Nichols, and a sequel to *The Price of the Phoenix*. Sondra and Myrna have been in great demand as guest speakers at various *Star Trek* conventions, and have spent a lot of time working with both professional and aspiring writers on their *Star Trek* and other fiction. Sondra and Myrna were brought together by an article of Myrna's, "The Spock Premise." Myrna moved from Colorado Springs to Baton Rouge, Louisiana, where Sondra lives with her husband, Alan, a professor of electrical engineering at Louisiana State University; their young son, Jerry; her mother, Mrs. Anna Hassan; and their German shepherd "Omne," named after the villain in *The Price of the Phoenix*. Sondra's background includes a B.A. and an M.A. in history, while Myrna has a B.A. in philosophy and psychology.

FOLLOW THE BOLD SAGA OF LUGH OF THE LONG ARM BY
KENNETH C. FLINT

The tale of Lugh of the Long Arm is among the greatest of all Celtic myths. Now this mighty legend comes blazing to life in a new retelling filled with all the fire and magic of the ancient bards.

☐ **RIDERS OF THE SIDHE (24175-3 • $2.95)**

Out of the mists the Fomor came to enslave Eire, a dread race of twisted men ruled by an inhuman lord: Balor of the Evil Eye. But a champion came from out of the sea, a youth called Lugh, sent to Eire to fulfill an ancient prophecy . . .

☐ **CHAMPIONS OF THE SIDHE (24543-0 • $2.95)**

The evil lord Balor and his dark druid Mathgen send the traitorous Bres with an inhuman army to recapture the isle of Eire . . . and Lugh rouses the de Danann warriors for the final battle for the throne of the High Kings of Tara.

☐ **MASTER OF THE SIDHE (25261-5 • $2.95/$3.50 in Canada)**

The de Dananns prepare to battle to the death with the now-desperate Fomor . . . while Lugh leads an intrepid band of champions on a daring assault against Balor and Mathgen's tower stronghold.

Also by Kenneth C. Flint

☐ **A STORM UPON ULSTER (24710-7 • $3.50/$3.95 in Canada)**

The legend of Cuculcain, Ireland's greatest hero, and Meave, the flaming haired warrior queen of Eire, whose dreams of conquest became black visions conjured up by an evil enchanter.

All the above titles are available wherever Bantam Spectra Books are sold—or use this handy coupon for ordering:

The long-awaited new novel from
Hugo and Nebula Award-Winning Author

DAVID BRIN
THE POSTMAN

Here is the powerful story of a post-holocaust
United States, a shattered country slipping into a
new dark age—until one man, Gordon Krantz,
offers new hope for the future . . . using a symbol
from the vanished past.

THE POSTMAN—available November 1985 in
hardcover wherever Bantam Spectra Books are
sold.